Praise for

'This swashbuck
The Times

'Wonderfully drawn characters and a terrific pace'
Jess Kidd, bestselling author of *The Night Ship*

'A poignant depiction of true female friendship, and a really good adventure story, beautifully told'
Frances Quinn, author of *The Smallest Man*

'A cracking read . . . Fascinating, complex characters and a real page-turner!'
Liz Hyder, author of *The Gifts*

'Bonny & Read has it all. Adventure, atmosphere, sizzling suspense and unforgettable characters – a brilliant debut!'
SD Sykes, author of *The Good Death*

'A deftly told tale of the complexities of friendship, female identity and freedom, featuring two remarkable women determined to define their own destinies . . . the pages turn themselves'
Anita Frank, author of *The Lost Ones*

'What a debut! A fabulous, dangerous sea-shanty of a story'
Katie Munnik, author of *The Aerialists*

'A wonderful story, so beautifully told and absolutely gripping to the very end'
Emma Carroll

'Walker's book is a warm and wonderful tribute to these timeless women, with intriguing detail of the period and the pirate life'
Lisa Redmond, Historical Novel Society

BONNY & READ

JULIE WALKER

HODDER

First published in Great Britain in 2022 by Hodder & Stoughton
An Hachette UK company

This paperback edition published in 2023

1

A CIP catalogue record for this title is available from the British Library

Paperback ISBN 978 1 529 39572 3

Typeset in Adobe Caslon Pro by Manipal Technologies Limited

Printed and bound in Great Britain by Clays Ltd, Elcograf S.p.A.

Hodder & Stoughton policy is to use papers that are natural, renewable
and recyclable products and made from wood grown in sustainable forests.
The logging and manufacturing processes are expected to conform to the
environmental regulations of the country of origin.

Hodder & Stoughton Ltd
Carmelite House
50 Victoria Embankment
London EC4Y 0DZ

www.hodder.co.uk

For mam and dad. For all the books, the stories, and for everything else.

PART ONE

Anne

Chapter 1

Charles Town, South Carolina , 1718

It has been a filthy hot day, the night following suit. The sluggish silence is shattered by the sounds of a loud argument at the Cormac house. Moments later, to the music of breaking glass, Anne tears from the French windows, skirts bunched in her hands, long red hair streaming behind her as she races like a March hare across the lawn, the sounds of pistol fire ringing in her ears as she runs full pelt for her life, ragged-breathed and laughing as vitriolic obscenities are hurled at her.

Her father, the source of the fury, takes repeated drunken aim at the darting figure from the open doors, his only child, thank God, married without his knowledge or blessing earlier that day. And to a servant, of all things, this lesser person running in the wake of his dashing bride, sheer panic on his face as the gunfire continues, a hand held to his bleeding arm, where, against all odds, one of his father-in-law's bullets has glanced its target.

This is typical of James Bonny's luck – something that his new wife will know soon enough. But for now she feels the exhilaration of chaos, the proximity of death, and the freedom of being Anne Cormac no longer.

'You whore! You are your mother's daughter, and none of mine!'

Her father's aim is not helped by a brandy-soaked afternoon and the insult of sudden betrayal, as he screams things to the running figure that a father should never utter to his only girl, things to terrify a man like James Bonny.

'You think you'll get away so easily?'

There are torches close behind, the smell of cordite in their nostrils, the thick air catching at their throats as they run, the cushioning grass soon giving way to the sharpness of parched soil as they reach the boundary wall.

The roused servants have let loose the dogs, thinking perhaps that their master has disturbed thieves in the act, and the fugitives hear their snarling pursuit, drummed up by the mad excitement of William Cormac, who agitates the men and beasts to do them great harm.

The dogs are fast and are already snapping at James Bonny's ankles as he frantically tries to climb beyond their reach, while Anne is halfway over the wall using a creeper that she has climbed since she was a child, her underthings on shameful view for all to see. After everything he has endured, it is almost her father's undoing. He falls to his knees, holding up his hands to the heavens and wailing:

'And will you show your arse to the world too?'

She hauls herself to the summit eight feet from the ground and salutes her father with the requisite number of fingers before swinging her legs over to the other side and, using the overhanging creeper, drops, landing unscathed and unladylike onto the road beyond. She is soon joined by a breathless and sweating James, who falls like bad fruit beside her, his eyes wide at the raw memory of recent insults to his person.

'You smell worse than the dogs, James Bonny!'

Her eyes are dancing, her face burning from her exertions, but he does not appreciate the joke. He had not realised when they married this morning that she was clearly quite mad.

'So that was your idea of breaking it to him gently, was it? Jesus, woman, I nearly lost an arm.'

He holds out the limb in question to show her the scratch and suggestion of blood, already dried.

'Sure enough, it wasn't your arm I was worried about.' Her glance and filthy smile suggest a softer target, and he rests his hands there to protect his treasures. 'Besides, it was broken as gently as it needed to be, for we don't need his money now that we have each other.'

James's look suggests otherwise and she sees it at once. Her smile hardens; a hardness that will be difficult to shift. He will not be the man to do it.

But at that moment the shouts of men and yelping of dogs on the other side of the gate grow louder at the unmistakable sound of a key turning in the lock.

Anne grins at James, eyes flashing.

'We're not clear of this place yet. You'd better hope for your sake that you have breath left in you.'

Anne hops from one foot to another, pulling stained satin slippers from her feet, before she sets to running again in earnest, throwing the shoes behind her into a ditch.

Chapter 2

It is only when they are lost in the chaos of the port, breath slowing and sweat flowing freely, that they are able to slow down, sure now that they are not being followed.

James looks at his new bride without affection as she takes stock of this new situation.

'And what will become of us now? There is no money since you have ruined everything ...'

Anne doesn't listen to him finish – there is no need. He has killed her infatuation dead, and all that is left behind is the inconvenience of legal obligation. That she has saddled herself with a man like James Bonny, she will have time and cause enough to regret, but for now there is the immediate future to consider.

It is inconceivable that the affair has gone sour after so promising a start. Stolen glances across a neighbour's drawing room; he forward and insolent for a mere servant. As the men retired for drinks, Anne had entertained herself with the footman with the indecent smile. The velvet uniform had suited him, though he looked better out of it; he had not been shy, and nor was she. He had bundled her into a cupboard only a week back with whispered promises, warm breath and lips upon her face and warmer fingers beneath her skirts, urgent and eager. In her haste to leave home, and their mutual delusions about the other, Cupid had smiled upon them.

But in the few short hours that they have been joined in the eyes of God, Anne has found her husband disappointing in more ways than one. He is less exciting than she had expected; it's clear that their escape has been more terrifying than exhilarating to him. He is far less appealing now that the smiles and flattery have stopped. It is unfortunate that he is also more stupid than she had hoped.

That he has managed to disappoint her in such a short space of time amazes her; that she is not the rich prize he hoped for amazes him. They are well matched, indeed.

James is still waiting for an answer, his face red from exertion and temper, while Anne is pricked by feelings of dislike.

'We shall go to sea, then. You'll get work soon enough, but after today it won't be here.'

She will remember later how full of hope she still is, and curse herself for it. But here and now, their passage on the merchant ship is bought in exchange for the gold cross and chain Anne had worn for her wedding that morning. It had been stolen especially from her mother's jewellery box as she slept off her daily dose of laudanum, prescribed to cure her of sadness. It is an affliction Mrs Cormac has suffered from since she met Anne's father, and will hardly improve now.

The ship is handsome against the horizon, ripe with promise. All ties with family, home and propriety now severed, Anne climbs the gangplank with great hopes for New Providence, the jewel of the Bahamas, she hopes. James follows sullenly in her wake.

Chapter 3

The ship slips from port, the increasing dip and crest as she pushes out towards the expanse of ocean driving Charles Town further behind. The promise of the voyage, of a future not yet made, is all that Anne needs for now as she breathes in salt air, listening to the boom of waves against the hull as *The Betty* forges ahead.

Anne is interrupted by one of the ship's mates, a hairy man with a cleft lip, who tells her gruffly to move as she is in his way. Against her better judgement, she follows the path her husband took earlier, descending into the twilight of the deck below down rickety stairs. The underbelly is lit by occasional lanterns, its air damp with sweat and scented with spices.

They have been allocated a hammock each in an inhospitable corner of the lower deck. James has already taken to his, his back stubbornly turned towards her, a convenient deafness having taken hold of him when it comes to his new wife.

Anne is distracted by the creaks and groans of the hull now that she is beneath sea level, the weight of the dark ocean beyond. She grips the rough rope of the hammock for balance before climbing in, allowing herself to be rocked and swayed by the motion of the sea.

As the hours pass, Anne sleeps, dreaming of open expanses and glittering horizons, unaffected by the sickness that repeatedly wrenches the insides from James. She wakes refreshed and finds him ill and miserable. Were he someone else entirely she might have felt quite sorry for him. As it is, she is glad of it.

Anne leaves her husband bemoaning his lot, spittle trailing from his mouth from the latest evacuation, a man bereft of hope as well as breakfast. He is a sorry sight and a poor excuse for a man – but it is no one's fault but hers that she is no longer a free woman in the eyes of the world. Her greatest hope is that he might fulfil his newly repeated promise and die of seasickness.

Anne reminds herself that the adventure of leaving her old life behind has begun. She has cast off ladylike things, and is ready to make her way in the world. She does not wish to be bound by the limitations inflicted on her as a woman, and certainly not as her father's daughter. She is sure there is a life out there that can be created in her own image. What that might be exactly is a little vague, for she was always better at action than planning – but all in good time.

'New Providence.' Anne enjoys the shape of the words as she whispers them to herself. No doubt a paradise of coconuts and palm trees, ripe with opportunity. A pirate port once, but lawful now that the British government has taken control once again. Its cut-throat reputation is old news – the last mass hangings of pirates two years back saw to that. She knows, for she has read about it (the newspaper reports taken and kept folded in an unread book of devotions), but she would like to think that something of the spirit remains.

She has already made up her mind to part company with James once they hit dry land, for marital separation is a difficult thing to achieve in the middle of any ocean. She therefore bides her time, mulling over plans of what she might do to keep body and soul together once she reaches her destination.

Anne prefers to remain on deck where James is not, lying amongst sailcloth and rope as she keeps out of the way of the working crew. From this position, she is able to marvel at the myriad stars that reveal themselves as darkness falls, stars that have always shone upon her but never as brightly as they do now.

The most seasoned of the crew is one Ezekiel Moore. He is as wrinkled as a walnut, wisps of white hair shooting from his scalp, and the way Anne looks up into the night sky, transfixed, stirs a fierce protectiveness in him. Ezekiel had a daughter once, lost to time, and he fancies a similarity in Anne against the blue-black of the sky.

He settles himself on the deck, lights up a pipe and speaks once the tobacco has caught and pale blue smoke rises.

'I can tell you more about them if you like? The stars. There's more to the sky than you'd think.'

After a moment of hesitation, she nods and moves closer to join him, sitting cross-legged just as he does, transfixed once again by the star-studded sky.

Ezekiel tells her that the stars belong together, and points at the constellations: the bow and arrow of an archer, the paw of a bear, the pole which anchors them all. Anne cannot remember having seen them before, but the patterns fall into place before her and she reframes her world beneath the shimmering sky, dotted with stories.

'And the brightest, that is your Pole Star. Look out for him and you'll be all right. Now isn't that a thing?'

As the days pass Anne is happy to spend her time on deck, as far away as she can be from James Bonny and his overwhelming self pity. And she is learning. Ezekiel shows her how the stars can be used to navigate, tracing patterns in the air with roughened fingers, weaving stories and tales from the night. She listens and watches carefully, willing herself to absorb this information, to keep it safe.

'Such a pretty girl – you've no reason to be on your way to a place like New Providence.'

She turns to the sea-worn face, sees the moon reflected in his eyes. 'We must always be on our way to somewhere.'

He considers it for a moment and then roars, for 'laughter' does not do the sound justice. 'Pretty and a philosopher. Now there's a dangerous mix – god help your husband.'

She turns away again, eyes flickering upwards, and addresses the sky.

'God needn't worry himself on my behalf.'

Chapter 4

The journey continues and a sea change takes place in Anne. The salt air calms her. The shriek of gulls is music. The fall and tilt of the ship as it makes its way across the restless ocean become her core, balance shifting so her bare feet are planted on deck as if she were a tree grown from it.

She becomes familiar with the shifting colours of the sea, from blue to silver to black, and the play of light upon it from sun, moon and cloud. She begins to understand it too as the long days stretch one into another; learns to listen, to sense its mood, and is shown how to respond with sail and tiller and wheel, for she has made it her business to learn from the willing crew. And she is good.

Anne begins to know the ship: the groaning complaints as it powers over the fathoms of water beneath, the demands for attention that are met with scrubbing, scraping, oiling, and patching by the patient crew, as attentive as a mother to a newborn. She has taken to wearing trousers and a shirt bought from the ship's carpenter, for they are more practical to scale masts than dresses ever were, drawing amusement but never direct comments from the crew. There is something about her that prevents it.

James has also spent his time productively, slumping into a depression which he self-medicates with plentiful quantities of rum. He has barely spoken to his wife on this their first (and last) trip together, watching her sullenly through bleary eyes as she learns her new trade of sailor.

But, for what it's worth, she remains honest to her marriage vows.

Her skin takes on a red tinge, which tips over to a freckled nut brown in its unaccustomed exposure to the sun, tightening and peeling, until her old skin sheds like a snake. Her hands and feet have begun to toughen too from exposure to rope and wood, so that it is inconceivable she ever travelled anywhere other than barefoot.

Anne has almost forgotten that there is an agreed end to this journey when New Providence reveals itself through an unseasonal mist.

'Landfall ahead!'

Her heart becomes a stone, the clouds slowing above and shutting out the sun momentarily. There is a reluctance as she remembers herself, and why she is here. In poor temper, Anne searches out her drink-sodden husband, a sorry sight in the same clothes he left in, tucked tightly behind a coil of rope, hands wrapped just as tightly around the neck of a bottle.

'I had thought you might make yourself useful.' Her voice is free of softness.

'Then you thought wrong'.

He takes another swig, each now wordlessly daring the other to react. Neither does and they continue to glower at one another in silence as the ship slips into harbour.

The sounds of the sea are swallowed by the urgent noise of civilisation – yells and shouts from ship and shore, the groans and scrapes as the ship meets shallow water, the high-pitched calls and cackles from rowboats as the local ladies of a certain persuasion offer themselves up to fresh meat. The anchor drops and pulls them to a halt. There is a sudden flurry of activity, jobs to be done, cargo to be readied for offloading, the crew going about their business as they always do.

Anne stands to the side, watches as busyness flows around her, an imp of worry on her left shoulder talking of hardship, of want, and of the simple decision to return to Charles Town with all its wealth and comfort. She listens momentarily, before she shoos it away like a fly, for backwards is not a direction she likes.

The ship is soon a waking dream as the newly-weds find themselves back on land, their sea legs uncertain, unused to stillness after so long. Mister Bonny's continuing inebriation hardly helps.

They have little luggage, for Anne has exchanged her mother's pearl earrings for a shawl and a few necessities to make her journey and immediate future a little more comfortable. Most of the remaining credit James has pissed out long since, so they are travelling light. She once again wears the dress she fled in, it feeling strange now for it belongs to another life she has left far behind. Anne has kept the trousers and shirt for they speak of far more than a brief voyage now ended, and packs them up in the shawl for safe keeping.

New Providence is not South Carolina, that much is clear. It may no longer be a pirate port, but it is far from polite. Their first impression is of urgent chaos as men, women and cargo are offloaded, boarded or traded. The town is indifferent to them, noise and stink rising as the sun arcs overhead, the searing heat raising sweat and tempers, dust billows up in clouds as the swarm of people and animals go about their business together in narrow streets that close in around them. The town would swallow them whole; their wits are the only thing between them and it. Lucky that Anne has enough for them both.

She clutches a piece of paper with the name of a tavern – a parting gift from Ezekiel Moore – telling her of the place that will put a roof over their heads for the last few coins she has left from her stolen dowry.

She and James make their way down a darkened alleyway, he several steps behind, past a butcher's shop, where a thick pool of blood and miasma of flies line their way. They push through a cluster of painted women touting their wares half-heartedly in the sickly heat and take directions from a one-legged beggar to the Lucky Dog tavern, buried in the winding backstreets. The inn is rickety from neglect, its lurching gait matching her husband's. Anne, grim-faced, holds on to her remaining coins.

A few boards bound together serve as a door, and Anne pushes it open and steps inside. The place is busy with a glum crowd, the landlord barely looking up from his tankard as he listens to her request for lodging and shows them to a tiny room upstairs. It is gloomy despite the blazing sunshine outside, the floorboards creaking, the noise reminding Anne of the ship and so giving her some small comfort.

'You're lucky – it only became available this morning – the last lodger died in his sleep.'

Anne looks briefly alarmed as the landlord moves to reassure her.

'Only knife wounds – nothing catching. God rest his soul,' he adds hastily, to show his respect. He has rented rooms to the dis-possessed for years and knows they have no other choice if they have ended up here.

Anne glances around the tiny space. It's somewhere she would not have let a dog sleep before, but she is tired and there is always tomorrow to find somewhere better.

'We'll have it. But we will need new straw for the mattress.'

He huffs at this unreasonable demand – the blood has long since dried in the stifling heat – but is mollified by the money she places in his palm before dismissing him.

'We will be down shortly for supper.'

And so married life for the Bonnys begins. James is asleep on the filthy straw before the landlord has pulled the makeshift door to. Anne surveys the space wordlessly, wondering what on earth she has done.

Chapter 5

James Bonny is sleeping off another gutful of beer in their tiny quarters, the miserable hole that has become home despite her best efforts, her money running far short of this town's demands. James is of no use to anyone, least of all her, and so she does what she has always done – she falls back on her own resources. Anne wraps herself in her shawl, leaves the tavern and walks boldly through the streets, familiar to her after only a few days, eyes darting for opportunity as she goes. Poverty is a novelty that has already worn thin, and she will have none of it.

A job is clearly out of the question, and she cannot think this place capable of charity. Anne does not have a plan as such, but she is alive to luck when she sees it. Ahead of her is a sailor, prodigiously drunk, his coin purse in plain view on his swaying midriff. She walks quickly up behind him, smells grease and gin as she unhooks the bag from his belt. She is clumsy and has to try twice to remove it, but he is too far gone to care, though the jostling knocks him on his backside, much to his confusion.

Anne walks away, flushed and breathing hard, fully aware that she has been watched by two street girls; but they see something in her – the pinch of hunger perhaps – that makes them turn away and mind their own business. They are all too familiar with hunger themselves, and if he is too stupid to mind his own property, then the fool deserves all he gets. They have seen nothing.

Anne feels better now that she has money again. She has not eaten since the previous day, her stomach hollow and grumbling at the uncommon assault. Food was always plentiful in her father's house, and it is the one thing she misses now, though she can feel from the weight of the stolen bag and the coins within that she will be able to eat her fill and have some left over for tomorrow. James Bonny can fend for himself.

Fate waits for her at the waterfront. She follows the salt nip of sea air and as the narrow alley opens up to the familiar chaos of the port once again, she sees The Mermaid Tavern, the smell of roasting meat reaching across the expanse with beckoning fingers.

The barmaid nods in acknowledgement and points to a table near the door, which Anne takes quickly, unusually self-conscious under the gaze of so many men who pause to look, making no attempt to hide their leering. She takes out a large knife from her skirts that she had acquired from a careless crewman on *The Betty*, and places it on the table in front of her, finding that this makes almost all the clientele lose interest in her at once.

The same barmaid stands before her, smiling.

'I was going to ask if you needed help, but it looks like you've brought your own.' She nods at the weapon.

Anne pats it. 'She and I will be fine together. Better still if you will bring me some pork and a beer.'

Her mouth weakens as she says it, and the barmaid leans close, her face softening.

'I'll bring you some bread too. On the house.'

Anne is grateful but embarrassed too, not being used to kindness or sympathy, and finds herself alone again to look around her.

The inn is a memorial to lost ships and dead sea captains who gaze down from their gilded frames, frowns frozen in time. Drownings, murder and occasionally old age have taken their toll on each of the painted men, their names crossed through in the great ledger in the sky.

Beneath them, the pewter bar they knew so well is worn thin, shining from years of perched elbows as drinks are drunk and the world, such as it is, put to rights. If you had suffered as we have suffered, they seem to say, but the living continue to drink, oblivious to their mortality, as the living tend to be.

There is an anchor, leaning awkward above the card tables, and ropes, fishing nets, rum bottles, and seashells as big as a man's hand strung up above as if the drinkers are under water. The place is strangely soothing.

A plate of stew and a tankard of beer appear before Anne, but it is not the barmaid who brings them but an extraordinary figure of a man, dressed for a carnival. His eyes are deep brown, set in a startlingly handsome face.

'It's not right that a pretty girl like you should buy her own supper. Please, be my guest. My name is Jack Rackham. Captain Jack Rackham.'

He places a stress on the 'Captain' and smiles to complete the effect. Without another word, he places the plate in front of her and takes a seat by her side, whipping the tail of his red coat out behind him with a flourish, the gold buttons catching what little light there is to catch in the place.

She has not taken her eyes from him and although he does not meet them for a moment, he is well aware of her attention, of the effect he has created.

'I should eat it before it gets cold. It is slightly more palatable that way.'

The eyes twinkle and Lord help her if she doesn't blush, dropping her eyes to the plate of already congealing meat in her confusion. But it is food nonetheless, and she takes up the spoon with undignified haste, cramming the stew and bread into her mouth as if each bite were her last.

He is surprised at the intensity of her attack, for she has not yet lost the bloom of recent privilege – her skin supple, hair with a sheen that can only be attained through determined brushing by maids. But the eyes are a little sunken, the face thin, and the looseness of her waistband tells him that food has become something of a luxury of late.

Jack assesses this with the practised air of a man who is alive to weakness; he has taken advantage of less. But there is something about her – a strength – that intrigues him, and warns him too.

It is not long before the plate is empty. She smears the last of the bread in the gravy dregs, stuffing it into her mouth as she reaches for her tankard to wash it down.

'I take it that New Providence has not been kind to you?'

Her eyes are guarded over the lip of her tankard as she drinks and lowers it slowly to the table.

'I am doing just fine for myself, and will do better still given time. I am deciding my next step is all.'

He moves his hand close to hers before noticing the knife and withdraws it quickly to rest on the table as if that was the intention all along.

'I have no doubt about it. And what will that next step be? I should imagine you would make a fine wife for a man.'

She snorts and turns her head away.

'I have tried that already. It is not all it is made out to be.'

He laughs and she turns back, annoyed, but he holds up his hands in surrender.

'I apologise – I meant no offence. But there are very few men worth marrying, as I understand it, and marriage is a state guaranteed to put an end to the tenderest of feelings sooner or later. And how long have you been in such a state?'

She looks as if she will not answer, but her face relaxes.

'Not two weeks, and here I am accepting food from another man.'

He smiles, as she does, and his hand finds hers, the knife forgotten.

'And I am very glad you did, for these hands should not have to see a workaday life. These hands should be put to kinder use – Miss…?'

'Bonny. My name is Anne Bonny.'

She is under no illusion what the 'kinder use' is he refers to, and she is glad of it. He has brought out the devil in her, and he has fed her, which is more than James Bonny has done. That he is a captain is no small part of this, for it speaks of wider horizons and adventure, while her husband speaks only of a filthy room and disappointment.

'So what, exactly, are you captain of?'

'Myself only at this point in time. I had a ship – a fine one at that – but the governor's pardon was too good an opportunity to miss. I was a pirate, if it should not shock a young lady such as yourself.'

It does not. In truth, it thrills her. He has her full attention now, her eyes caressing him.

'I should have hated to continue to offend His Majesty with my choice of profession, and besides, I like my neck just as it is. A rope around it would not suit me.'

She leans in, her eyes on his. 'So tell me – how many men have you killed?'

He looks surprised and smiles, his voice dropping.

'Now why would you think I should admit to such a thing as that? Should you not ask me instead of my lawful life on this island?'

'I doubt it would be entertaining. I should rather hear stories of pirates.'

He leans back, studying her, and is silent for a moment, but it is not his natural state. He cannot help himself.

'There are certainly plenty of stories …'

He leaves the sentence unfinished, a trail of breadcrumbs that she follows greedily.

'And has this new lawful life given you what you wanted?'

The tavern leans in to listen, dark and heavy.

'It is not my ship or my former life, that is the truth.'

His mind is clearly elsewhere, on his former ship, no doubt.

She knows she has him.

'And what would persuade you to return to that life?'

He surveys her like a map until his eyes return to hers.

'I might be persuaded by a woman such as yourself.'

She lets her hand caress his, lightly.

'And what is to stop you borrowing another ship now, save for your aversion to hanging?'

He is not used to being spoken to like this. She sits before him, pretty and dangerous, exposing the thoughts that have whispered to him in his sleep, like some she-devil. If he was a wiser man, he would leave; send her back to her husband to let what will happen, happen. As things stand, she is none of his business. But there is more to life than simply living it and she has reminded him of an ache that has never quite gone away.

'I have a room here at the tavern. Perhaps you would care to join me there?'

She does not need to be asked twice. They rise from the table, the barmaid winking with exaggerated knowingness as they pass.

Anne follows her captain up the creaking stairs, the darkness ahead pushed back by the lantern he carries. She is so close she can smell the warm salt smell of his skin. Proximity makes her shiver, despite the warmth of the place, and it is all she can do not to reach out and touch him.

He pushes open the door to reveal a room with cushions, and paintings, with a window open to the sea beyond, a dishevelled four-poster bed at its centre. She watches him place the lantern on the table, its wick spluttering, and turn to move towards her. Her lips parting in anticipation of his kiss, her breath becoming shallow as his arms enclose her. She enjoys the moment and reciprocates with corresponding enthusiasm – something that surprises and delights him in equal measure.

He wastes no time in unwrapping his prize, and she hers, and they fall to the bed in an awkward and furious embrace. Their coupling is fast and efficient, he boarding her with little finesse, but she is grateful that she is no longer hungry, and the fact that this man is not James Bonny. They are soon finished with one another and he rolls off her with a languishing sigh.

'Quite the thing, aren't you, Miss Bonny.'

She props herself up on an elbow, her flesh glistening, sweat-damp, in the lamplight.

'I think it's time you called me Anne.'

Chapter 6

It does not take Anne long to persuade him of a plan – she is as persuasive verbally as she is physically. She is right, of course. Once a man has stolen one ship, every ship is an opportunity in waiting, if they only have patience and a little luck. He knows of a crew – of course he does. The governor's pardon granting all pirates immunity from death if they give up their former profession has brought relative peace to Caribbean waters – and deathly boredom to those it cast into civilian life. It was always just a matter of time.

A pirate life stays with a man, is an urge that demands satisfaction. Jack will have little trouble in assembling a decent crew from the leisured men of New Providence with only a few murmured conversations, he is sure of it. His master and quartermaster first, and the rest will follow.

The governor could not have imagined that the lawful and proper environment he has created is so close to moral collapse. It has taken only a woman like Anne – though she is quite a woman – to plant the seed in the fertile ground of Jack's imagination. She is the spark to his tinder, and he is fully aflame.

As for Anne, she has found what she was seeking. It does not suit her to stay still, and the prospect of an ocean voyage with a man like Jack Rackham is everything she needs for now.

More dishevelled than she was earlier, she hurries from the tavern, promising with kisses and bright eyes to return that night. There is no time like the present, for she knows that enthusiasm can dull if left too long with reality playing upon it.

The streets seem different to her now. The people are mere bystanders to her urgency, she impatient as she pushes through the crowds, slowed briefly by the weight of them. Sweat pulses from her brow, streams down her back and her legs, forming rivulets with the juices which flowed from her so recently, the tingle of it putting a steel in her heart for what she is more than happy to do.

James Bonny is awake for once when she returns to their room, though he has not dressed and is slumped on the straw mattress. She takes this in in one cold glance as she begins to pull together her few belongings into a pile – a hairbrush bought from a pedlar, a pewter plate kept from her supper, a coat left over a chair by a distracted lady.

He stirs and props himself onto an elbow to look at her disdainfully.

'And have you brought your husband his dinner?'

His tone does not help him, but it is one he has learned to adopt in his self-pity.

Anne does not look up as she folds the coat into a pack and throws it across her shoulder.

'I have not – and will not be doing so ever again.'

He does not have time to reply as she flings open the door and heads for the stairs. Limp and useless, he stares after her – and realises at once how sorry he is that she has gone. He really is very hungry.

Chapter 7

The moon has hidden itself behind rainclouds, thunder grumbling overhead. It is a perfect night to steal a ship. There are twelve of them rowing through the drenching rain towards *The William*, a sloop and a good one if her drunken captain, John Ham, is to be believed. They have left the old man asleep and snoring face down on the table they dined at together, paid for by Jack in prior compensation.

There will be no fight, for there is no one aboard, and no chase, for they have left the town asleep, much like the captain himself. He has only himself to blame for the loss of his beloved, for his loose words and carelessness over such a fine vessel.

The presence of a woman has surprised the motley crew, for everyone knows that women are bad luck at sea. But they push this from their minds – they have committed to their captain, who must know better; and besides, this woman belongs to him. They keep their grumblings to themselves, for they have had a gutful of civilian life and its boredoms. They are ready again for adventure, whatever that might mean.

They draw alongside their new ship, the slap of water against wood the only sound apart from the cloaking thrum of rain. The youngest of Jack's crew, Patrick Carty, lassos a beam and undulates up the rope. He disappears over the side as the others gaze upwards at the hulk, until a rope ladder is thrown down and clatters against the side of the ship. Anne is first to ascend, the rungs, slick with rain, pushing themselves away from her in silent protest as she struggles to control it.

She pretends not to hear the sniggers of the men as she brings the thing under control, but is glad of the trousers and shirt she has changed into. The climb done, she hauls herself over the side, landing solidly on the deck. She feels the thrill of the sea once again, the ship moving in time with the waves beneath as if dancing, and of James Bonny left behind. Anne is free once again.

Patrick goes about the further business of ship stealing, the other men following quickly behind. It is only minutes later that a small crowd of breathless figures are stood alongside one another, the distance from Anne a chasm. Jack is last to ascend, appearing on the deck with an ungainly thud before dusting himself down and addressing the men.

'You know the drill. Mr Fetherstone – take four of the men and check for unwanted passengers. Mr Bourn – the anchor if you will. The rest of you – keep your wits about you until we reach open water.'

James Dobbins, a rigger, carries a bundle in his arms – a small black cat swaddled in a blanket. Now they are aboard, he unwraps her, cooing and speaking to her gently. He looks at her with soft eyes and whispers to her, though she is mostly indifferent, wriggling to release herself from his grasp until he places her on the deck. She disappears without a backward glance, slipping silent and curious below decks, where rats and adventure await.

The anchor is pulled in, with considerable effort, before the prow is turned toward open water. Slowly, the ship begins to cut her way through the waves, the land falling into relief in her wake, small and unreal as a doll's house.

There is no cannon fire for their leaving, no hue and cry. They have got away with it. The wind fills the sails of the *Revenge* (as she has been renamed, *The William* not suiting her new purpose at all), ready to take them far away from the complications of New Providence and out to sea.

Jack busies himself with the men, reviewing, repurposing and staffing the ship – a man to each task. It is only when the island slips fully from sight that they laugh and shout, the men smacking one another on the back, loudly congratulating themselves on their boldness.

The storm has headed inland, lightning illuminating the place they have left behind. As the downpour begins over land, the ship heads out towards the vastness of ocean, and keeps going.

Jack pulls Anne to him and kisses her hard before looking down on her face, shining and expectant.

Look what I have done! he seems to say.

That is all very well, but what will you do next? her eyes reply.

But he does not see it, and, triumphant, turns to watch the men, his crew once again, readying themselves and their ship for the great unknown before them.

Chapter 8

New Providence

The loss of *The William* is sorely felt. Old Captain Ham bemoans the theft of his ship and his livelihood to anyone who will listen, and those who would prefer not to. On finding her gone, he had torn his wig from his own head in anguish and thrown it into the harbour, where it sank, waterlogged, in the wake of the long-gone vessel.

Governor Woodes Rogers has heard, of course, the bad news invading the civil calm of his offices through the agency of a hesitant and whispering servant. The governor's verbal acknowledgement is not necessary as his quickly purpling face shows. With a heavily scribbled note, he sends immediately for his men so that they may all share his outrage, for he does not yet trust his voice.

Governor Rogers has seen active service; he is no mere penpusher. The battle-scarred governor lost the lesser part of his jaw and teeth twenty years since to pirates – a gunshot wound to the face that he survived, Lord knows how, so he has a personal score to settle. His face has sunken and scarred around the old wound, making him permanently sour in look, and the stuff of nightmares for those of a sensitive outlook. It suits him to be seen this way for it lends itself to the respect and distance from his colleagues that he expects.

He does not have long to wait as nervous officers arrive, knowing his temper and wincing at the anticipation of it. All the while, he feels the humiliating slight of the pardon thrown back into his face by Jack Rackham and his crew, whispering and taunting him as the minutes pass. It is a personal affront that he feels keenly, the details turned over repeatedly in his head. He will be a laughing stock, and he imagines Rackham leading sneering crowds in their disdain of him. He clenches his fists and brings them down violently as he speaks, wishing that Rackham's face was beneath them.

'The first ship lost in years, and lost to a pirate at that! The pardons for those aboard, I need hardly say, are void, and their lives are forfeit on the orders of His Majesty the King!'

The words burst from him in exclamation marks, and there is a respectful murmuring for their geographically distant monarch, heads bowed as if His Majesty might be there watching them from behind the curtains.

He will show them, he thinks, as he rubs at the place where his jaw used to be, the searing red of his pain visible as he closes his eyes against it. A common robber and pirate – he's damned if he'll let him get away with it – and opens his eyes again to the rank impertinence of Rackham's continued absence.

'A proclamation shall be issued this very day – they shall be known as pirates and enemies of the Crown and her colonies!'

He pauses, allowing the weight of his words to sink in. Only then does he lower his voice, the lower tone all the more unnerving.

'I will have him and I will make him pay.'

His men have no doubt, for his suffering has made him a monster, in more ways than one. God have mercy on Jack Rackham and his men, for you may count on it that the governor will not.

'My promise to the people of Great Britain – and to the people of these islands – was that I would keep these waters safe from common thieves like Rackham. We shall make an example of him, make no mistake! Where is Captain George?'

A whisper of a man with close-set eyes steps forward from the crowd, the man beside him jumping, startled to suddenly see him there. The governor himself is unfazed.

'George – I want you to bring me this man and his crew. We'll make a spectacle of it, of course, an event that will remind others like him that we are not to be trifled with.'

In his mind, he fondly remembers details of a favourite hanging that he itches to replicate – that of Captain William Kidd. The governor's connections had granted him a front-row seat to watch the devil hang back in London. The rope had broken and Kidd had been forced to mount the scaffold for a second time to meet his maker. He had lost his swagger the second time, by God.

Kidd's gibbeted remains had hung on the river for years afterwards – an ingenious flourish that impressed the governor so much that he has borrowed and imitated the spectacle of decoration – his personal contribution to law enforcement in these godforsaken islands.

'I could do that, sir, but I have it on good authority that Sir Nicholas Lawes, the new Governor of Jamaica, as you know, has a group of men on standby for just such an event. Might I have your permission to contact the governor, and his man Captain Barnet, about this matter?'

Governor Rogers winces visibly, for he does not wish to make his mistake known to such an elevated man as Sir Nicholas. But what choice does he have?

He smiles thinly. 'As you suggest, Captain George. Let us save our pennies and use this little task force of our esteemed friend. But I shall write the letter to him myself.'

There is suddenly a commotion towards the back of the room, all heads turning at this unaccustomed intrusion. The assembled men part to let through two soldiers who are dragging a bedraggled James Bonny between them. They release his arms and he slumps to the floor in exhaustion. He is considerably thinner since Anne left, for he has had to live by his wits, of which he has few.

Governor Rogers looks expectantly at the men as he raises his handkerchief to his nose to repel the smell of this newcomer.

'Well?'

The first soldier nudges the prisoner and nods towards the governor.

'Go on then—'

Bonny stays mute, looking as if he would like to disappear from the trouble he finds himself in.

The second of the soldiers kicks him, and he curls up into a ball with a small cry.

'Tell the gentleman what you told us or there'll be more where that came from.'

Bonny looks at his attacker with wary eyes before turning his attention to the governor, holding out his hands towards him pleadingly.

'You've got to believe me that I had nothing to do with any of it!'

The governor sighs deeply, for he often hears this from prisoners before they are sentenced, before they feel the weight and might of the British justice system that he holds in his hands. But after the day he has had, he is in a mood to play – a cat with a mouse – before he sends this creature to the cells.

'Nothing to do with what?'

'Well – the ship. Anne went with him on the ship – *The William*, Your Honour, sir – but she betrayed me as a husband with that fucking pirate!'

He clamps shut his mouth as he realises his language may not be entirely appropriate for the company, but he has caught the governor's illustrious attention. Perhaps this man has something to tell him after all.

'You're saying your wife has been abducted by Jack Rackham?'

Bonny gulps and starts again, tears welling in his eyes at the injustice of it all.

'She went as free as a bird, when it was my right to have her stay and deliver the dowry I am owed. Her father – William Cormac – owes me a dowry and I demand my rights!'

The exertion seems to be too much for him as he slumps back to the floor miserably. All eyes are on the governor, who is clearly shocked.

'Do I understand it correctly that you are the … son-in-law of Mr Cormac of the Carolinas? Do not lie to me, sir, for he is a greatly respected man and a friend of this colony …'

'It's no word of a lie. I was married to his daughter Anne not two weeks ago – and look at me now!'

His dander is no longer up. They have no choice but to look, and find themselves disgusted at the sight. The governor is ashen.

'And I am to believe that Anne Cormac has become a pirate? Of her own free will?'

Bonny nods miserably.

It is common knowledge that daughters of great men should embroider and give birth, not cavort with villains. What has Cormac allowed her to become – to first marry this person in front of him, and now to run away to become a common criminal?

The governor turns stiffly to one of the soldiers.

'You, man – get the prisoner a glass of wine, for he has almost expired. And something to eat – there must be bread for him?'

The soldier nods, confused by the sudden change of fortune in the man he has so recently assaulted, wondering how this will sit for him later when his superiors hear of it, while James Bonny brightens perceptibly at the promise of sustenance.

'You, sir – get up from the ground, for a relative of William Cormac should have more respect for himself! You are a disgrace, though we shall overlook it for now while you tell me more about your recent marriage. Her name is—?'

'Anne Bonny. My wife, if it pleases you.'

It does not please him, it does not please him at all. He cannot understand for a moment how a specimen like James Bonny can find himself married to the daughter of someone like William Cormac, but all in good time.

He turns to Captain George, grimacing.

'It seems that I have an addendum to my letter, George. We have a female pirate as part of this crew and the end of days may be nigh.'

The governor turns back towards Bonny, now sat at a nearby table setting about the newly arrived food with the manners of a pig.

'And when you are quite finished, we have some talking to do, Mr Bonny.'

PART TWO

Mary

Chapter 9

Plymouth, England, 1701

Mary's mother huffs, kneeling, her mouth full of pins, as she transforms her wriggling daughter into a boy. Her long brown hair has been cut away earlier to much screaming and will be sold (as all hair should be) for a few extra pence. The costuming now being done is a little more subdued in volume, thanks to the sugarplum Mary has been given to eat, the hard smack across the head she'd got for her earlier bellowing having had little effect.

Mary sucks angrily at the rare treat, eyeing her mother who kneels at her feet, doing her best to adjust her dead brother's breeches.

'But why do I have to be a boy?'

Her mother looks up briefly in annoyance. If Mark were still here, he would do as he was told. Though if Mark were here, she would not be on her knees, about to brazenly deceive her mother-in-law.

'Because as a boy you will have an easy life. Your granny's money will keep coming and you'll be warm and fed.'

Mary looks at her slyly. 'And will you be warm and fed too?'

Her mother bristles but chooses not to respond.

Mary is just getting started, the draught at her neck where her hair used to be pricking her into irritation.

'And what about if I tell her that Mark is dead and that you have told me to pretend to be him? Do you think she will still send money?'

She is rewarded with a sharp slap across her face that throbs hotly where the fingermarks show.

Her mother's face is suddenly directly in front of hers. 'Now you listen to me. A crown a week is a crown a week and let me tell you, you little witch, that there are other ways to earn money like that, and for the likes of you and me they are not pretty ones. Your granny doted on little Mark—'

Mary begins to whine.

'But why didn't she dote on me? I could climb trees better than Mark, and throw stones better—'

'Because …' She pauses, stabbing the pins with unnecessary force into a cushion tied to her wrist. She needs to make this plausible whilst maintaining her dignity. She cannot tell her daughter that her granny is not her granny. That Mrs Read the Elder has only supported them out of embarrassment since her son ran off to sea (easily done in Plymouth), abandoning his unwanted wife and baby son to resume a life of carefree adventure.

That said wife, abandoned and lonely, found company and herself pregnant again with a new and unexpected female burden that Mrs Read the Elder would take no time to realise could not possibly be her son's. It stands to reason that it must be Mary who is the dead child, for as far as her grandmother is concerned, she has never existed.

'Because life is hard, Mary, and things are not always as we should wish. But should granny ever come here, you are Mark, and sweet and not yourself at all. And it is better than us being thrown onto the streets, which would be what would happen to us. Is that what you want?'

Mary – or Mark, as we should now call her – screws up her face as a collar is put around her neck like a noose.

'But is it not a sin to lie?'

Her mother sighs, exasperated, and pulls the collar tighter.

'It would be more of a sin to kiss goodbye to free money, and that's the end of it.'

But Mary has not quite finished.

'But what if granny should want me to live with her instead of with you?' she enquires innocently.

Her mother snorts and yanks viciously at the collar.

'Then I shall tell her it would break my heart to part with you, God strike me down, so don't be getting any ideas.'

Mary has heard stories of her granny, a severe woman afflicted by religion, and on weight of consideration decides that she will play along for now. She sucks at the dregs of the sugarplum, scowling at dark thoughts.

Chapter 10

Plymouth, 1717

Mary is almost sixteen when the news comes that her grand-mother – or rather, Mark's grandmother – is dead. Her mother's eagerness at having the letter read to her by a gentleman of her acquaintance turns to dismay as she realises that the money is at an end. Mrs Read the Elder, being a godly woman, has left her earthly possessions to missionaries bound for Manchuria (wher-ever that might be), hell-bent on converting the heathens.

When the letter has been read and re-read (the gentleman becoming increasingly impatient; he has not come to Mrs Read to read letters), the abandoned widow sets herself to swoon and wail in turn, much to the gentleman's annoyance.

Their financial resources exhausted, it is less than a week later that Mary finds herself bundled off to work as a foot-boy to a French lady nearby, for Mrs Read is both enterprising and well connected in town. The respectable widow and her fine young son are well known to those who would offer charity, and once again Mrs Read has found herself greatly in need of charity.

Madame Dupont is sympathetic towards the younger woman and her son, for she too has been abandoned by her handsome sea captain of a husband in this most dismal of places. But her sympathy goes only so far, for she has had few outlets for her frustrations since the sharp exit of her beau capitaine, and she believes it to be her right that others should pay for the injustice of it.

Enter young Mark. The other servants are glad at his joining the sombre household, for they are happy to think that they have now taken their share of Madame's bitterness, and someone new will now be at the sharp end of it. A new toy for their mistress to play with.

Sure enough, whatever Mark does is received poorly. He is accused of carelessness, clumsiness, and disinterest – all of which are true, of course, but Madame sees it all. No mistake is too small for her to miss, or to comment on loudly in richly accented tones.

'Garçon, idiot! That is not how one serves soup. I wish to eat it, not to wear it!'

Madame punctuates every admonishment with a slap to the ear, and Mark thinks less than fondly of his mother whenever she does so. It cannot continue like this, and so he changes tack. He could, of course, become better at his job, but that is not what occurs to him first.

Mark has a way with words, for he has learned the art of flattery and deceit from the best. He decides to become more of himself rather than the cowed and servile creature his mother had encouraged him to be to keep the old lady on side.

Over the coming weeks, Mark is cheeky, and smart, winking at the old lady when he sees her watching. And, remarkably, it begins to work.

No one has winked at Madame for some years, and she realises with a start and tear or two that she has missed it. Not least because young Mark Read is rather handsome – in a rough sort of way.

Madame Dupont's frozen defences built up over so many lonely years begin to thaw in the presence of young Mark. Within weeks, she is seen to smile on more than one occasion, hiding the unexpected upturn of her mouth behind a fan. He becomes something of a favourite, and finds that the increasing ease of his life is greatly preferable to what it was before. Madame becomes less demanding of his services as footman-in-waiting, and he relaxes into this new world with pleasure.

With his status of favourite, the other servants begin to treat him more kindly, hoping that they too might benefit from Madame's increasing good mood. The cook ensures that he has his pick of leftovers from the lady's generous table, and the housekeeper turns a blind eye to the odd missing coin when he returns from errands with local merchants.

Perhaps Mark would stay in this position indefinitely were it not for a growing impatience to be up and at the world. Perhaps he would stay too were it not for a growing friskiness in his mistress that is inappropriate for her advancing years, a friskiness that can only end in disappointment for the lady.

He has managed to escape her fumbling at his breeches on more than one occasion. He is horrified to see that his mistress lets an elderly bosom slip out of her low-cut dress as she takes her breakfast in his presence one morning, coy and embarrassed, of course, that she has allowed such a thing to happen in front of such a young and virile man.

He all but runs from the room on the pretext of some remembered errand, frantic to erase the image of the bosom, great gulps of Plymouth air required to return a sense of wellbeing.

It has been a good enough existence, but this is the last straw. Madame would be greatly surprised by the content of his breeches, and his income come to an abrupt end. He cannot allow that to happen, for it is all he has between himself and the streets. And he has seen enough to know that the streets must be avoided at all costs. His mother will not help, he knows, and this is his chance to break with her for good.

Mark Read has always planned ahead, for life is not easy, and so the following day he takes the money he has been given for the vintner (for his mistress enjoys her wine), puts it into his pocket, where it sits snugly, and heads towards the docks. If it was good enough for the man he assumes was his father, a life at sea is good enough for Mark Read. Even if he is a woman.

Chapter 11

That Mary – or Mark – becomes a soldier is inevitable. She has quickly found that life as a sailor is a tiring one, and a poorly paid one at that. The ship's first port of call is Holland, where she escapes her obligation to the British Navy under cover of darkness, the lookout snoring like a farm animal as she leaves. She cannot help congratulating herself on her cleverness as she slips away into the anonymity of the port town and quietly takes a small room at one of the many inns for a day or two.

The following morning, news of Mark Read's absence makes the captain lose his famous temper. He sends out his men to hunt down the deserter, determined to drag him back to face his punishment to the full extent that Navy law allows, but he is nowhere to be found.

Mary lies low on Madame's stolen money until the hue and cry dies down and the short-handed ship is forced to leave port without her. Mary is beholden to no one but herself once again.

The money will not last long, that much she knows, so she must find another way, for poverty instils a strong sense of practical necessity. Hunger and want do not suit her. The comforts bought by her grandmother's money, and by the French lady with her wine and silks, they spur a hungry mind to solution. If that adventure is partner to what she needs to do, then so be it. She has never been one to shy away from a challenge, after all.

There is a war in Flanders – she has heard enough talk at the inn where she is lodging. Wars need men to fuel them, she knows well enough, and it is as good an idea as any.

Still dressed in her naval uniform and her mind made up, she approaches the recruitment tent in town, the officers smart in their army uniforms against the brown and greys of the civilians.

'Want a life of glory, lad? Well, you've come to the right place!'

They pour her an ale and are happy to spin tales of riches and honour that wait at the front. She declines to share her true name of course, but Mark Read is as good a name as any out here. It is not long before, dazzled and a little drunk, for the ale keeps coming, she signs up as a soldier.

The following day, she starts the long march to the training camp in the countryside with a ragbag of other recruits and is welcomed gruffly, as all young men are to the military. She is given a new uniform, a sword and pistols, and with that she finds herself a new home in the tents amongst a sea of eager faces.

She throws herself into the drills with more enthusiasm than skill, her energy threatening to take out the odd eye or slice a limb from those she would fight alongside, but her determination wins out. She practises long after her fellows have been dismissed from their training, lunging, slicing and parrying with imagined enemies with swarthy faces. If she is here to kill the Spanish, then kill them she will, whatever they are supposed to have done.

It is only a few short weeks in, her sword skills thankfully improved, that she is allocated a unit and sent to the front.

'Your time has come, lads!'

She is curious to get to it, though the long march towards combat is gruelling in itself. She is buoyed by her fellow soldiers and their talk of sweethearts left behind, wives abandoned and lovers yet to be found. They may march on their bellies, but their loins drive them on too, something she makes a determined point of closing her eyes and ears to when they barrack together at night.

A few days later, they know they have arrived, mud churned slippy underfoot, the unmistakable smell of blood and decay in the air. The horrors of war await, but for now she falls into line, is commanded to advance with her troop, and prepares for her first taste of combat.

She hears the battle before she sees it, with explosions of cannon fire, the metal clang of sword meeting sword a hundred times over, and the screaming voices of men in anger, in fear, in pain. The troop reaches the brow of a hill and they see what they have heard – Hell on earth – the valley seething with men fighting for king, country, money and dear life.

Blood and bile flow freely as men below are cut down like cattle, their comrades and enemies fighting on over them, stamping the dead and dying into the ground they will soon become a permanent part of. The few cavalry horses still alive rear up on hind legs, rolling their eyes at the horror and stupidity of it all, this great work of the master species that drives them forward into death.

There is a shout – 'Troop – advance!' – and Mary finds herself running hard down the hill, exhilarated, sword held high as she swings it down into the arm of a black-haired soldier no more than seventeen, he tearing his head around to look death in the eyes, his own wide with fear and pain as she wrenches the sword back up into his throat and cuts a broad red smile before he falls, heavy, to the ground. For a second, she pauses – for it is that easy to kill a man – but another of his comrades is running towards her, sword primed, and she is forced to dispatch him too, stepping swiftly to his left and plunging her blade up through his jaw into his head.

He looks startled for a moment before falling, with Mary almost falling with him, so keen is she to keep hold of her sword. She has to brace her foot on his thin chest to pull it out, the gore of it shocking her briefly until she reminds herself that she is a soldier now.

She wipes the sword as best she can on the dead man's tatty uniform, and turns back to the battle, striding forward to make her presence felt.

Chapter 12

Breda, 1718

Months in, and she has lost count of the men she has injured and killed. If she felt any trace of remorse, it is long gone now; she is numbed and efficient like the other soldiers of her platoon. Their numbers are depleted daily, the roll call of the dead ever growing, new faces arriving to fill the gaps they leave. She does not try to remember their names until they return from their first day of fighting intact, for she has learned the effort is wasted.

There is no elegance to war. Each day, cannon fire decimates the enemy before the men move forward and hack away at one another, creating horror. It is sickening, but she must survive. And so she does as they do, with as much violence as she can muster. And she finds she can muster a great deal of it, though the weight becomes heavier on her shoulders. Perhaps the glory comes later.

They fight for every inch of ground for someone else's cause. She cannot rid herself of the rough music of battle, of the explosion of cannon and small shot that play hellishly whether she is there or not. She picks her way daily through the dead, bloodied and still, lain in the same ranks and order as they had advanced. Crows wheel black overhead, before landing heavily, claws out, pecking viciously at unseeing eyes.

The dead bodies have no further need of the earthly things, so they are freed of the encumbrances by the men, human parasites all, who travel with the Army wherever they go. These lesser men strip the dead soldiers of clothing and belongings, their own finer feelings long since buried in the mud of Flanders, eyes as dead as those killed. But it makes for a decent living as they sell the plunder back to the soldiers, and the circle of life continues.

She avoids the infirmary tent, for the horrors there are almost worse than the battlefield: limbs lost, minds gone, open flesh that festers, exposed innards, the stench of decay cloying and sweet. She cannot bear to see it, so she closes her eyes and mind to it.

The detachment helps – it is a matter of survival. She has dealt with the deaths of her comrades in many guises each day, and it gets no easier. She marks off new names daily in her roll call of loss. So many dead, but she is still here, still breathing, still fighting as she needs to do. She does not recognise what it is, this slow creeping thing that lies heavy on her as she closes her eyes and sinks into its arms, thinking nothing as sleep blacks out the grim reality.

Through all of this, she has kept herself alive, has not become the scattered thing she might have been. She has not cut open her own throat as she has seen a man of her own platoon do when the living nightmare of waking becomes too much to bear. She has not retreated into madness as some of the ashen, stumbling men who hold out their hands pitifully to God knows what, the unlucky living. Her strength has saved her from the worst of it,

but she is still human. There are times when she has found herself
crying tears she did not know she had, and she wipes them away
quickly for she is a soldier now.

As it sometimes does, salvation comes in the most unexpected
of ways. She returns to her tent after another long day, filthy and
exhausted, to find a new tentmate unwrapping a piece of pungent
cheese that makes her mouth water at the smell of it.

He acknowledges her and grins.

'A present from my mother. We will not go hungry – you'll
have some? It's good.'

She sits down on her bed, staring at him, for her stomach feels
odd. It must be the smell of the cheese.

'I'm Arno. Pleased to meet you – your name?'

She has to think for she seems to have forgotten it, though
perhaps she will find it again in his eyes, deep blue and fringed
with long lashes. She cannot remember seeing such long lashes on
a man before.

'Do you speak English?' Arno nods, uncertain, willing her to
speak, wondering if perhaps his new bunkmate is deaf, or simple,
until she suddenly remembers herself.

'Oh – Mark. My name is Mark Read.'

He grins and her stomach flips over. It is not the cheese.

'Pleased to meet you, Mark. You can tell me about yourself
while we eat.'

Over the coming days, she is forced to acknowledge that she
does not feel for him as a fellow soldier feels. Arno is an oak tree
of a man; his face is kind, his nose broad, his smile lopsided, and
he talks to her of his mother, of the cows on their farm, of his
hopes of a buxom wife and wholesome family if God wills it. She
has almost forgotten herself as Mary, but as she watches him talk,

drawn to the shape of his mouth, a kernel of something buried forgotten inside her breaks open and blossoms.

It is accompanied by an inconvenient stirring in her loins. She is appalled, for she knows that a soldier cannot do this. A soldier must show discipline. Though she cannot help seeing that his shoulders are a sculpture, and his lips … She gives in, of course, as warm blood courses through her veins, and to certain other places too whenever she thinks of Arno. Nature will have its way, and so will Mary. So much deceit and make-believe and she will be undone by her sex.

As a soldier, Arno is brave enough, though not so brave as Mary. She has stayed by his side, fierce and protective, for days of fighting before the inevitable happens.

He had almost died that day, she stepping in before him and taking a blade to the thigh before he carried her to safety. A mere flesh wound, as luck would have it, that is soon bandaged, and Private Read dismissed back to his tent. They are tired, but grateful to be alive.

Mary has been powerfully reminded that the threat of death is ever near, and the urgency of living a real one. Her feelings, she accepts, are far from comradely as she watches Arno undress by lamplight, the glow caressing his bare chest, the muscular shoulders, the curve of his perfect backside. There is only so long she can bear it. And there is no time like the present.

Mary begins to undress, but not secretly as she has done to date.

Arno has assumed that Mark Read was particularly shy, but what is that to him? He has no interest in seeing another man naked. He is therefore confused at this sudden change of heart, but more confused still to see that Private Read has breasts – and then, as he lowers his breeches – praise the Lord! – he has other corresponding parts too.

Arno drops to his knees in supplication before this vision, ready to grab her – for it is definitely a her – by the quivering buttocks for balance as he investigates this delightful surprise. But she places her hand against his forehead, holding him at a tantalising distance.

'You will see that we cannot continue to be bunkmates as we were, but what you see before you is for my husband only. It is only fair that you inspect the goods, but what do you say?'

As proposals go, it lacks romance, but he would say anything at this precise moment, would run barefoot through the battlefield unarmed to find a priest from somewhere – anywhere – for a soldier starved of female company is nothing if not committed. He would go this very moment, but that would mean tearing his eyes away, and he has no intention of doing that. And then a flash of inspiration.

'In the morning – the captain maybe?'

She smiles as he nods eagerly and asks hopefully.

'A little taste?'

She does not try to stop him as her future husband sinks, grateful, into her thighs, and sighs as she thinks of the wedding to come, and the faces of her platoon when they realise that she is Mary once again.

Chapter 13

The unexpected announcement the following morning sends her platoon into uproar, a festive spirit to rival any Christmas, as the captain, having quickly recovered from his surprise, promises extra beer rations for the men, and a fresh egg each for Mary and her Arno. They have taken the news well, the men, that one of the best of them has been a woman all along, whilst some wonder wistfully why they could not have the luck to have been Mark Read's tentmate.

Arno is impatient to be wed, for Mary will not consummate their union until she is legally married in the eyes of God. The captain good-naturedly holds the ceremony, saying that he hates to see one of his best men lost to marriage, but if she will insist on marrying her Flemish boy, then so be it. There is a great deal of laughter at this, with much back slapping for the newly married man, and cheering too.

Mary smiles demurely at her new husband, clasping a bouquet of daisies that has been found by the men that morning for her, miraculously spared from the mud of the battlefield. Arno kisses his new bride with enthusiasm and hastily sweeps her away to make their union official, to the cheers of the troop.

There is no question of Mary continuing to fight, of course, for now she has exposed herself as a woman, propriety must prevail. But the captain is a good man, and is genuinely sad to lose her. He and the men make a collection for her and her new husband – a modest sum but honestly meant, and enough for the newly-weds to put a down payment on an inn near Breda Castle. The Three Trade Horses will serve as winter quarters for the regiment, and is close enough to serve men going to or returning from the front, where Mary can bring them beer, comfort, and home-baked pies.

It is the first home she has had of her own, and Mary grasps it to her heart. It is a simple building, dark wood panelling throughout, but is a miracle after all that she has been through. Mary loves it from the first moment.

The inn is more than either of them could have hoped for, and she and Arno run through the few rooms wide-eyed, dizzy with their good luck. It will take work, of course, but they have one another and perhaps this is what happiness looks like.

It is remarkable that she has come out of her previous life mostly intact, but for a cut sinew in her hand, shot wounds to her thigh and a tattered ear from a shrapnel fragment. Her ears ring too from the noise of cannon fire, and will ring for a long time to come, but they have left the battlefield behind.

It takes time to adapt to this new peaceful life, not least because of the new encumbrance of skirts that she has to learn to wear for the first time now she is a woman. They are a ridiculous invention, and Arno has to contain his laughter as she practises walking, face clouded in ill temper and concentration, her legs stifled by bunching petticoats, floor-length hems ready to trip her and break her neck as she barges into stools and sends tankards flying.

'I am taking up more space than I should for all the wrong reasons,' she tells him, scowling, and he can contain his laughter no longer.

She still finds herself waking at noises in the night, reaching for her pistol by instinct. But slowly, slowly, with Arno by her side, kissing her neck as she works in the kitchen, becoming fatter on civilian rations, she begins to breathe again. Her breathing slows, and the headaches stop. Mary has kept the secret of herself for so long that it takes time to remember what she once was. Arno helps, soft and patient, as she emerges from the habit of so many layers of deceit. Her new life is a good one and she will not need to hide herself or to lie to him. Every day is a blessing.

She misses her old troop, but sees familiar faces from time to time, catches up on news, of those dead, or hurt, or gone mad. The sadness is tempered by this place of her own, where she works with Arno, who falls to the work as if he had been born to it. There is a contentment here that she has never felt before, being busy, offering comfort to those in need, of providing something worthwhile. The inn sees a steady flow of soldiers who have heard of this strange woman who served as a soldier, and want to see her for themselves so they have something remarkable to tell their friends. They are not disappointed.

'Mark Read I was, and Mary Read I now am. One and the same!' she tells them all, her pitch practised and polished over time.

To feed her customers as they deserve, Mary has made herself the mortal enemy of chickens and pigeons. Her own livestock serve her well enough, but pigeons have learned quickly to avoid her on her outings, armed as she is with pistols, a good eye and better aim. She returns each morning, hessian sacks weighed down with plump bodies of dead birds that she sets about plucking and gutting with gusto.

She has a recipe handed down from Arno's mother (her own mother having been unfamiliar with kitchens), and she employs her untested domestic skills for the benefit of her patrons each day. It is unfortunate that she is a terrible cook. The pies are nasty, the pastry tough and burnt, a challenging chew to it, but they are hearty at least. The soldiers have little choice, and it is just as well it is not the food that brings them in.

Arno is sad each time she begins to bleed each month, and she is sad for him. He kisses her and her belly, and says with great seriousness that they must try harder.

'And how much harder?'

She is all innocence, his face breaking into a lopsided smile as she bunches her skirts in her hands and runs shrieking – though not so fast that he can't catch her.

And then, afterwards, as they lie together, content, he laces his fingers through hers and looks into her eyes, searching.

'It will be all right. Everything will be all right.'

She wants to believe him, but it is a dream of a happy life and cannot last.

It is only months into this great adventure that Arno falls sick with a fever, brought from the front no doubt by one of the men. It is a cough at first, then exhaustion that sends him to his bed. He is not easily stopped, and she knows then to be worried. As she watches him laid low, she feels a terror that she has never felt before.

She grasps his hand to her heart.

'Don't leave me. For God's sake, don't leave me.'

He shakes his head, his face shining from sweat. 'As if I'd ever let anything take me from you.'

He thinks it is nothing, but Mary knows different. There has been too much good for it not to be balanced out by pain and loss. She watches the sickness take hold of him, beating him into silence, his eyes wild and staring. She sits with him, his hand held in hers, but after three days, he does not wake up at all, trapped inside himself as she whispers to him.

'Please don't leave me. I have never wanted anything but this.'

His answer is a thin paper rattle of inhalation, a rasp as the used air leaves him. Mary lies alongside him, her body wrapped around his, but he slips away from her while she sleeps.

It is too cruel, to wake up, to find him gone. Her Arno. She shakes him in rising panic, cold and lifeless, howls, and thinks she will go mad from the pain of it. She is still wild with grief when a passing neighbour, a farmer with muddied feet, runs in and tears her from her dead husband.

Kind but awkward, the stranger tries to calm her until finally, finally, she slumps back, panting from the exertion of it, the bed covers pulled around her in protection.

'I could not keep him with me. I tried, but I couldn't do it.'

And she falls to sobbing again as if it will never end, the man a helpless spectator to her misery.

Chapter 14

Breda, 1719

The grief is muscular and relentless, hitting Mary in waves, an invisible assailant. It sits on her like a blanket, taking her breath and startling her awake, panicked and breathless in the dark.

Arno is gone, and she is left behind. It hits her hard, over and over, an emptiness that keens at her like a starving baby. She pulls herself together as best she can and soldiers on as she has learned so well, for what choice does she have? She must continue to offer a temporary home of sorts for men in need of respite, or the oblivion found at the bottom of a tankard, until they are forced to return to face death once again in battle.

But the shape and texture that were her days before have gone. There is a flattening, the colours leached, the world duller than it was before. And she knows it is because the world, or this small part of it that knew him, mourns Arno too. But it is at least a comfortable pain, with her own four walls, and a fire, and enough bread to eat. Things could be worse, she tells herself numbly. And still the grief howls silently at her.

The officers have long since written the names of the fallen on the wall behind the bar for her, the list growing longer each month. The marks mean little in themselves, but she knows the names mean something to someone and so she bears witness for them, lighting a candle every night when she is alone again as if it were a church.

Now that it is Arno's turn, she asks the officer to mark his name with a cross beside it, much as he made his mark on her. And so, each morning and the end of each day, she can touch what she has left of him, a name on the wall that she cannot read.

She spends a silent moment with them all each night, her lost comrades, before she retires to an empty bed, placing her hand upon Arno's pillow before she falls into a fitful sleep with dreams of death and loss. If there are tears, they are hers to shed, she has earned them, but they leave her empty. The dark unnamed thing from the battlefield has crept into her bedchamber and she does not have the strength to fight it anymore.

Life continues, though it is ragged at the edges now. A new routine forms – as it always does – until it is Peace, in the end, that undoes her. Fewer soldiers arrive at her door, the slow trudge past of men returning home with their lives, at least, intact, some dead-eyed after all that they have endured. Before long, there is no one – to feed, to bring beer to, to swap stories – bawdy or otherwise – with the woman who was once Mark Read.

Within a matter of weeks, she finds herself for the first time alone in a strange country, an expanse of flat green land as far as the eye can see. There is nothing but silence. The emptiness gnaws at her as she peers into the bluest of skies, peppered by sparse clouds. She tries to push all thoughts of sorrow, hardship and death from her mind – and why shouldn't she try? They will find her again soon enough, and she will be ready for them. Men may have their strengths, but Mary more so.

And so, with her money dwindling, and only ghosts left behind to keep her company, she kisses the name of her dead husband one last time, says a silent prayer for the lost souls of fallen comrades, and closes the door of her tavern for good. She does not look back – it's not in her nature – and, walking, heads towards the nearest port, her eyes bright with unshed tears. She has a mind to try her hand again at sea, and has kitted herself out in her husband's old clothes to do it. They will let her travel unremarked, and besides, men's clothes suit her remarkably well.

Chapter 15

For now, a low weather front of depression presses at Mary's temples and whispers dark things to her as she tries – and fails – to sleep. She is sure she has begun to see her dead husband sit silent in the shadows when she stops to rest, a wrenching reminder of her loss. Without him, the darkness sings, what does she have? And she has no answer for it, just this strange feeling of sinking, of her mind blank and brooding.

The moon is swallowed by black clouds, and she forces herself wearily to her feet. If her own thoughts will not leave her be, and sleep refuses to come, she may as well press on towards the sea. But it will not give up on her so easily, and she feels the dark, dragging thing follow her. She walks faster, thinks that if she moves fast enough, she may leave it behind, but he is persistent. The black dog of her mental torment paces himself, knows that there may be hours or days at a time when she is lighter and thinks that she is free of him. But he will be there still, and she will feel his breath on her neck, and she will sink again.

So on she goes, one foot in front of the other, resting only when she becomes too exhausted to continue. She thinks of Arno, for he is always there when her eyes close, a terrible comfort, for she will never hold him again.

It takes days – she is not sure how many – but soon the clean salt smell of sea air, familiar and long missed, greets her before she reaches the port. It is a kind of hope. And when she finally arrives at the port town, its dense hub of buildings and bustle of people a welcome relief after her long and solitary walk from Breda, it is easy enough to secure work.

There are several wigged men at desks, sat in front of their ships, and she chooses the youngest of them, a man of perhaps thirty who sits frowning at the ledger in front of him.

'I am looking for work on a ship.'

He looks up at her, surprised. He had expected to send out some of his crew to cosh and drag back the drunk, the stupid and the unlucky to man his ship, but their work will be lighter by one by the looks of things.

'Have you worked at sea before now?'

She nods. 'I have, but most recent I was a soldier in Flanders. I expect it will be much the same.'

He is delighted to find an experienced man, and encourages her to make her mark quickly on the ledger before she changes her mind.

'And your name, sir?'

'My name is Mark Read.'

He stands and shakes her hand.

'Welcome aboard, Mr Read. You are now a crewman of the English Navy ship *Margaret*.'

And so she finds herself a common seaman once again, and she sees the truth of her new arrangement soon enough. The pleasantries of recruitment over, the unpleasantness of daily life in the Navy begins. The others cannot believe she came willingly ('You're out of your mind, man'), for the press gang came for them, finding themselves sobering up on the deck of a ship far away from port. It is the only time most of them will curse their drinking, their oaths of teetotalism wrung out of them by the anguish of forced work and temporary sobriety.

She keeps herself to herself, for they are a motley crew, a sorry lot, for who else would be found drunk and senseless in port towns after dark? A sullen discipline is soon established as they are held in check by threats of beatings and worse. The threats would happily be followed through too, handed out by the captain and his senior officers, less sadists, of course, than obedient servants of His Majesty the King.

Mary – or Mark, as she is once again – is a good enough sailor, for she has become accustomed to military discipline, and so escapes the sharp end of Navy life. It is a strange relief, to be barked at, to be given tasks to complete, to hand over responsibility for herself to something bigger. She keeps her head down, tries not to think of the man she left behind in the cold Breda soil. It is easier during the day, but at night he creeps into her thoughts unbidden, her black dog with them too, whispering to her of loss and the end of love.

'Where did you go to, Mary? When you said you'd never leave me ...'

It pulls at her, though she tries not to give in. Her only thought now is to get herself to the New World, to start all over again, but she knows that to do this she must keep the secret of herself from her fellow crew.

She has found quickly that the confines of a ship are harder than a battlefield to keep herself disguised. There are no latrines here to slip away quietly to, but an open hole at the heads. She tries not to look at the rise and fall of water passing swiftly below as she feels dizziness take her, but once seated, it is both bracing and a relief to give in to nature's needs. But it is risky, and she cannot afford to be found out as a woman.

She has spent a day holding herself to bursting, until darkness when she comes up with a plan. She breaks her silence to barter for a piece of horn that she covers with a scrap of leather, fashioning it into a detachable thing that she can piss through. There is such a satisfaction in it that she wonders how she ever did otherwise, and the crew learn to avert their eyes when Mark Read pisses, for he is unnecessarily showy, whistling as he does so.

But only a few days later, she finds herself with a bigger problem still. When she bleeds, it reminds her that Arno did not get his rosy-cheeked boy, but also that she lacks rags to deal with her unwelcome visitor. To avert suspicion, she lets it be known to the gossip of the ship that she has the pox, and curses the imaginary lady of easy virtue, Poll, who had passed it on for the price of a penny or two.

She elaborates on their glorious liaison to the great entertainment of the men. The crew accept it, of course, for who has not known a Poll of their own, and grimace or nod in sympathy as they thank their lucky stars they have avoided the same fate. For those who have not been so lucky, she is welcomed into a fraternity of bleeders, each natural in their own way, though hers most surprising, should the truth be known. While the others scratch, curse and suffer, rotting slowly from the balls up, she holds at the ache in her belly, and whispers 'sorry' to a dead man.

And so, slowly, she begins to settle into this new way of life. The routine is useful, and she has learned the ropes. She was a better soldier, of course, but a wage is a wage and body and soul must be served.

The thing she misses most is fresh food, for she was spoiled with her pick of it in Breda. But food is at a premium on long voyages such as this, and what is available to the crew is far from good. Ship's biscuit is both plentiful and unpleasant, the other men showing her how it must be tapped against the table to get rid of the beetle larvae within before eating. ('They're only beetles – they taste better than the stew.') Even then it almost defies consumption, and goes down fighting every time, chewed relentlessly until finally giving in and slipping down her throat.

She swills it down as best she can alongside portions of salted meat at each gruff gathering around the swaying dinner table, fashioned from an expanse of wood suspended by sturdy ropes to the beams above. It keeps its balance against the swells of the ocean beneath, but it takes practice to get right. To stop food and drink spilling and running away.

Salted meat and dried biscuit give every man a powerful thirst and this need is answered by a generous allowance of beer and rum, the one aspect of this new life that shows generosity. The Navy has learned how to keep its crew in check, for a drunk man is easier managed.

It is almost three weeks before they reach the Tropics, and she has accepted her new life as it now is. She notices a shift in temperature first, the warming breeze unexpected as she goes about her daily duties. The colours here seem brighter, as if the sky has washed itself clean of European murk. Above them now is a never-ending blue sky, faintly streaked by thin clouds. The heat becomes a given as the days progress.

The unrelenting heat becomes ever-present, but it does not suit Mary at all. She does not know how to deal with it, for she has never known sun like it. She continues her duties as if she were back home, but it soon becomes clear this is a mistake. After a day working on deck in the full glare of the sun, she finds herself red-faced and woozy.

While the men laugh pitilessly at her, a kinder soul points her in the direction of the ship's doctor, a small man with a thin nose who peers at her through wire-framed spectacles.

'You must help me – my head is thumping and my skin is burning. What is wrong with me?'

He glances at her and allows himself to smile – a rare enough occurrence in his job.

'Welcome to the Tropics! An Englishman with English skin is your problem. The sun is fierce here and will continue to burn you if you don't keep out of its way. I should suggest you see if the cook can spare some pig fat, for it may help the blisters.'

'And if it doesn't?'

He smiles again, enjoying himself for once.

'Then, Mr Read, your will redden further, the blisters will burst, and then you will shed your skin like a snake. You may thank your country of birth for it. And for God's sake, man, cover yourself and stay in the shade as sane men do.'

Alarmed, for she has a vivid imagination and sees herself transformed into a monster, she goes to find the cook at once, a fat man with a bald head who does not look like he subsists on the usual Navy rations.

Mary barters for the pig fat, generating great hilarity, as her skin has reddened and tightened further, as if her entire hide had shrunk on her back, with she about to burst from it. The smell of the stuff that she smears over herself makes her gag as she tries to go about her business, miserable and irritable at the lack of sympathy and overt hilarity she encounters from everyone, leaving as she does pools of bacon grease and sweat wherever she works or sits.

She has decided that she does not like the Tropics at all, and who can blame her? As the days drag on, she experiences a kind of torture at the constant, inevitable sun. It does not relent and she finds herself daydreaming of fog and cold and honest rain, for a lifetime in England and Holland could not have prepared her for this. The sniggers of her crewmates at her misery ('Might I warm my hands at the fire of your cheeks?') does little for her temper.

The unyielding heat finds its way into the darkest corners of the ship, thickening the very air, leaving her craving the cold of an autumn day, or the gloom of a wet afternoon. Without these familiar visitors, the days and weeks roll on together into one, the yellow brightness of sunlight straining her eyes. Even the evenings, with their slight relief of cooler breezes do little to pacify her.

But slowly, over a matter of days, the fiery red of her skin begins to subside. The easing pain means the balm is no longer needed, and so – to her great relief – she smells less of bacon. The experience weathered, her journey continues, as journeys do.

Mary has become familiar with the routine of the ship, the domestic chores, the friendships forged by close proximity, the rough camaraderie of mealtimes. There is a pattern to it all, as comforting in its way as the steady rise and fall of the sea itself.

They can travel for days without seeing so much as another speck on the horizon, so vast is the ocean around them, and she finally comes to find some comfort in the limitations of the ship, having made a kind of peace with the climate. She begins to think of what she might do next, to haltingly imagine a future for herself without Arno beside her.

It might continue like this forever, were it not for something else following them. Far out at sea, with nothing more than seagulls sighted for days, and a ship has begun to track them. It begins as a speck on the horizon, but as the hours pass, the distance between them shortens. This other ship is fast, Mary thinks. Something about it makes her stop what she is doing to watch.

It is close enough now that she can see an English flag, but every fibre of her knows that something is wrong. The skin on her back begins to crawl. Her instincts have kept her alive so far, and so she knows to trust them.

She leaves her post and walks quickly across the deck, approaches the forecastle uninvited and sees Captain Harker addressing a press of fawning officers. She interrupts, voice more high-pitched than usual in her apprehension until she remembers herself as Mark Read.

'We are being followed, sir. Should we make ready?'

She points at the approaching ship, her sense of unease growing. But while the officers watch her in amusement, the captain does not. He is greatly annoyed by the interruption of the excellent story he was telling the men, his face curling into an exaggerated sneer.

'Do you understand who you are addressing? I have eyes in my head, and can tell you that there is no threat from an English ship. But if you show such insolence again, you will be flogged for it. Now – back to your station, Mr Read.'

Mary does not doubt the threat for he is as cruel as he is pompous, and so she retreats back to her station as instructed. But discomfort stays with her, and she knows to listen to her gut. She watches the other ship and thinks of the sword and pistols stored in a sea chest below decks. They alone give her comfort.

Tam Weir, a young Glaswegian lad, appears by her side, for he has been watching Mary in her distress. His face is thick with concern.

'D'ye think we should worry?'

He waits for Mark Read's answer, for he likes and trusts the man. He is the closest thing he has ever had to a friend.

'I think we should, Tam – there's something not right. Get yourself to the crow's nest – it will keep you out of harm's way. But let's hope I'm wrong.'

He does not wait to hear more and scuttles off, panicked, leaving Mary alone to watch the approaching ship. Mary is rarely wrong.

It is not much later, as the other ship grows ever nearer, and hails are sent and ignored, that the captain's façade begins to crumble. Nerves show themselves as he paces, barks increasingly urgent orders to his officers, who in turn scurry around like ants under a spyglass. It does them no good, for by the time Captain Harker has accepted that the threat is real, a black flag showing a skull and crossed bones has replaced the Union Jack and the pirate ship is upon them.

PART THREE

Bonny & Read

Chapter 16

Jack Rackham has watched the English ship ahead through a telescope, and instructs the crew through Mr Fetherstone, who passes on orders and musters the troops.

Anne has had her instructions ('You will stay behind the men, let them fight, and you may join us only when it is over'). She nods at Jack, and he assumes her acquiescence. He does not know her at all.

They have taken smaller ships in the prior months, but this will be her first boarding. She can barely remember a life before this ship, for this one is as natural as breathing, and she is fully part of the crew. Anne has learned from their earlier raids, and now she is ready to join them. Firstly, there is spectacle to be created to intimidate and confuse the other crew before swords ever meet. The men dress themselves in their brightest clothes. Mr Howell pulls on a red soldier's jacket that he tells them all loudly was gifted by a former shipmate on his way to the gallows. The same story is told before every raid, though the others do not seem to mind, and he polishes the buttons fiercely until they glare and flash in the sun.

The other men tie bright ribbons and scarves around heads and sleeves so that the fabric will catch the wind, blurring and shifting their shapes into spectres in front of terrified eyes. Anne chooses not to elaborate on her usual outfit, for a woman with a sword is confounding enough. Jack is the brightest of them all, in his trademark red frock coat, kohl drawn thick around his eyes to emphasise the madness he will feign.

The *Revenge* has an advantage from the stiff breeze and gains ground against the ship in front, ignoring the signals sent with increasing urgency from up ahead. Anne wonders if they have any idea what is coming, of the chaos to be unleashed upon an ordinary day, and watches the pirates as they gather their weapons, draping themselves with blades of varying lengths, and multiple pistols.

She feels a sudden nakedness without one of her own and looks around until she spots a stray pistol laid on a barrel. Picking it up, she weighs it in her hand and feels a satisfaction in the cold curve of its handle. She slips it into her shirt without a word; if it had been hers, she would not have been so careless with it, and so it becomes hers by right.

Jack hands Mr Fetherstone a black flag with something approaching reverence.

'Let's show them who we are, Mr Fetherstone. It is time.'

The British flag is lowered and the black flag raised in its place. It is soon flying above them, a grinning death's head that speaks of what is to come. It is only a thing made of fabric, stitched lovingly by Jack himself, but it casts a dark spell.

Anne finds herself transfixed by it, an assault against the blue of the sky, as it looks down upon her with sightless eyes, rippling in the wind. She shivers, and for a moment feels a pang for the men they are about to meet, recognises the fear that this horrible thing is meant to instil. She forces herself to tear her eyes from it, but the feeling remains, the skull still staring down blankly upon her from above.

They are almost alongside the other ship now. It is bigger than their usual fare, but she trusts that Jack knows what he is doing. Anne sees the frantic activity of those men aboard as they – too late – try to assemble cannons and fetch weapons, having seen the pirate flag raised as a gesture of war.

She does not expect the lurch and tear of timber against timber as the ships meet. Ropes snap and sails tear, the sound terrifying and loud. And suddenly all hell breaks loose as the pirates roar, a cannon is fired, and pistol shots follow, grappling hooks deployed, a clamour as they howl like animals, teeth bared as they pour across onto the unprepared vessel, sailors scattering in terror, a few foolhardy men who try to stand their ground cut down by heavy swords, the air suddenly thick with the iron smell of blood.

And Anne is amongst them. She picks up a sword, swings it clumsily, for she had not expected the weight, did not realise there is a skill to it that she does not possess, and she suddenly finds herself face to face with one of the foolhardy few, a squat figure with a face of pure fury, who steps forward, sword poised to split her skull open until he falters, blinks and steps back, sword falling to his side.

'I'll be damned.'

There is something odd about the voice if she chose to hear it, but now is not the time.

Anne presses the blade slow and hard against the man's throat and forces him to his knees. 'That you will be. You'll regret having lowered your sword. Maybe I should slice you open ear to ear for your trouble, what do you say?'

Mary sees that Death has come to claim her in the guise of a woman. The pirate's green eyes blaze with the madness of battle. Her red hair hangs freely beneath a black tricorn hat and has gathered in sweaty ringlets about her face. And she is dressed as a man, just like her – a white shirt, ill-fitting and spattered with blood, breeches held up with a thick belt. Pistols and knives are strapped about her, but the sword is her biggest problem.

She is vanquished, and yet Mary's heart soars. To have someone try to kill her shakes the black dog from her back and wakes her from her slumber of grief. This is what it is to be alive – she had almost forgotten – blood pumping, breath ragged. And there stands her redemption – another woman, a she-devil, and why on God's earth is she here? – ready to cut her clean open. Mary begins to laugh, for the first time in a long while, and finds she cannot stop.

Anne pauses, mightily confused at this sudden change in mood, her sword held less certainly at this maniac's throat. Other pirates turn to watch this madman rock with his own mirth so hard that he falls to the deck under the weight of it.

Finally when the laughter subsides, and Mary remembers herself, wiping her eyes dry with a filthy sleeve, she looks up at Anne.

'What exactly is so funny?' Anne is disconcerted.

Mary is herself again, feels herself stirring somewhere deep and hidden inside. She had forgotten that there is more to living than not merely dying, and cannot for the life of her understand where she lost this shining thing. She recovers herself long enough to answer, shaking her head in amazement.

'You're a woman.'

'I am. And do you have a problem with that?'

The green eyes blaze wilder than before, and a blade glints at her throat. Mary shakes her head, still smiling.

'No problem at all.'

Anne lowers her sword and steps back to observe this oddity in front of her. Mary finds it hard to believe her own eyes, that there is a woman here – she has never seen anything like her! - and that she is clearly a member of the pirate crew. It beggars belief, but here she is. Though she has precious little experience with a sword.

'If I were you, I'd practise handling a weapon before you point it at a man. It's a dangerous business you're at, but stabbing yourself should not be the way to get hurt.'

Anne bunches her free hand into a fist, determined to do this madman some kind of harm, but Mary beats her to it, pushing the blade aside and sitting back on her heels to get a better look at this strange apparition before her.

Anne still struggles to comprehend this creature at her feet. 'Stand up. You have guts, I'll say that for you. The captain will want to meet you.'

And with that, the extraordinary figure of Rackham, like something from a carnival, appears, looking down on Anne's quarry.

'I see you have survived our Anne. I must congratulate you for it, for she is a fierce one.' He smiles stiffly, before turning to Anne. 'Though I see that you had forgotten my instructions.'

Anne glowers as Mary leaps to her feet with a lightness she had forgotten, and salutes. From the corner of her eye, Mary thinks she sees a shape like a black dog leaping over the side of the ship, yelping, before he swims frantically away, his head bobbing amongst the waves. *And good riddance to you, you bugger*, she thinks.

The rest of the pirate crew have lost interest and go about the important business of plunder as Jack looks her up and down.

'And your name?'

'They call me Mark Read. Able seaman. Not bad with a weapon either.'

'Well, Mr Read, I hope you shall join us. And we'll open up our invitation to the rest of the crew and see if anyone else cares to join us.'

Mary smiles. 'I shall be glad to join you, for you never met a more scurvy bunch of rogues and bullies than these. I am sure I will find your company more pleasant.'

She can barely contain her excitement at the chance of joining this woman and her crew. To sail with another woman – it is unimaginable.

Jack grins broadly, hands on hips, as Mary leans in to Anne, whispering loudly.

'We women should stick together.'

Anne is startled, but cannot unsee it now. She looks Mary up and down slowly as if to reassure her eyes before she begins to laugh. She suddenly understands this sailor's reaction.

'Another woman – here?'

It could not be more unlikely. It is thrilling.

'What an unlikely pair we are.'

Mary smiles, her body relaxing, and Anne suddenly sees the softness of the woman beneath the uniform. Only a keen eye would have found her out.

Jack has overheard and his brief triumph is frozen on his face. He did not see it, for he had not expected it. And besides, Mary's hair is cut close like a man's, her complexion grown ruddy and freckled under the relentless sun during her voyage to the Indies. But what can he do now when he has made such a public display of taking this man – or bloody woman, another of them! – onto his crew?

Harker's men have heard, of course.

'Sweet Jesus – no wonder we have had this luck with a woman aboard. It is unnatural!'

The old lag who spits this out has Anne's weapon turned upon him in an instant. His old age has been hard won after long years in the Navy, and he suddenly sees it all flash before his eyes.

'Unnatural you say, and yet here you are at the end of my sword as if it were the natural order of things.'

The proximity of the blade to his eye means he cannot avoid seeing her point of view, and he swallows visibly.

'I meant no disrespect ...'

'I couldn't care less for your respect.'

Her sword carves the air for want of flesh before she becomes bored of the game and turns back to Mary, who watches her with a smile. She is extraordinary. Anne had thought herself an aberration, but here is another just like her. She stares, and Mary stares back, an apparition that might disappear in a puff of smoke. But she doesn't. She is flesh and blood, and she is here. She should not be here, but here she is. A woman dressed in men's clothes – Anne has seen nothing like it – and it thrills her.

'And what should I call you?

'You can call me Mary. It used to be my name, after all.'

Anne cannot help smiling, a lightness taking hold of her that does not fit with this place at all. She has so many questions jumbled in her head and doesn't know where to start.

But now is not the time. Captain Harker, thoroughly defeated, is dragged on deck by two of the bearded pirates. His jacket is gone, worn now by one of Jack's men who is far too fat to wear it well, his shirt torn and bloody, his dirt-streaked face boasting a swollen and blackening eye. Anne holds a pistol to him, safe in the knowledge she will not need to use it.

Jack steps forward, stands astride, looking down on the defeated captain before grabbing his face painfully, forcing him to look at him.

'Hiding then – not a good look for a man. Not your day, is it, Captain – what shall I call you?'

The man looks at him through half-closed eyes, pain and the glare of the sun preventing him doing more.

'My name is Captain William Harker of His Majesty's Navy ship *Margaret*.'

'Well, Captain Harker, I am here to unburden you of your cargo. And you shall help me offload it if you value your fingers.' He taps his sword on the man's knuckles to emphasise his point. 'Now to allow my protégé to continue.'

Anne's eyes narrow as Jack turns to her again, his authority proven.

'Be my guest. What will we do with the prisoners, Anne?'

Irritation is clear in her voice. 'They can join us or be left here without provisions.'

Jack makes a show of weighing up her words. 'She's right, you know, boys. Though leave them enough water to see them through the day – we're not savages, after all. We must all strive to be fair and decent men – even the women amongst us.'

He smiles thinly at his own joke and turns to the defeated crew who regard him sullenly.

'My name is Jack Rackham. I thank you for your cargo, and you can thank us for sparing your miserable lives.'

He waits as if expecting a response, but there is none.

'We're to leave you in peace now, but we have carved out a fine life for ourselves and I have a proposition for you. Aboard the *Revenge* there's food enough to go around, a share of the spoils for every man, and enough rum to leave you senseless each day. If you want a taste of it, and are willing to fight, you are welcome to join our crew. Speak to this man here if you are game.'

He places his hand on the shoulder of his master, George Fetherstone. Having pointed him out, Rackham turns his attention to Captain Harker's cabin, indicating with a motion of his head that Anne should follow.

Tam scrambles with surprising speed from the crow's nest where he had hidden himself. Mary nods in acknowledgement as he approaches them cautiously.

'You'll join us, won't you, Tam?'

He nods, for he will not leave his pal, but confusion is written on his face.

'Cin I still call yi Mark?'

'My name is Mary, so call me that.'

The rest of the crew watch on, murderous, as Jack returns with Anne, his pockets suspiciously full.

Mary and Tam stand apart from their former crewmates, Tam taking great care to avoid their accusing eyes. Jack smiles at his dishonourable, eager face.

'Get what you need and come aboard. You're a pirate now.'

Tam moves clumsily under the cold gaze of his crewmates as the pirates strip the ship of all remaining useful items, from rope and candles through to food and drinking water. They work as efficiently as locusts, theft coming easy to them.

It does not take long, but Jack has not quite finished his performance.

'We should like to thank you for your cargo and for your belongings. Remember that you have met with Jack Rackham and his men, but that we leave you with your lives. We wish you a pleasant day – or at least what is left of it.'

He bows mockingly, smiling at his own cleverness, as Mary approaches, Tam in tow.

'And now we go?'

He nods. 'And now we go.'

Their departure is as sudden as their arrival. The *Revenge* is soon a speck against the sky as the depleted Navy crew, dazed and shaken, begin to pick up the pieces of the day. There is the grim task of swilling blood from their decks, and the sewing up of wounds. Their captain sits in a heap, head in hands, a broken man.

Chapter 17

'So yer a woman, then?' Tam Weir's face is contorted in confusion as he stares at Mary.

'Not much gets past you, is there, Tam?'

'But you were a man. And now yer a wo-man?'

Mary nods, barely suppressing a smile.

'Life is confusing, Tam. Best just accept it.'

He sets to processing this unlikely news as he and Mary follow their lumbering crewmate below decks. They make their way through the cramped bunks, the assorted belongings of the men, and newly stolen cargo crammed into the too-small space.

'This will do you.'

The man stops abruptly by a hammock suspended in the midst of the sleeping quarters and jerks his thumb towards it.

Mary takes the opportunity to leap into it.

'Good enough for me.'

He grunts at her, Tam stands staring at the back of his head, eyes level with the folds of a neck ingrained with greasy filth.

'Can yi tell me—'

But he is already gone, retreating into the faltering gloom beyond the lantern until only the suggestion of him is visible.

'Too slow. You know how this goes – just find yourself somewhere without a sea chest, and hope the natives are friendly.'

The young lad looks nervous, but Mary has already turned her back, eyes closed, for it has been a tiring day.

A number of the hammocks are occupied despite the early hour – the men exhausted, no doubt, by their recent exertions. Unfriendly faces turn to look at Tam, and he averts his eyes for fear of inciting some incident or other, his face flaming red.

John Howell, a large man with a huge neck, steps into his path, barring his way and bringing him to a standstill. He has led a colourful life, if his scars are to be believed: a deep zigzag from right eye to mouth makes it look like his face might split in two at any moment. He pushes his face into that of the boy.

'Bet your crewmates are gutted you're gone.'

Tam stammers, looking for words that aren't there.

A couple of crewmates watch on to see which way this will go as his tormentor cups a hand to his ear.

'What's that you say? You'd like to be buggered by me and the rest of us? You filthy little toad.'

The men laugh, and Tam looks as if he would like to disappear but waits for wherever this torture will lead.

'Leave him alone – I'll speak for him. If you want a fight, I'll give you a fight. Though if I were you, I'd take some snuff instead.' Mary pours herself upright from the hammock and stands her ground eye to eye with the scarred man, holding out a peace offering in the shape of a pouch. 'It's damn good snuff.'

He looks her up and down and leers.

'Another woman on board. Well Anne is spoken for, but you – not yet. I have some ideas on how you could make friends with us.'

She does not flinch, but squares up to him, her tone weary.

'I do not want to hurt you, but keep at things as you are and I will gut you like a fish.'

'Now that's not very friendly—'

He steps forward but is stopped by the unexpected tension of a dagger against his belly. Mary lets the blade nick the fabric of his shirt and scratch the skin beneath.

'Well?'

She places more pressure on the blade so that the tip of it draws blood.

He puts up his hands in surrender and steps back, a queasy grin on his face.

'No harm meant. It was just a joke.'

Mary lowers the blade without smiling.

'But no one is laughing. I am always armed, so my promise stands. And I have a short fuse. Just – as I suspect – have you.'

There is laughter at this and she leans in towards Mr Howell, who flinches.

'Now *that* is a joke. Now piss off before I stick this up your arse.'

She produces her old friend the leather-covered horn and holds it in a way that leaves little to the imagination.

Mr Howell wilts, but his crewmates are enjoying the exchange too much to let it drop.

'Take her up on her offer – for it will save John Davies the bother later.'

He colours and turns on his tormentor at this unexpected turn.

'I've told you before. We were catching rats.'

New voices from the crew join in this new sport.

'A strange way to catch rats if you ask me.'

'Jesus, we have eyes in our heads, more's the pity.'

'You won't catch many rats with the noise the pair of you were making.'

John Howell makes one last attempt to save his dignity.

'It's an insult to my wife's memory, saying filth like that.'

'Does his arse look like your wife's face? That would explain it then.'

Anne is stood unseen in the shadows. She had been ready to step in to offer Mary her protection but sees, with great satisfaction, that Mary does not need it. Mary can take care of herself, and will.

The crew roar with laughter and Mr Howell slinks off in an embarrassed huff. Mary watches him leave and addresses the crew.

'I am here for myself only. You will treat me like a crewmate and we shall get along very well. And if you have other ideas – well, I served my time as a soldier and could fillet any one of you. It is no idle threat.'

She puts away the horn, and pulls out the pouch once more.

'Now who will take some snuff?'

A smile breaks out across the face of Samuel Teague, a giant of a man, as a mallet of a hand reaches for the pouch. The huge fingers take more than a generous pinch and he shoves it up his nose, snorting loudly.

'It is good snuff, you're right about that. I thank ye – but why bother yourself for a gangling tripe of a lad like him?'

He nods towards Tam, who has shrunken back as far as he is able in the shadows.

'We've all been gangling tripes in our time, and I am paying my dues to the useless in the hope he may prove me wrong.'

Mr Teague slaps his new pal hard on the back, causing her to almost topple forward. It's all Anne needs to see and she removes herself silently from the scene.

Tam does his best to salvage some dignity for himself.

'I widnae git on the wrong side o' him. Even if he's now a her.'

He has confused himself again, and withdraws to repeat it more slowly, over and over, until it finally makes sense, while he is ignored by his new crewmates as they settle into a companionable silence.

The smell of food tells Mary that it is time for supper. She follows the smell, Tam trailing close behind as if trying to be invisible, until they reach the mess. Heft and malignance are everywhere. Fists like hams, necks the width of thighs, tattoos and scars helping identify the owners. But what did she expect of pirates?

Thomas Earl, the carpenter, and the doctor, Mr Mayhew, sit at the end of the table, absenting themselves as best they can from the general rabble. The noise of aggressive camaraderie meets them. There is no sign yet of the captain or Anne, though two dozen sets of eyes, curious and hostile, rise to meet them.

With as much indifference as she can muster, Mary takes her place at the end of a bench and reaches for a piece of ship's biscuit before motioning for Tam to do the same. Only when he is seated, sneaking into his place does she look around her.

Noah Harwood, the cook, sighs in annoyance and stands, his own food uneaten.

'I suppose you'd be wanting stew?'

John Davies, a bald man with folds of fat masquerading as a neck, speaks.

'She won't be saying that once she's tasted it.'

There is laughter around the table, the tension easing, as the sullen cook slops stew into a pewter bowl and pushes it in her direction. Mary nods.

'I'm sure it will be better than Army or Navy rations.'

The bald man's mouth gapes open, displaying the rugged landscape of his teeth.

'The King is taking women as soldiers now? We're more fucked than I thought.'

Mary pushes away her plate and stands slowly, her spoon suddenly an inch from his eye that widens in alarm.

'A decorated soldier. Now, shall we be friends, or should I scoop out your eye?'

There is no time for him to reply, for Jack and Anne appear.

'Getting to know this miserable bunch, I see. There's time enough for fighting, but let's at least wait until we've eaten. What do you say, Mr Davies?'

John Davies pushes the spoon away from his eye and stares at Mary.

'You'd have done it.'

It is not a question, and Mary does not answer. She takes her place again and spoons the stew into her mouth with an appetite that surprises her. It's a long while since she's eaten her fill of anything, and she's not one to pass up an opportunity. It's as bad as they've told her, but she's had worse.

She glances at Mr Earl, but he has kept his eyes down all along, as if he were deaf and his food fascinating. Mary recognises the hesitation, the refusal to engage, and decides she will get to know him better.

Anne sits down by Jack, the men wordlessly moving to allow them space. Noah Harwood places dishes of stew before them with more care than before as Anne meets Mary's gaze. They observe each other curiously as Jack speaks.

'We have two new recruits, lads. We have Tam Weir and Mary Read. And they are both welcome.'

There is a murmur of agreement, though hardly an endorsement.

Jack continues. 'They will work with us and fight alongside us, and they will take their equal share. We shall have our new crewmates sign the Articles.'

Mary looks up expectantly, and Jack obliges.

'Our code of conduct. Your signing the Articles will show that you pledge your allegiance to me and to the ship. And your right to a share of our spoils. You're not in the Navy now – we pay you your fair share.'

She and Tam look surprised but happy as Jack continues.

'Mr Fetherstone here is our master and shall put you to work tomorrow, but tonight we eat and drink.'

There is a lacklustre cheer from the men who continue at their plates, but Anne catches Mary's eye, smiling.

'Well, you are unexpected. I had not imagined finding another woman serving on a ship.'

Mary grins back, stew showing in her teeth.

'And nor had I. It must have been fated.'

They observe one another, eyes glittering as they drink the other in, but Jack does not like being ignored.

'Fated or not, you are welcome to our crew. You will be pleased to know that you are sailing with a captain who once served with Blackbeard himself.'

The good-natured groans and eye rolling from some of the men suggest this is not the first time he has told the story.

Jack holds up his hands in mock surrender. 'I know, I know. The boys have heard this on one or two occasions before. We have been together for so long most of us that there are very few stories left untold.'

Mr Harwood, the cook, speaks.

'You should tell them about Captain Vane, Jack – we haven't heard that one for a while.'

The men laugh, and Jack joins in graciously.

Anne leans forward to Mary, whispering.

'Jack led a mutiny and took Vane's ship. Cast him adrift in a rowboat, if you can believe it. Some of this lot have been with him since then.'

Mary's eyebrows shoot upwards.

'You were part of a mutiny?'

Anne shakes her head.

'Not me. I was never part of his previous crew.'

Jack continues.

'I merely wanted to let Mary and Tam here know that they are in capable hands. This crew has taken many ships, and we will take many more.'

There is a cheer at this, the men raising their tankards, for it is a very good toast.

Jack turns back to Mary.

'You will find us fair as long as you are willing to work. You said you served as a soldier? That's hardly women's work.'

Anne winks at Mary and cocks her head towards Jack. Mary nods in return and puts down her spoon to give her story the attention it deserves.

'I joined up in Breda and fought there until I let myself be found out as a woman. I was one of the best soldiers they had.

Not sure how many men I killed, but it was plenty. Just so you all know.'

She looks around the table with an unwavering stare, daring any of the men to contradict her, but no one does. She is clearly not one to lower her gaze for anyone.

It is Anne who answers.

'You were one of the only men to fight back on that ship, so I don't doubt it. Did you hear that, Jack? – a woman and yet a fine soldier too. Who would have thought it?'

Jack ignores her sarcasm and flicks his frock coat out behind him in an exaggerated show of disinterest.

'Then we must try not to provoke you, and look forward to your fighting our next battle on our side.'

'Thank you, Captain. You won't regret it.'

He realises he is not convinced.

It is lucky that Anne's curiosity takes over. She leans in.

'So what makes a soldier from Breda join a ship?'

Mary feels a stab of loss, but swallows it down.

'The war stopped. And my husband … died.'

She has not spoken about him for so long. The word feels awkward, wrong in her mouth. To her horror, she feels the prickle of tears.

Anne sees it too late, and knows that she has been the cause of it. Her voice becomes gruff.

'This is talk for another time. For now, we drink to you and Tam.'

She raises her tankard, glancing across to see that Mary has met her gaze, her eyes soft in thanks.

'To Mary and Tam!'

The crew raise their tankards and Mary is grateful for the small kindness. There will be another time to talk to Anne about Arno. She will make sure of it. After all, women must stick together.

Chapter 18

Waking from a deep sleep the following morning, Mary finds herself alone below deck, her hammock swaying gently to the rhythm of the sea. She jerks herself into wakefulness and tips herself from her bed, rubbing her eyes as she rushes to join the crew above. It has just gone first light, but the business of the ship is already in play.

The day has brought with it blue skies and empty seas. The men are at work already and she observes the assembled pack of cast-offs and undesirables that she will now sail with.

Jack sees her look around with something like dismay and seems to take pride in her discomfort. He ensures that Anne hears as he speaks to her.

'I see you are familiarising yourself with the crew. We were lucky to intercept a cargo of villains from Newgate prison – bred from the very filth of London – bound for the plantations. They were eager enough to join me rather than be worked to death for the profit of rich men. And the rest are old friends.'

He glances at Anne, for her father was just such a rich man, but she has grown selectively deaf.

The master, George Fetherstone, breaks off a discussion with the cook and approaches Mary.

'I've been told you have been with the Army. So I suppose you know your way around a cannon?'

She nods.

'Then we'll put you to work. It's been a while since they've had a proper looking at, so don't hold back.'

He leaves her to it, which suits her, and she is soon lost in the mechanics of it, and the smell of warm grease. She has kept her men's clothing, for who would go about this work in skirts, but no one remarks upon it. The unnatural has become commonplace for the men and they no longer recognise it as anything other than the way of things.

As Mary works, Anne takes to the rigging, hauling herself up through thin air, ropes digging into the flesh of her bare feet that curl around the rungs. And when she pauses for breath below the crow's nest, she surveys the ship below and the bustle of the crew beneath her. Her eyes are drawn to their newest recruit – another woman! – and she watches as the men keep a wary distance from her.

Anne is just as surprised that Mary is here but cannot bring herself to show it when she is with the crew. She has always sought out the company of men, other women never having interested her much, but Mary is not like other women. Still, she does not have a way to speak to her – she has not had the practice – and would rather stay silent than say the wrong thing.

And, likewise, Mary watches Anne when she thinks no one is looking. She watches Jack, earnest with his quartermaster, laughing and back-slapping with the men in his own world. And there is Mary, alone in an orbit of one, driven and meticulous, absorbed by her work as she goes about the cannon.

Some of the men eye Mary askance, suspicious, watching for some hidden motive in her application to the job. Perhaps she has religion, and that is the root of it. But there is none. The cannons are hers to care for, and she will do so as well as she can. Their lives may depend upon it after all, and she will not entertain distraction. There is time enough for that when the light starts to fade and the working day is done.

Chapter 19

Work for the day is finished and a cool breeze picks up as the evening draws in. Lanterns are lit around the ship as darkness closes in, and after they have eaten, the men are drawn to them like moths. They fall into their routines as they sit to play cards, to talk, to tell stories, and to listen to the music of the fiddle player, Joshua Hands. He plays a range of sentimental tunes, which please the men no end, move them even to tears, and he will sometimes receive a coin or two once they are drunk enough.

Tonight he plays and sings 'Lowlands Away'. His voice is sweet and the song well known, steeped in enough sorrow to stir the coldest of hearts. As he begins to sing, the noise on deck quietens to let them listen.

> 'I dreamed a dream the other night
> Lowlands, lowlands away me John
> My love she came, dressed all in white
> Lowlands away ...'

Tam has brought his pipe and tobacco with him and is puffing away happily as he watches two of the men in deep concentration at their game of cards. Mary, meanwhile, finds a coil of rope to sit upon, and leans back, watching the orange-red sunset.

Anne is suddenly stood before her. 'I need hardly say it, but you are not like the other men – and I'm grateful for it. I have been in the company of men too long.'

Mary nods.

'Much as I like the company of men, it has its limitations.'

Anne smiles, and Mary indicates that she should join her. Anne lowers herself to the deck alongside Mary like a cat, her ease and elegance showing itself in her movements.

'The guns have never looked so well as they do now, thanks to you. The crew are as work-shy as they come, though I hadn't realised how much until now.'

Mary thrills that Anne is here. She has so many questions, so many things she needs to ask her.

'I should hardly neglect the weapons that will keep us safe and make our fortune, should I? Though this crew is not like any other I've known.'

Anne cannot find the words to ask the questions she has. She still has so many things she wants to know.

'I thought that all sailors must be as lazy as this. You are showing them what work really means.'

Anne does not look like she has struggled in life. Mary sees that those hands are still soft, the calluses new.

'They are a sorry lot from what I've seen.'

Mary has seen the world. She has done things that Anne had never dreamed of, had never thought possible for a woman. She could have killed her back on that ship, but she didn't. Mary is remarkable, and Anne knows she is unworthy of her. It is not something she has ever felt before. She leans in towards Mary, her voice lower.

'I don't understand how you lived among men for so long without being found out?'

Mary drops her voice.

'There was no reason for any woman to be aboard – and most of them lack the imagination for anything out of the ordinary. And I was careful – I learned that in the Army.'

'I cannot think how you managed it. I know myself that there are … practicalities.'

'I should introduce you to my friend the horn, who helped me piss stood up like a man. As for bleeding – well, I let them think I had the pox. Wasn't on my own with that, I tell you.'

Anne laughs at the audacity of the woman. She is remarkable.

'This is not a conversation I expected to have at sea.'

'That would make the two of us.'

Mr Hands' song is coming to an end.

'And then I knew my love was dead.

Lowlands away …'

There is a smothered sob from Titus Oates and a smattering of applause about the deck before Mr Hands turns his fiddle to play a happier tune by far.

Jack is stood before the women, Tam Weir at his side. He nods at Mary.

'Mary. Yourself and Mr Weir are to join me in my cabin this evening. Food and drink to welcome you before we have you sign our Articles.'

Anne nudges her conspiratorially.

'Mr Harwood has roasted a pig. It's the best you'll have tasted.'

Mary grins.

'I like this place already.'

Jack walks across the deck, the women following. He swings open the heavy panelled door to his cabin and steps inside, his arm sweeping across the room. The smell of tobacco greets them.

'Make yourself at home. This is life at the Frontier, and we make of it what we can.'

The ship's master, George Fetherstone, is waiting inside.

'Our legal witness. To ensure everything is done fair and square.'

Despite his attempted nonchalance, it is clear that the captain is proud of his cabin and keen that his guests should acknowledge it. Although cramped – the beams of the ship closing in above them to narrow at the ceiling – the last of the day's sunbeams stream through a row of windows at the far side of the room, framing the shifting sea beyond.

The interior is obviously a working one – a sturdy desk, a wooden chest with a solid lock upon it, and a small rectangular table at the centre covered in maps. Every last surface is strewn with papers, bottles both full and half drunk, and random treasures.

The captain uncorks a bottle and drinks from it directly, the air suddenly pungent with red wine. Anne moves behind him to open a small creaking window and a cool breeze whispers in. Mary is grateful for the shifting air as she casts an eye over the haul.

There is a whale's tooth, a foot or more long, an ostrich egg of similar size, a gilt box and silver candlesticks. Loose gems in winking reds, greens and blues shine seductively in the low light, a gold ring with diamonds, and silver buttons. There is a small wooden chest bound in iron, the keys worn close at Jack's waist she notices, and Mary wonders what is inside.

Her attention is drawn by a 'Wanted' handbill that hangs on the reverse of the cabin door. There is a poor sketch of Jack's face, and a few words offering a substantial sum of money for his capture. Mary may not be able to read the words, but she knows what it is.

'I see that you are a work of art, Captain.'

He grins.

'That's fame for you, my likeness in every shithole in the Indies. Did you know you were in the company of a celebrated man? My mother would be proud that her son would someday be worth two hundred pounds. Would no doubt have sold me for it had she lived – God rest her soul.'

The affection in his voice is obvious.

'Well here's to your continued freedom, Captain!'

'Indeed. I'll drink to that!'

He pours a generous measure of claret into a crystal glass before he remembers his manners.

'Care to join me?'

Mary and Tam eagerly accept his offer, as Anne and Mr Fetherstone join them at the table, filling their own glasses as they do so.

'Got a thirst on you there, I see. Drink up while it's there, for who knows how long we'll live beyond today, eh? Don't let the bottle stand still.'

They raise a toast to that, but Jack has not quite finished.

'What do you think of that, then?'

He inclines his head towards what at first seems no more than a black cloth, but as he turns it over a picture reveals itself of a human skull with the grin of death upon it, sat upon a cross made of two bones. He is mightily pleased with the thing.

'The Jolly Roger. My calling card and my own design. We raise it so they know they have met with Captain Jack Rackham. And, the way I see it, if we keep death flying high above us, it is less likely to creep up on us as we go about our business.'

Mary grimaces.

'Well, he's not pretty, but if he's a good luck charm, I'm all for it.'

They drink again as Mr Fetherstone opens the Book of Articles to them with the reverence usually reserved for Bibles. The book is bound in rough brown leather, worn and fading at the edges. It has clearly seen some use.

'It's how we run *Revenge*. What we all strive to do, and what we must not. How we settle disagreements, punishments for transgressions, and what we pay if you lose an arm, leg or eye. Mr Harwood – our cook as you'll know him – has done very well from it.'

Jack grins, his teeth flashing, as the quartermaster finishes his piece.

'As Mr Fetherstone says, it is all of those things. Even pirates must have rules aboard ship. And, for yourselves, what this will give you is my guarantee that of the spoils we take, we share and share alike – though for my part, I have two. I am captain, after all.'

Mary has not expected such consideration, such fairness, for it is not how life works, or not as she has known it. Strange that she has had to join a band of pirates to be offered such a thing.

Tam is slower to understand than Mary, but even he looks delighted at the promise of what is to come. As if the jewels alone were his – and he is lost in dreams of himself as a rich man, crowned in gold and carried aloft by his old crewmates who had shown him nothing but contempt, they cowed and miserable.

'You'll sign?' says Anne, doing her best not to laugh at Tam's silent raptures.

'That we will.'

Mary takes the quill first.

Anne watches as she hesitates before making her mark in the book, a slow and deliberate cross. It is a shock, for she had forgotten that women do not read and write. Or, rather, women of a class beneath her own. A flush runs up her throat, the memory of the privilege she has cast aside so lightly sharp and unwelcome.

But Tam is being shaken from his lovely waking dream by a smiling Mary, and he follows suit with his own cross in the book before they set to drinking in earnest to their shining future.

Chapter 20

The evening has ended well. They have seen off too many bottles to count, and their bellies are full. They have two new crewmen, a useful addition in such uncertain times, and though Mary might be a woman, she is at least a capable one.

Anne has taken herself to the red-curtained bed at the back of his cabin. Jack smiles to himself, knowing that she is waiting. It is a good life he has given them here. He removes his coat, belt and breeches, and lays them over the back of a chair, resting his pistols on its seat. He scrapes the chair across the floor until it is next to the bed, for a man should never be further than arm's reach from his pistols.

Dressed now only in his shirt, he draws the brocaded curtain aside to reveal Anne, naked and waiting for him, propped up on her elbow. She smiles, fully aware of the impression she is making.

'I had thought you had forgotten me.'

There is a look in her eyes that says she knows otherwise.

'As if I should be able to do that.'

He climbs into bed alongside Anne and kisses her. She is willful, but she is pretty with it. He takes a curl of red hair and winds it gently around his finger.

'You should have listened to me aboard that ship. You might have been hurt.'

She smiles and kisses him back.

'But I was not. I am a pirate, and besides, I have my handsome captain to protect me.'

'Handsome I may be, but you risked too much. I do not want to see you hurt. You are lucky Mary dropped her sword.'

A wave of irritation. He sees it in her face and feels his hopes for the remaining evening deflating. He recovers himself quickly.

'Though she is lucky you did not kill her where she stood, of course. I had not thought to see a woman with a sword such an appealing sight.'

The look is gone, the misstep recovered. He is pleased to feel his hopes rising once again.

Anne lies back on the bed, lost in thought, her eyes a thousand miles away.

'Mary is a world unto herself. A soldier and a sailor – I could never have imagined it. The stories she must have ...'

Pleased though he is with his new crew member, he does not want to continue the conversation just now.

'You did well to win her for us. Very well.'

Anne's eyes turn back towards him, and she sees that his attention is all for her. Those eyes, those lips.

'And how will you show your crewman how well she has done?'

He pretends to think for a moment before rising to his knees and looking down. A broad grin stretches across his face.

'It seems that I am all present and correct. Prepare to accept your captain's most sincere thanks.'

She squeals in delight as he launches himself upon her – though she will not forget how he doubted her.

Chapter 21

The men have no reason to converse with a woman, and so do not bother to do it. But over time their words and behaviour reveal who they are – whether they mean to or not.

Mary thinks about what little she has been told about them. They could not be anything other than convicts, with heavy brows, sunken eyes and arms like hams. They roam the ship with lumbering gait, grunts making for conversation, glares for challenges. Like clumsy dancers, they skirt around one another, irritable and wary, punishing hands forming fists, itching for the contact with flesh and the crushing of small bones.

No doubt the men make for excellent pirates, for avoiding execution or death through overwork gives a man an appetite for life. His Majesty did not have this in mind when he sentenced them to transportation. Did not imagine the strange loyalty this would breed towards a pirate captain like Jack Rackham.

Mary does not have to wait long to see her new crewmates at their most natural. In a matter of days, she has witnessed a beating over a misplaced dinner bowl, a knife fight over stolen tobacco, and an attempted strangling of John Fenwick by John Davies over a game of dice. Two days later and the fingermarks can still be seen clearly in the bruised and swollen flesh of

Mr Fenwick's neck. Casual violence, petty theft and breaches of trust are daily events.

These are not faces one would wish to find together, but here they are, the stuff of nightmares, confined to the ship as crewmates. But it is not just the faces. Their hands are gnarled and calloused from ropes and bare-knuckled fighting, their spirits deadened, with animal instincts and dull eyes that only come alive when money or violence are at stake. They are a sorry lot compared to army men, but they are her crewmates now, and so Mary must come to know them.

George Fetherstone is the ship's master, Richard Corner the quartermaster. They are honest men and sailors both since the King saw fit to pardon them for piracy. They have sailed with Jack for years, and he would trust them with his life. And there are precious few people Jack trusts with anything.

Thomas Bourn, a bald man from Cornwall, is their boatswain. A man of little ambition and less intellect, he became a Navy man by way of the press gang following a hard night's drinking, and has been at sea ever since. He does not much mind the work as it has turned out, but he prefers to be part of a pirate crew. There is more money in it than he ever saw in his Navy days.

Noah Harwood, the one-legged cook, is cheerful at the pension of 400 pieces of eight he received for the loss of his left leg on Jack's previous ship. 'If they'd have taken my eye I'd have a ship of my own by now,' he tells her brightly. As it is, his lesser state has made him a seacook, and there are men whom he knows to be far less fortunate.

John Howell is the man with the zigzag scar who she saw off on her first day aboard. His jaw is off-centre following a brawl, masticated food on view for all to see when he eats. He was one of the Newgate men, sentenced to deportation for cutting off the fingers of a gentleman who refused to relinquish his watch.

John Davies, the man she had almost blinded, is a swabber – for he is not trusted with anything requiring more skill. He is a man so fat, his skin struggles to contain him, his pendulous belly swaying to the thud of his walk. His hands are slabs for breaking things. A Newgate man too, he had stolen a collection box from a London church, and bludgeoned the parson's brains to custard when interrupted.

John Fenwick, the man with the strangle marks on his neck, is one of the riggers, though Anne has called him out already as a gobshite and a misery. He is determined to share words of wisdom whether they are wanted or not. He drags dark clouds of temper with him about the ship, and is not well liked.

Titus Oates is the ship's gunner. His hair is an unruly tassel of knots and tats. Ears that burn red with temper, his crewmates have learned to remove themselves when they see it. He too had known Newgate, after he had beaten his wife half to death as he had drunkenly decided the baby she carried was not his. Neither she nor the baby survived to bear out his theory.

Patrick Carty is the ship's mate and the youngest of the crew. He is apprenticed to the master, boatswain, carpenter and gunner and has not experienced much of life. No doubt his current tenure will cure him of that. Poverty has driven him to sea, much as many others before him. He is an explosion of red hair and freckles that have spread and merged in the Caribbean heat.

Samuel Teague seems a decent sort of man, though Mary is advised to count her fingers after shaking hands with him for he was the most prolific of thieves back in England. He would be there still, happily emptying the pockets of the unwary, had he not pinched a pocket watch from a magistrate. This unfortunate slip had cost him a harsher sentence than usual from the enraged gentleman in question.

Owen Mayhew is the ship's doctor, taken by the pirates along with Mr Earl from a military ship. There is little difference in the doctor's duties, though he does not have to hide his fondness for drink here. He is sodden by breakfast, reeling by supper, and well oiled at all times in between. Smudged spectacles sit on the end of a thin nose, yellow eyes peering, in and out of focus, at anyone unfortunate enough to be one of his patients.

Tom Earl, the ship's carpenter, is a gentler man by far, and does not share in the excesses of his crewmates. But a sober man is one to be suspicious of, and the crew are often seen to threaten, cajole and pour drink into him until the carpenter is insensible and their suspicions are allayed. He will suffer horribly for it tomorrow every time it happens, but at least it grants him a peaceful night of unconscious sleep.

'And what about James Dobbins?'

He is the only one Mary has not been able to find out and so she has asked Anne's help, for she is very willing to give it. Mr Dobbins is a large man, mild-looking, and another rigger.

'Be nice to his cat and you will be friends for life.'

Mary comes to know him soon enough, for she is partial to cats herself. She learns quickly that he cannot bear cruelty to mere animals, though he is less concerned what happens to people. He is a heady mix of violence and sentiment. He tells her happily how he had throttled a man until he grew limp in his hands for kicking his Alice, a mewling scrap of fur then, against a wall when she was only a kitten. And he has loved her fiercely since he picked her up so gently from the ground where she had fallen and held her to his heart, broken, bleeding but still breathing. His girl.

Every day, Mary sees Mr Dobbins whispering secrets into Alice's soft fur, stroking her velvet ears, and feeding her the tastiest things he can find. And she has stayed with him, mercurial and indifferent, as only cats can be. Her green eyes melt his heart still, and a bloody good thumping is waiting for any man stupid enough to raise a hand to her ever again.

The whole crew carry themselves armed to the teeth even when they go about their daily work on the ship, with daggers and pistols strapped to them, swords being too clumsy for everyday. The captain himself wears two pairs of pistols in a sling he has fashioned from yellow silk, and Mary has asked him why.

'I like to carry more than one, for great English workmanship being what it is, they are as unreliable as hell.'

'But to wear them while you eat and sleep?'

Jack lowers his voice as if sharing a confidence.

'Would you trust these men an inch? We are amongst thieves and murderers, Mary.'

Chapter 22

The ship ploughs on, the rolling and clanking within in harmony with the groans of her hulk against the vast ocean beyond. Her timbers are lined and uneven, a face wrinkled by time and experience. She has seen such things and endured. She has become older, more experienced, tougher, though she is not as pristine as she had been once. She is to be treated appropriately, and respected for it.

There is always work to be done. Decks are swabbed, ropes are hauled, sails patched and fixed, rot is driven out, pumps worked. For the essentials of sustenance, Mr Harwood goes about his business at his galley stove with poor rations of dried beef and pork that he does his best to boil, cheese gone hard as rock, ship's biscuits laced with weevils.

The men avoid fish where they can, those slippery things that glint and glide through the water beneath, barely seen. If it comes from the sea, no man should consider eating it – with the exception of turtles, of course, for they are known to be tasty. That said, a body must be fed and they have known harder times when fish became necessary.

Mary's first expedition as a pirate is a practical one. Anne has explained that when they are near land and it is safe to venture out, the men go to the islands in search of fresh water. If Mr Harwood is lucky, the landing party might bring him a bird or two, perhaps even a goat or wild pig. The cook has, by necessity, become handy with a knife, burying it deep into any poor thing's throat before he bleeds it and goes about his butchery. Beggars can't be choosers, he was always taught, and he makes the best he can of the scant things he is given to work with. In the circumstances, he makes a fair go of it and no one has mutinied because of his food yet.

The men from the landing party have headed off into the undergrowth to hunt four-legged prey. But before she can join them, Mary is distracted by bird calls overhead, and is delighted to see a large flock of wild pigeons in the fruit trees nearby. She is not to know that it is the right time of year for them to fly over Tortuga, but it is good news for her, if not for the fowl.

Mary pulls out her pistols and takes aim with both at the cooing trees before she fills the startled air with gunfire. The pigeons squawk and panic, with more than the occasional bird falling to its doom as Mary continues her assault. The ground is soon littered with the corpses of dead birds, for they have grown fat and slow in this land of plenty, and Mary cheerfully seats herself under a shady tree and sets about plucking the unfortunate creatures before she bags them up for the cook.

Mr Harwood is delighted by her haul, and makes a point of dismissing each of the other men who return with lesser game.

'See – this is how you fill a cooking pot!'

The men look at their haul askance, having only been able to catch themselves a scrawny goat between them. They had been full of their own bravado and cunning until faced with Mary's success, and mutter gruffly in response as they leave the carcase to its new owner, now slightly shame-faced, and melt back into their usual roles as invisibly as they can.

Mr Harwood cooks the birds well. They are plump and sweet, the smell of them making mouths water across the ship long before they are ready. Then, at supper, the crew are able to gorge themselves until they can gorge no more, personal pride forgotten in the bliss of full bellies. Pigeon meat tastes better than it ever did in Flanders since Mary has been taken out of the equation of cooking, though she tells herself that it is merely a different bird. It could not be anything else.

The guns receive their care and attention too, with Mary making it her daily business to check they meet her exacting standards. The ship's gunner is Titus Oates and while he is pleased to have to do less because of her proficiency, he is less pleased that Mary makes such a good fist of it. He is less pleased still when the captain comments on the transformation of the weaponry, shining and sleek as it has never been before, and Mr Oates masks his displeasure as simple indifference while nurturing a sizeable grudge in private.

The ship is armed with four mounted guns on the main deck and two swivel guns on the rails for close combat, and Mary knows every inch of them. She has taken the task on as her own as she is the best man for the job, and they have never been so battle-ready.

When the day's work is done, Mary is pleased to see that not all semblance of military order is ignored. Lookouts are posted at the topmast head, watches agreed with the men taking their turn.

'Be sure to keep a good lookout, lads.'

Business done, Jack turns his attention to the serious matter of the hour.

'Take your grog and be happy, lads. Curse the King and damn the governor!'

Jack leads by example, to rowdy approval from the men, draining a cup before refilling it generously from the bottle. Joshua Hands takes up his fiddle to play a lively jig as the cook gamely starts to dance, his wooden leg keeping time more or less, as Anne begins to sing along, not too badly, and the crew go about multiplying their debts at dice or cards.

John Howell snatches food from the mouth of John Davies just as it is about to be chewed, much to his own amusement, while John Fenwick begins to tell stories of mermaids to Tam Weir and Patrick Carty, their eyes huge as they listen to tales of wonders and strange creatures that the other crew have long grown weary of. The men drink to the Devil and to themselves, and are happy more or less.

But not Mary. She will partake of a pipe, as had become her fancy in Flanders, but the rest of her coins are stowed in her sea chest, beneath Arno's shirt where it will be safe. Mary stashes her tobacco there, counts her money, carefully places it alongside buttons torn from the frock coat of an officer, and a spare cotton shirt, all precious in their way.

She spends quiet moments where she lays her palm flat on her dead husband's shirt and feels the comforting shift of coins beneath whispering of freedom to come, and a life still to be lived. This will become another inn, another Three Trade Horses that she will run. Hers alone if she must.

Mary is happy to take part in the life of the ship with its hard drinking, casual violence and blasphemy, and more so than Anne, but she stays herself. The woman she is has been hard won, and she will not dilute herself for anyone. She steers her own ship, and it concerns her that Anne does not. She already sees that Anne trusts too easily, does not look to see beyond the surface of anything. But Mary sees it all. She thinks that she will keep herself apart just enough to make sure it stays that way, for she knows bad luck is only ever a breath away.

Chapter 23

Still, Mary is fascinated by Anne. She cannot help herself as she follows Anne at a distance, watches her, making her self-conscious and clumsy.

Anne tries not to notice, but cannot for the life of her remember how to go about her business, or to put one foot in front of the other, when her watcher is there. Jack finds it greatly amusing.

'You have an admirer. Watch yourself – she might enjoy the company of women in unnatural ways. Though I'm sure I could learn to tolerate it, if you were so inclined.'

Anne looks at him witheringly.

'Your imagination is more than I had given you credit for, but I hate to disappoint. I have no more interest in her in that way than she has in me. She is a crewman, and a good one at that.'

'Well, a man can hope. An able seaman will have to suffice. Why not show her the ropes, since you refuse to show her anything else?'

He walks away, clearly pleased with himself, oblivious to the vile poison Anne is pouring down his gaping throat in her mind's eye, leaving him convulsing and green-faced.

Mary joins her. 'We have stories to tell one another, don't we? I had thought myself alone in this, and yet here you are. Comrades in arms. Now isn't that a thing.'

Anne smiles, unable to share her delight at her inclusion. If she has ever thought that she did not need anyone else, she knows it now to be nonsense.

'You're lucky I didn't cut your throat back on that ship. I've not had anyone laugh before at the end of my sword.'

'I think we both know you've never had anyone at the end of your sword.'

Anne considers taking offence before Mary bursts out laughing, and she cannot help but join in.

'If you were as good with a sword as you are in the sails, you'd be a terror and no mistake.'

'When we met, I might still have killed you. At least allow me that.'

'You might have cut your foot off. That's the worst use of a sword I've seen in a long time.'

Anne knows it is true but still feels the slight.

Mary continues.

'I can teach you a thing or two that would keep us all safe.'

Her pride is wounded, and this sounds suspiciously like work. Anne has never been keen on work.

'None of the men here practise anything, and yet they've come to no harm.'

'They are hulking brutes and could kill with their bare hands, but we cannot. Not everyone will drop their sword as I did when I saw you. I can teach you if you like. It's not a natural thing; to make a sword your own takes practice, and I would say you've had precious little of that.'

Mary has a point, and Anne still smarts as she remembers that day, the sword swinging wildly in her hand. She would prefer not to repeat it, and especially not in front of Mary.

'This is your living now, and you must keep yourself alive. I should consider it a favour, for the sake of my own body parts.'

It is not a discussion, and Anne knows it. Perhaps it is easier to accept the help of another woman – one who has kept herself alive, and more. Anne only has the protection of a fond captain – and that cannot last forever. She has no real abilities of her own.

'It is a handy thing, learning how not to be killed. But you'll have to work for it.'

Mary sees Anne's hesitation.

'As capable as you are fierce. Now wouldn't that be a thing.'

Anne feels herself giving in to Mary's cajoling, relief mixed with resignation, as she is handed a sword.

'There is no time like the present …'

And so they begin. Anne is impulsive, aggressive and bold but leaves herself open too often to recourse. Mary nips her with the tip of her sword at each parry at first, taking care for now not to hurt more than her feelings.

'There, and there.'

Mary's movements seem effortless, flowing around Anne like water. It annoys her hugely.

Anne becomes more reckless, not least because the crew make little effort to hide their amusement at these women playing at sword fighting, but all she is rewarded with is ever more nips of the sword, the last of them tearing a small hole in the breast of her shirt and skin beneath.

'For God's sake, how do I stop you doing that?' she asks angrily as she wipes the annoyance of blood away.

'Now *that* is the right question,' says Mary as she lays down her sword, indicating that Anne should do the same.

There is a moment's hesitation as Anne considers thrusting her blade into Mary's throat, but only a moment.

'Please …' says Mary, smiling, guessing the thoughts crossing Anne's mind until she too lays down her weapon. 'I will teach you the laws of close combat, and show you how to keep yourself out of harm's way. It's a dance worth knowing, believe me.'

Anne does believe her, and so they continue their lessons, the men greatly amused as the women parry against phantoms, each taking it in turns to watch the other, Mary instructing and adjusting Anne as she goes. Anne becomes more sure of herself as the days go on – of when to push forward, when to fall back, when to step aside to avoid her teacher's sword. And the slow lessons begin to pick up their pace over the weeks, swords reintroduced, the ring of metal against metal a now common sound. The men begin to lose interest as the women are now more evenly matched, though Anne does not yet have Mary's strength, built up over months of active service.

Work continues – cannons cleaned, sails sewn, decks swabbed. And after work is done, the women practise their swords until sunset, when they catch their breath in close proximity and share stories about themselves, their hands a whisper away from one another.

Mary tells Anne about her time in Plymouth, about Flanders, but not about Arno just yet. Mary prompts Anne for her story too. Anne hesitates but then, slowly, tells her about her father, her mother who yearns only for happy death, about the plantation and the wealth she has walked away from. They are more different and more alike than they could ever have known, and the more they know, the more there is to learn.

Over time, Anne's shoulders grow stronger, her arms grow leaner, and she takes less nicks and gashes more through ability than charity. Until one day she parries and catches Mary on the arm with her sword, cutting a deep gash.

Mary laughs in delight and drops her own sword to the deck to throw her arms around Anne, she panting and triumphant, as Mary's blood runs down Anne's back and soaks into her shirt.

'And now we are true brothers in arms,' says Mary, and Anne glows in the light of her praise.

They continue to go about their duties every day, and to their practice, and learn one another's nuances through familiarity. Anne has become as good as any man on board in combat, perhaps even better, and one day she hopes she will be as good as Mary.

Mary, pleasantly exhausted by her training with Anne, is unimpressed to see a lack of similar effort from the men. Instead of drills, there are dice. Instead of practice, there is drinking, fighting and sleep.

Jack has seen her puzzling at his crew, and cannot let it rest.

'I can imagine what you are thinking, but we have luck on our side.'

She looks at him doubtfully.

'Luck is a fickle thing.'

'They get their practice when we board a prize. There is no need for tactics – this is not the Army, Mary.'

And she concedes that he is right. This is no well-oiled machine. For all its faults, the Army has preparedness and discipline. Here just a belief that brutishness will win the day, for there is plenty of that in evidence.

A man who applies himself to the arts of battle, teaches his body what it must do for him, cannot be compared to a cheap cut-throat or cutpurse who did not even have the wits to outsmart the law.

Of the men who had avoided death at Newgate, who had been fated to die a slow death on the plantations, there is at least a strong will to survive, and to take whatever they choose, whether it is there for the taking or not – their crewmates amongst them, for there is no honour amongst thieves.

Jack's men may choose to trust him implicitly, but Mary does not. She knows better than to do such a thing. She appraises him coolly and it unsettles him. What he has to offer is mostly seen on the surface, but Mary sees straight through to his core. Jack suspects all too well that this is where his ability is thin. And he is not pleased by the reminder.

It is a slow drip of discomfort that pools and sours. What was he thinking – to bring another woman on board? If Anne had begun to weaken in his eyes, Mary has straightened her back. There are two of them together now, a partnership in the midst of his crew. It has thrown him off-kilter, and he does not like it.

He has watched Anne at her lessons with Mary, though he has tried not to let them see. Anne had shown more will than skill at first, but the women have sparred together, hour after hour, day after day, and she has gotten better.

Jack has been surprised, and not a little appalled. Mary has been an excellent teacher, demonstrating, correcting patiently, laughing delightedly as her student occasionally bests her, Anne beaming at her success and at her friend.

But it does not end there. The swordplay continues, and picks up in pace. Anne's stamina improves, as does her determination to master her weapon. It is weeks later, the seasons having shifted from spring to summer, and Jack realises that Anne can fight almost as well as Mary now, and Mary is the best of his men.

Mary has made Anne a better man all round. So what does that make Jack?

His little experiment has taken on a life of its own, and God alone knows where it will end. The Big Man upstairs plays his cards close to his chest, but Jack suspects it will not end well.

Mary notices him watching as she sharpens her cutlass and winks. He replies with something less than a smile, a ripple around the mouth that he hopes gives nothing away.

Chapter 24

Mary has been accepted as one of their own. Anne has never known anything like her, had never considered that a woman could exist who was less constrained by her sex than herself. And yet here she stands: vulgar, loud and magnificent.

But Mary is just as curious about Anne, and has endless questions for her when they are together, which is often.

'You were married before Jack, then?'

Anne looks as if she has smelled something unpleasant, curls her lip.

'His name was James Bonny. His name was the only good thing about him, so I kept it.'

Mary looks greatly amused.

'You needed to marry him to find out he was a waste of skin? I should explain the birds and the bees to you ...'

Anne is vaguely annoyed, though at herself or Mary she could not say.

'I had sampled the goods and decided it was enough, for I had imagined him a much better man than he was.'

'And I bet you have damned your imagination to hell and back many a time since. Optimism has been the downfall of many a good woman ...'

Anne grins.

'You've mistaken me for a good woman, for I left him drunk and naked in a boarding room in New Providence before I stole a ship with Jack.'

Mary's eyes widen before her face catches up and she explodes with laughter.

'Well, Jack is very well made in his person – I can see why he would turn your head.'

Anne snorts.

'I had too much beer in my head when I saw him or he'd not have turned it at all.'

'Well, I cannot say that I'm immune to a uniform myself. Married my own bunkmate, having bitten my tongue and more until I couldn't bear it any longer. His name was Arno. He was a better man than James Bonny was, that's evident enough.'

Mary's face clouds.

'He died of a fever back in Holland. I gave him a good burial, for there was nothing more I could do for him.'

Anne does not know how to answer. She tries to find words, but Mary's face has begun to crumple.

'I left him behind, Anne.'

Anne has not had a husband worth remembering, but can see Mary's pain well enough, raw in her face. And when she starts to cry and cannot stop, Anne holds Mary to her fiercely, the wetness of tears warming her chest. The words come now like a benediction.

'You did not leave him. You carry him still in your heart and your memories, and now I will know him too. He could not have had a better wife than you.'

Mary lets herself be held, her tears soaking into Anne's shirt. It is a while later that she pulls away from Anne and wipes her eyes.

'You think so? That I was a good wife to him, that he would forgive me for what I had to do?'

Anne looks her straight in the eyes, her gaze softening.

'I know it.'

Mary becomes still and quiet, and Anne holds on. The space between them thickens, lengthening until, finally, Mary breaks the silence.

'At least you have Jack.'

Anne looks off into the distance. She had thought the adventure enough at first. And Jack is still well made. But from what Mary has said about Arno? Well, that is something different again. She had not even thought to consider it.

'Yes. I have Jack.'

There is nothing more to say and they sit, watching the fixed stars above them while the ship passes below, slick and silent in the darkness.

Chapter 25

Anne has been unmoored. She finds herself in uncharted waters. Anne has never felt responsibility for anyone other than herself before, but she feels it keenly for Mary. It is a new and shining thing that spurs her to restless action. She remembers Mary signing the Articles with a cross all too well, thinks of the way she has described Arno with such tenderness through the dark shared hours of the night. Anne knows what she must do.

She asks Jack for paper and a quill, which he grants with some bemusement, and makes use of his empty cabin as he goes about the day's business. In the strange silence, she devotes herself and the following hours to writing down, word by word, what Mary has told her about Arno. How he looked, his manner, how they met, but most of all how he loved Mary and she him. And when she adds the dot of a full stop, she sits back. She is satisfied with what she has written so far, but is not quite finished.

Anne casts her mind back to the art lessons of her youth. She clearly remembers the despair her tutors (for there had been many) had shown at her disinterested attempts at capturing the likeness of anything on the page. Her lack of care had shown itself all too well in the smudged and ill-realised efforts at still lives of flowers and fruit. Her portraits had been distracted and lumpen, each face much like the other. But she knows she can do better, for now she has a reason to try.

Haltingly at first, she takes the quill and draws a curved line on the page, the length of her thumb. She follows with a mirror image on the other side, before she measures the span as she had been shown so often (and thought forgotten) and sketches in eyes and a nose. She takes particular care about the eyes and lashes, for Mary had spoken of them as if they were carved on her memory. The mouth follows, smiling and firm, before she begins the curl of his hair. Mary had closed her eyes, smiling, when she had described how it had framed his face.

Finally, she sits back and surveys what she has done. It is no work of art, but Anne has done all she can. Her hands are splashed with ink, an outward sign of her labour. She is awkward when she thinks about sharing this with Mary, but has already determined to do it. The pages are meant with kindness, though Anne has had little practice at such a thing.

It is later, when the day's work is over that Anne seeks Mary out, as she always does. She is nervous as a suitor as she holds the paper out to Mary.

'What is it?'

'It is for you.'

Mary takes it uncertainly and opens it, staring at the image on the final page.

Anne begins to speak, uncertain.

'It is Arno, or at least I tried. I wrote down everything you said about him, and tried to draw him too. So you always have him with you.'

Mary is still and silent and Anne thinks, her heart lurching, that she has made a terrible mistake, wonders if it is too late to snatch the thing back. She should have set fire to it, or thrown it overboard. She has broken something fragile and irreplaceable, she knows it. What did she think she was doing?

Mary takes Anne's hand and kisses it softly. She lifts her face towards her and Anne sees now that she has tears in her eyes.

'Thank you. You have brought him back to me.'

Thank you. No one has ever said that to Anne before, and she melts.

Chapter 26

The ship stalks the trade routes, awaiting prey that always comes. There are naval ships too that must be avoided, an inevitable game of cat and mouse that will sometimes see *Revenge* retreat to a safe cove or inlet for a while. The opportunity taken to refresh their food and water supplies until the coast is clear and they can set sail again to lie in wait for their next prize.

A few years back, things would have been easier, but there are fewer safe havens for them now. There used to be towns where the pirates were welcomed with open arms and treated like kings, but that all changed as the governor tightened his grip of law on the Caribbean islands. There are still places, but they are only whispered about now by the pirates for fear of discovery, lawless places, their every sense and whim indulged while they are on shore, a place where they can live life furiously as it were meant to be lived before the money runs out and they are forced to set off to sea once again.

It is still a decent living. Perhaps not the riches that there once were when the pirates roamed free, when every merchant was forced to plan losses of entire ships into his balance sheets as a matter of course, but it is better than any living on shore. It is better than any honest living anywhere.

And there is always hope that unexpected treasure will be found. A chest of rubies or sapphires from the strange countries of the East. Bags of coins, all glorious gold and silver, from deals successfully done. But the pirates are happy to take whole cargoes of whatever they find and sell them on themselves, at less than market price of course, to a few dubious merchants of their acquaintance. They are scavengers and make the most out of anything they acquire in the shadows of the law.

There can be weeks between raids, for at this time of year too there are storms and hurricanes that threaten the islands, and sensible merchants will avoid a voyage where they can. But there is always money to be made, and greed can be a powerful incentive in risking the routes even at this treacherous time of year. And the pirates lie in wait for them.

Mary does not have to wait long for her first taste of piracy. A Spanish galleon has been spotted and the pirate crew are ready. Mary is already watching their prey as they sail ever nearer, her eyes sparkling.

'You're ready, then?'

Anne has joined her, her eyes fixed on the ship ahead.

'Born ready. And in Breda I fought the Spanish too. It was meant to be.'

'You have your sword and pistols ready?'

Mary turns to Anne with a look of disapproval.

'You do remember who you're speaking to, don't you?'

Anne holds up her hands and backs off laughing as Mary adds:

'Just remember what we've practised. We will leave them with memories worth keeping.'

She knows she has nothing to worry about so long as Anne keeps her head.

Jack has taken to the forecastle to address the crew. He is, she notices, more heavily armed than usual.

'Fortune has smiled on us again, lads, in the shape of a boat full of Spaniards. I know you will give them a good English welcome, and look forward to counting our plunder. Good hunting!'

There is a roar of approval at this as Joshua Hands picks up his fiddle and begins to pick out a familiar tune:

'*Farewell and adieu, to you Spanish ladies ...*'

There is laughter and the odd cheer for this, as a number of the men begin to join in loudly.

'*We'll rant and we'll roar like true British sailors*
We'll rant and we'll roar along the salt seas ...'

Mary finds herself whistling along as she checks her pistols for the third time, and glances towards Anne to see, with satisfaction, that she is doing the same. The inspection meets Mary's approval, and she devotes herself again to watching the enemy ship as it approaches.

They are just minutes away from the galleon when the *Revenge* raises the black flag and the Spanish crew are plunged into panic, as they are meant to be. Anne is by Mary's side once again and they wait with the rest of the crew, Jack ready to lead the charge. Then the tear of wood against wood, the lurch of the enemy ship and the charge begins.

The pirates spill over onto the deck of the Spanish ship, roaring and cursing with swords held high. There is little resistance, much to the women's disappointment, as they find the only sailor who holds a sword up, it trembling like a sapling caught by a breeze.

His eyes widen as Anne and Mary advance and he falls to his knees, his eyes transfixed, his sword clattering to the deck as he does so.

'*Mujeres?*'

It is a question and an expression of hurt all at once.

Anne nods slowly and his face collapses as he holds his hands up to the sky.

'*Santa Maria!*'

He makes a sound like a hiccup at the indignity of it before he starts to wail uncontrollably.

Anne and Mary glance at one another.

'It means "Holy Mary".'

Mary smirks.

'Tell him I just go by the second part.'

The ship is efficiently stripped of its cargo, sacks of gold coins being a welcome part of the haul. Mary has taken a uniform jacket from one of the officers in blue and yellow brocade, and is already wearing it as she clambers back on board *Revenge*, proud of her first plunder. Anne too wears a Spanish uniform jacket, and Mr Corner wolf whistles and laughs as the women return.

'I had thought us boarded by Spaniards!'

Mary twists and turns to show the uniform off to better advantage.

'Thank God only English, but don't we fill them better than the Spanish men did?'

Revenge sets sail again, the crew jubilant, the vanquished crew left dumbstruck and bewildered in their wake. But before they are out of earshot, Joshua Hands picks up his fiddle and resumes his crowd-pleasing song:

'*Farewell and adieu to you Spanish ladies*
Farewell and adieu you ladies of Spain ...'

There is laughter as the pirates begin to join in the shanty, each voice lending strength to the others.

'*We hope in a short time to see you again!*'

Anne puts an arm around Mary triumphantly, her face beaming.

'We did it.'

Mary hugs Anne back.

'My first spoils. Spanish gold!'

'Don't forget your new jacket.'

'*Our* new jackets. And what fine jackets they are. I think I shall sleep in mine tonight.'

'What fine soldiers we must be to have taken them.'

There is the suggestion of a question in Anne's voice, but Mary sees that her earlier concerns are happily forgotten.

'That we are.'

Anne beams at this and Mary is glad to see it. She throws Anne a heartfelt compliment.

'Not just anyone could make a man cry without touching him, you know.' Mary mimics the sailor, cruelly accurate.

Anne laughs. 'Next time we'll do more than just make him cry.'

Chapter 27

The spoils have been divided amongst the crew, and they are happy for a time. Mary thinks that the Spanish gold coins are the prettiest she has ever seen. They have been taken, bitten, counted and stored away in her sea chest. They are her hope and her future made real, and she feels a sense once again that she is making her way in the world. A woman with her pockets full has a right to be happy.

Mary is home. She was born to live this life, and has Anne alongside her. She feels a new contentment in being dwarfed by the ocean, by this unending expanse of blue as they work and wait. Now that she has space to be herself again, Mary feels the freedom of it. And it is wonderful.

She begins to fall in love with it all, just as Anne has done. Sea breezes salt the air, the taste of it on her lips and tongue. There are extraordinary colours that she has never seen before. She had not known that there could be so much beauty, a multitude of blues, greens, silvers and greys that she has grown greedy for, and holds so gladly to her heart.

And the fish. She had thought that all fish were grey as a Plymouth sky, but here, in this strange place, they are a carnival of colour. They slip through the water, glittering shoals that flash and dart in jewel tones, hundreds or more, glimpsed and then gone.

Now that she has slowed to the pace of the sea, there are new sounds to hear, too. The distant song of a humpback whale, strange and mournful, somewhere in the distance. The high-pitched chatter of playful dolphins as they race to stay alongside the ship, leaping and spinning across one another through displaced water. The frequent cries of gulls, and the flustered sound of their wings as they come to rest awhile in the rigging, white against the sky.

It is a strange sound like the harrumphing of horses that draws Mary to the stern of the ship, where Anne is looking down to the water. As her eyes adjust to the swell and fall, she sees a strange movement within the waves. Around the stern are twenty or so jet-black creatures, sleek as seals, their backs breaking the water as they swim together, emerging to snort loudly at the women before submerging again.

'Are they sharks?'

Anne is greatly amused to hear fear in her voice. She has not heard that before. Anne does not look up in case Mary sees her smiling.

'They are pilot whales. Not everything in the sea exists to cause you harm, you know.'

Mary is not so sure. She has not yet seen a shark, but from the tales she's been told of sharp teeth, dead black eyes and a sole purpose of tearing men apart, she is in no hurry to do so.

The largest of the animals rises above the waves, water spewing from a hole in its back. There is the harrumphing again, a question perhaps, as the smaller ones weave in and out, never far from the biggest.

The women stand together watching the animals play – the emergence of a sleek back there, a glimpse of a doleful eye looking up from the waves below, before they slip and slide out of view, surfacing a distance away.

'It's like they are watching us.'

Anne nods.

'I think we are as much a curiosity to them as they are to us.'

'I have never seen such a thing.'

She does not sound sure, but wonders how many more creatures are there that she knows nothing of.

'They may be a family. After all, it would be strange to think we were the only creatures to seek safety and comfort with others.'

The whales have begun to make their way back out to sea, and Mary feels a sudden pang of sadness at their departure. There is some truth in what Anne has said. And she is glad that she and Anne have the comfort of each other.

Chapter 28

Mary is always at Anne's side now. They are patient and curious with one another. Anne now knows what she does not want, but not yet what she does. She had never thought that it was for her to determine, but she is starting to see it is for Mary, in the gentlest of ways, encourages her to look and ask questions of herself. Mary has made Anne realise that she does not always mean what she says. It is a revelation to her, that the surface on which she has always skimmed has further depths.

Anne has always needed to feel that she is alive. She had thought she was merely outrunning boredom, but perhaps it is more. The chaos she has created throughout her life has been an urge she cannot suppress, a stubbornness that has led to rebellion against everything she has ever known. The thought that she can choose and create an alternative way of being for herself is brand new.

As Anne starts to look tentatively beneath her own surface, she begins to see unexpected things. A dark outcrop of doubt. A splintered shipwreck of fear. A yawning chasm of loneliness just beyond the shelf of her vision. She is more complicated than she had ever imagined.

Anne has always been a creature borne of frustration, and Mary is a feast for her. She has begun to feel sated and Anne is never sated. She has begun to wonder whether what she has now is enough, and it thrills her.

Mary sees more in her than Anne has ever seen in herself. Mary has held her up against the rest of the crew.

'You are the best of them, without the worst.'

Anne feels a little drunk on this new sense of worth. Of being enough just as she is, of not needing to chase the phantom of herself she had always thought must be the only version that might meet the world's expectations of her.

And Mary feels it too. The women have held up dark mirrors to one another, and seen something new. They are not alone in this world. Anne had never needed anyone else, or so she had thought, but now they have found one another ... They are two parts of a whole. They steady each other, and magnify one another. If they were remarkable apart, then they are more so together.

It is Mary who captures it, as she always does.

'I have never known anyone like you, Anne. I am glad we have met'.

And to Anne, it is everything.

Their monthly cycles find accord too. During their time, they are fierce mother bears, snapping and snarling at the men, who learn to keep a sensible distance when it becomes obvious they must. It is a monthly reminder of time passing that the men have been free of until now. It is a new experience for the crew to be so squeamish about blood, but in this case they are. Collectively, they are startled into embarrassment at this otherness, hidden in plain sight. It is wholly unnatural.

And it emboldens the women.

They are together as usual one evening when Mary asks a question.

'If either of us were to be captain of this ship, who would you keep as your crew?'

Anne is glad to hear that she is there in Mary's imagined future, and that they are equals. It tastes sweet. She folds it away inside herself and sets herself to the task at hand.

'We could not keep Jack. For if we are captains, we do not need another.'

Mary nods.

'Agreed. Which means our master and quartermaster must go. Too much loyalty to Jack.'

Anne nods.

'So we have three of them in the rowboat now. And Mr Fenwick?'

Mary snorts.

'It's clear we'd be better off without him. He'd be first over the side.'

'Into the rowboat?'

'Or the sea. No one would miss him, and I think the rowboat will become too crowded.'

They settle into their considerations with great pleasure, pointing out one man after another and submitting him to scrutiny and judgement. It is not long before they realise that were they to be captains of this ship, they should be crewing it with only Tom Earl, the cook and the cat for company. Tam Weir would be included for sympathy's sake.

The men are a little confused by the great hilarity that echoes through the ship, but dismiss it from their thoughts. Women are strange creatures, and sometimes best ignored.

Mary has become herself again, and is content. She has work to do (honest in its way), a full belly, and there are worse places to be than at sea since Anne is with her. Arno is still in her thoughts, of course he is, but her fancy cannot stay in Holland forever. Red blood flows in Mary's veins still. She has noticed that the ship's carpenter, Tom Earl, is thoughtful, and does not rush to fill silences like the other men do. He is capable – he had made the shortlist of her crew, after all – and she sees something other than the sea in his eyes. That he is blond-haired and rugged does not hurt either.

A carpenter is more important to the ship than their doctor, as she has often been told. The heat, the tropical rains, the constant exposure and wear, seams that warp and gape, wood that rots. So Tom is an important man, Mary thinks, as she watches him work one day, skilful and oblivious to her interest for now.

The uneven curve of the deck, the worn grooves of ladder rungs – Mr Earl is ever alert to the ship's complaints, patient in his treatment of her. He is as attentive as a nurse, understands her for what she is, soothing her when she breaks, patching when she is beyond repair and parts of her must be replaced. He honours every part of her, each broken piece kept safe and fashioned into something new so she lives on as dice, as toys, as trinkets that he sells to the crew. There is a kindness to his face, as well as skill in his hands, and Mary cannot help but notice it.

'She is a demanding mistress, and must be treated well,' he tells Mary as she watches him work a piece of wood with his knife. She is paying more attention than usual. She has noticed that he is never happier than when he works. He is different then to all the other men, and unexpected.

'How did you join this crew? You do not strike me as a natural pirate.'

He nods across to John Howell.

'I was travelling back to England when my ship was boarded by pirates. Mr Howell persuaded me with an axe to my wrists that I should like to join them, and here I am, with my hands intact.'

Mr Howell nods back cheerfully before returning to his sails, his large needle making its way roughly through the canvas.

Mary watches as Mr Earl works at the driftwood, removing layer after layer of it until a tiny doll reveals itself in the centre of his palm.

'For your child?' she asks, innocently.

He shakes his head, much to her pleasure.

'For Mr Teague, who has a little girl. Her name is Emily.'

Mary returns to her sea chest that evening and removes the precious document given to her by Anne. She takes the picture of Arno and strokes the line of his face with a finger lightly before she begins to speak to him with great seriousness.

'Now you were my love, Arno, and will always be so. But I am on my way to a new world without you. You taught me that the right man can make a woman happier than she ever thought she could be, and I must try to be so again. There is a man – I think you would like him. You must try not to mind.'

She kisses the picture of her lost love and places it at the bottom of the sea chest beneath his shirt, taking care to place the portrait face down. He may be dead, but Mary will feel more comfortable if he cannot see what she is about to do.

Over the coming days, Anne watches with amusement as Mary goes about her seduction of Mr Earl. She is far from subtle, and he is clearly alarmed by the attention. He tries to back away from Mary's enthusiasm, but where is there to go on a ship? Finally, she whispers something to him, for his ears alone, and he draws away from her in panic.

'I have no dishonourable designs on you, Mary.'

She smiles back filthily.

'But I have them upon you.'

Dismay is somewhat tempered by time, which leads in turn to resignation. He is a little afraid of Mary, as well he might be. That she dresses as a man is confusing, but months at sea will make a man tolerant of such things. Familiarity makes it more tolerable still. And within days, having put up insufficient fight against it, the inevitable happens.

It has been a long afternoon, the sun relentless overhead as the crew shelter in the shadows and rest as they wait for supper. Tom has resigned himself to his fate when Mary smiles at him warmly, whispering something unexpected in his ear. He knows he did not prompt it, and is in fact still a little bemused when Mary takes his hand firmly to lead him into the shadows behind the rum barrels to express her affection. They emerge a few minutes later, flushed and happier both.

It is a pleasant distraction from his work, and she is satisfied that the deed is done.

'And now we live together as man and wife. I have done it before and it has plenty to be said for it.'

She does not wait for him to answer as she assumes Tom's assent. Lucky then she has it for he has had time to come round to her way of seeing things, and he does not mind it at all.

And later, when they lie on the deck alongside the rest of the crew, Mary with her pipe, Anne sees that she lays her hand on his leg. She tries to smile at the sight, but finds that she cannot, her stomach tightening as she goes to seek out Jack.

Tom's crewmates have plenty to say about it, mostly unrepeatable and never said in front of Mary, and life takes on a new normality once again.

Mary tells Tom about her adventures, and Tom listens. Tom tells Mary of his travels, too, of the ships where he has served time, of the myriad strange creatures and stranger people he has seen from the four corners of this world. He is an education, a man who has seen more things than she will ever see. She gulps down the words greedily and waits for more.

And when he is too tired to continue and his head nods in sleep, Mary rests her head against his chest and breathes, lulled to sleep by the drum beat of his heart.

Chapter 29

The warm glow of Mary and her Mr Earl sheds a sickly light on Anne. Jack has lost his shine in its shadow. It happened so gradually that she had not noticed, but now she sees him before her clearly, faded and scuffed at the edges. She was infatuated with the man she wanted him to be, but he clearly isn't that man. Mary reminds Anne just how far her own feelings have cooled.

The Jack she thought she had known in New Providence – the man full of wildness and easy promises – has become distracted, his gadfly attention elsewhere. When they ran away to sea, Anne had not expected that they would end up taking fishing boats and small trading ships. She has questioned him about this more than once, and he has used up his small supply of patience with her. She smarts as she remembers their last exchange.

'It is a matter of survival, Anne, to replenish our food and water.'

'We should set our sights higher.'

His expression had slipped, a frown she had not seen before starting at his temples.

'We are happy to take what we can for now and keep to ourselves. If it is meant to happen, it will happen.'

'I had thought us adventurers, not petty thieves.'

The words were out before she could stop them, had she ever meant to. He looked as if he had seen a premonition. This is where it started. This is when reality began to set in.

There are yawning gaps between the adventures Anne had imagined as everyday things and the administration of a working ship. Jack is not fixed upon her quite so eagerly as he once was, for he has a ship to run, and he is not easily able to hold more than one thought at a time.

She knows that she is becoming waspish with him. He drives her to it, but she cannot help herself. The giddiness and rose tint of their early days is gone and she sees all too clearly that he is an ordinary man. Once Anne sees it, it cannot be unseen. She is no more capable of moulding Jack into the man she wants him to be than she is of flying.

She knows with certainty that Jack would not still be with her if they were on dry land, no more than she would be with him. But here in the middle of the ocean, they must get on with things until a better opportunity presents itself. What that might be she cannot fathom, so she takes her rum, heads to her hammock, and hopes to beat her thoughts into submission with drink and sleep.

But when she wakes up the following day, Mary is already there, eyes shining.

'Well, I have Tom.'

Mary waits, but Anne does not have words for her. A knot of something approaching jealousy has lodged itself in her stomach and grown steadily since yesterday. Anne is both dismayed and angry at its presence, for by ignoring it she had hoped it would disappear.

The thought of Mary and Tom scratches at her like nettles, the touch of it leaving her raw and open. She is not ready to share Mary with anyone, but it seems she is to be given no choice.

Anne tips herself from her hammock but cannot bring herself to meet Mary's eyes. She makes a show of searching for something in the darkness as Mary watches her curiously.

'You can't mind that me and Tom—'

'No.'

The word is sharp as a pistol shot and takes all air from the space between them. A season of emotions passes over Anne's face despite her best efforts, and Mary sees it.

'We will still be friends. That will not change.'

The word hits Anne like a fist and she feels herself reel with it. It is not so long ago that to have a friend would be an unthinkable thing. But now? How can it not change, this beautiful, fragile thing that has grown between them? There is no space for anyone else.

'You still have Jack.'

Mary leaves a question mark in the air. Anne pauses and looks her in the eye.

'We are no longer the novelty we were to each other. His attention has stalled, as has mine.'

Something withers inside Anne; it is one thing to think it, but another to say it aloud. Now it cannot be put back into its box again like the guilty secret it is.

'So you do not want him …'

There is a silence until Mary speaks again.

'Did you ever love him?'

Anne pauses before shaking her head.

'There was not enough time for it. He stole a ship for me, and I thought that enough.'

To her great annoyance, Mary starts to laugh.

'You're a strange one. To have lumbered yourself with a man you do not like – what were you thinking?'

Nothing. She was thinking nothing. She was carried along by a wave she had created, and now finds that she does not like where it has landed her.

'I liked him well enough to bed him.'

'But that is no reason to stay with him. The birds and the bees do not settle with every one they tup.'

Anne feels annoyance rise within her, and suspects it is directed at herself.

'But I do not know how to do it.'

Mary frowns.

'To do what?'

Anne falters.

'To make myself love someone. The way that you love Tom. The way that Tom loves you.'

She feels her throat tighten as she says it, and feels a blush spread up her neck. When she looks up again, Mary shakes her head slowly.

'That is not how it works. You cannot make yourself love someone. It is something entirely natural. It is so natural it is not always convenient and can feel like madness. It is a strange thing, but not always unpleasant.'

'But how do I find someone worth loving?'

Mary pauses, considering.

'Ah – now that's a different question. If I look around this ship, there is only one man worth having, and he is mine. So I would say to look beyond this ship, though that is not an easy thing at sea. As you are stuck with him, perhaps you could try harder.'

'To love him?' There is dismay in her voice.

Mary considers before she answers.

'Perhaps not that. But perhaps you could try to dislike him less?'

Anne smiles, pained.

'Perhaps I could try to do that. For a time at least.'

'Marriages can be made of less, let me tell you. Who knows – perhaps you will even come to like him again.'

Anne very much doubts it.

Chapter 30

Tom Earl's future is no longer in his own hands.

Mary has remembered her first ship's sentimental send-off from England; the teary grey-skinned women and their thin children, clinging to their mothers like tiny monkeys, eyes wide and uncertain as they tried to make sense of it all. There had been a fluttering of handkerchiefs and scraps of fabric as the ship left dock, the desperate women forgotten and the men grim-faced at their stations as they became part of the expanse of sea beyond.

'I shall not have you go to sea again. There will be plenty for you to do at home.'

Home is a strange concept and he takes time to remember what it means. A hearth of his own. A kitchen table. A wife and children. And Mary is telling him he can have it all.

Tom listens as she informs him of the inn they'll run in the Americas, the marvellous pies she'll bake, the rooms they'll let to the weary. It is an unexpected turn, this glimpse of domesticity in the middle of the ocean, but he finds that he does not mind it at all. Perhaps there is a life beyond this one, and a quiet one at that. He thinks, in fact, that he might like it very much. And there are worse things he could be called than Mr Read.

Tom has carved a wooden rose for Mary that she carries in her pocket, already smooth from stroking. It is as if he has given her his heart to carry, and she will treat it tenderly and keep it with her. When Mary laughs and Tom smiles back, it is more intimate than anything Anne has ever seen.

Anne feels her disappointment flex like a muscle, anger filling her stomach. She has done it again – allowing herself to believe that a man can answer her questions of herself. There is only herself to blame, and she needs to stop thinking. She knows just the thing.

She grabs Jack, much to his surprise, and suggests they meet behind the rum barrels. It has been a while and he is grateful, and clumsy for he has already been drinking. They meet together in the darkness, and quickly fall on one another, a mechanical act that leaves them both a little empty; Jack confused by what exactly is missing, Anne now quite sure.

She has seen the tenderness between Mary and Mr Earl, their foreheads close, the soft eyes, and knows this is lacking. Not lost, for it was never there, but to see it, to understand what this could be, is a deprivation, something that she has never had. There is a poetry between Mary and Tom and it resonates quietly.

Tom has seen that Anne watches him with Mary, has seen pain flash across her face. He does not quite understand it, but cannot bear the thought of being a cause of any level of pain to her or to Mary. But it takes some days for him to build up his courage, time that he takes to practise the words in his head. He has not spoken much to Anne but determines to do it now, for Mary's sake.

He sees Anne frowning at a rope knot that refuses to tie itself correctly and takes his chance.

'Anne – I would like to …'

She looks up as if he were that very same knot and he suddenly forgets what he would like at all. He stammers, which only increases her irritation.

'Well?'

The words so carefully chosen, and so well practised, have flown from his head and he is left with only blankness. He begins to panic and glances back towards Mary in the hope of finding inspiration. Her back is turned to him, lost in the work of the cannons, and he turns back to Anne.

'I just wanted to say, I will never hurt her, you know.'

His voice is gentle and pleading and she softens despite herself.

Anne takes a moment, and her voice is a warm balm when she answers.

'I know it.'

And Tom can smile again and breathe.

Anne knows that what she has with Jack is something overworked, grabbed and wrongly labelled as more than it was. And yet here, all along, in front of her is how it is supposed to be, easy, unconscious. Mary and Tom dance to their own song, and she finds herself dancing to someone else's.

She blames Jack, of course. Over the coming days, Jack learns to live with this growing discontent, Anne's disappointment, and he begins to resent her for it. He has not named it yet, this swelling sense of annoyance, but instead increases the rum ration for the crew and drowns his lack in alcohol. This, for now, is enough.

But storm clouds gather over Jack's brow too, and they will not blow away. Anne is not what he expected. Not yielding. Not unquestioning. She has not become his creature, as he had fondly supposed; she is built in no one's image but her own.

She is like no woman he has ever met, and Jack has met many women.

She is wilful and contradictory. A woman who would abandon her husband and take up with a pirate – and he has armed her, too. And here they are, trapped in the middle of the ocean, startled by the reality of one another and neither of them happy.

And now there is Mary, who has made Anne more like herself than she ever was before. The women look to each other first and not to him. He is the captain of this ship, and it is not right.

And he's damned if he can think of anything to do about it.

Chapter 31

News comes that a ship had been spotted. They are to follow and take her. With a new sense of purpose, the men go about the business of battle.

The captain is at the helm, keeping the speck in the distance in his sights, his officers at work with the crew.

Minutes pass, shadows moving across the deck, the ship ahead showing no sign of outrunning them. Aboard *Revenge*, attention has been turned to the sails, the old ship finding her wings and gathering speed, cutting through the sea like a knife and gaining on the hapless prey ahead.

They have transformed their quarters into a battlefield. The cannons, each as long as a man is tall, are wheeled into position, the men straining and pulling with great effort against their stubborn weight and the determined roll of the sea beneath. Powder, wadding and cannonball are rammed into the barrels as further supplies of the same are laid out alongside them. The fearsome weapons are set to peer bluntly through the gun ports, waiting their turn, the men now gun-captains and powder boys waiting grimly at the ready.

Whether the men work the sails above, ready the cannon or ready themselves, each has a part to play. Each checks their pistols and swords, each more heavily armed than usual. A taut silence accompanies these preparations, each man – and woman – alone with their thoughts, making peace with themselves for whatever might come that day.

The strange silence continues, the sounds of the ocean seeming louder as they wait. The doctor coats the floor beneath his butcher's table with a thick layer of sawdust for what will follow having already sharpened his blades.

The frantic activity of the crew ahead can be seen quite clearly, snatches of shouted conversation carried back on the sharp wind. The pirate crew are ready – and each man dressed for the occasion in his finery. Anne has adorned herself with scarves and ribbons just as the men have done, giving the scene an odd air of carnival. Mary is similarly attired, a wealth of weapons and grimness of purpose about her. Her Mr Earl, as always, is at her side.

The captain draws all eyes to him. He stands, the master of his domain, as his flag of the skull and crossbones flies above them, making all too clear their intentions to the ship, which is not now more than one hundred yards ahead.

'How are we, Mr Fetherstone?'

His voice is strong and clear and he soon has his answer.

'We are ready, Captain.'

He nods.

'Then good fighting, lads. Take your positions.'

A gruff voice shouts: 'Cannon – at the ready!' and the sudden roar announces the onset of battle.

The sails thunder as they catch the wind, the recoil and burn of the broadside scorches their nostrils.

The first shots tear a hole of three feet or so wide in the hull of the enemy ship in an explosion of flame as *Revenge* draws alongside.

'Let's make some mischief, lads!' shouts Mary as she leads the charge, screaming like a banshee, sword poised, the mad fiddle music on the deck of the pirate ship scoring their fury.

The men roar and follow her, wielding boarding axes and flint-locks against the unprepared crew, Jack finding himself some-where in the middle of his men.

At the battlefront of locked ships, a blur of weapon-wielding limbs push forward, the ferocity of the faces behind them a sight to behold. Anne and Mary are visible amongst them, their skill as swordsmen quite apparent as Mary slices down across the expanse of no man's land, taking half a man's ear as she does so, his scream distinct amidst the rising sounds of panic all around. He drops from view, holding onto his butchered ear as she presses home her advantage, leaping up to the side of the ship, and dropping down onto the enemy vessel before her, determined and single-minded.

The others need no further encouragement and follow, their roars deafening, as Anne fires two pistols full into the sea of unfriendly faces that presume to slow her progress. The weapons discharged and smoking, she casts them aside and leaps into the melee, eyes shining and sword readied, cutting powerfully at the throat of an officer, her first kill she notes with bloody satisfaction, he falling beneath her as she lands on the deck of the besieged ship, a board-ing axe whistling through the air behind her to land with sickening accuracy in the forehead of some poor soul ahead of her.

Jack is already amongst them, cutting and lunging at the belea-guered crew in a strange and savage dance. The crew of the mer-chant ship is a poor match for such a vicious group of brigands, though they make a fair show of it with swords and small firearms. But as Mary pulls her sword from the guts of a young man of perhaps twenty, his wide-eyed stare fixed upon her in surprise as he falls like a bloodied stone towards the deck, their captain steps forward, breathing hard from his efforts.

'For the love of God – stop. We surrender.'

It takes a moment or two for the instruction to filter through, but the British swords are lowered warily and finally dropped, the pirates pressing home their advantage with kicks, shoves, and the odd cruel swipe of a blade, forcing their captives together by the mast.

Jack strides over to the defeated captain, still breathing hard, Mr Corner with four other pirates sent to secure the rest of the ship.

'And what's your name?'

The man looks at him uncertainly.

'I am Captain William Spenlow of the merchant ship *Starling*.'

All eyes are on Jack as he makes a show of examining the man's coat, picking at the buttons of his collar with the end of his sword.

'And I am Captain Jack Rackham of the pirate ship *Revenge*. Now, would you say you're a good captain, William?'

Spenlow seems confused by the question and does not offer an answer quick enough for the pirate's taste. Without warning, Jack punches him hard in the stomach, causing him to double up in pain. His voice hardens and lowers.

'I asked you a question. I would suggest you answer it.'

He has rendered the man incapable of speech, though this does not concern him.

Anne steps forward, Captain Spenlow staring at her in confusion as he tries to make sense of a woman in such circumstances. He has heard rumours of Jack Rackham and his female pirates, of course, but to have one of them stood before him is quite another thing.

'Perhaps the crew have an opinion, since he doesn't have an answer for us?'

Jack turns to face the defeated crew.

'So, what do you say, lads? Is Captain Spenlow here a good man?'

Despite their predicament, a snort of derision comes from a red-haired man in the front ranks, though his crewmates try to silence him.

Jack is upon him at once.

'You have something to say?'

He looks Jack straight in the eye.

'He's a stone-cold bastard is what he is. It's a pity you didn't finish him off.'

Jack searches the faces of the men around him.

'And do you agree? Is this what you all think of the man?'

There are murmurs of agreement from some, subdued silence from the rest.

Jack turns to his audience once again.

'That's no way to treat a crew, is it? Do you know how we treat captains like William here?'

Anne has already forced Captain Spenlow to his knees, her sword hard at his throat as Thomas Bourn ties his hands at his back.

Spenlow's eyes are wide with fear.

'What will you do to me? I was a captain of His Majesty's Navy! You won't get away with this. We were expecting you, as will other ships to follow. Governor Rogers has taken a particular interest in you – as has James Bonny, a name I think you will recognise. You have a fine price on all your heads.'

Anne falters for a moment, her face suddenly ashen as Jack's expression freezes. It would explain the unexpected resistance encountered while taking this ship. But Anne is not to be wrong-footed for long. She will not be told what to do by this sorry excuse for a man. She will show him – she knows just how to do it.

She puts her finger to Captain Spenlow's lips as if shushing a baby, holding his eyes with hers and daring him to blink. Quite sure that she now has his full attention, she moves the blade slowly down to his stomach, and presses forward. He watches in fascinated horror as the blade sinks into his own soft flesh.

His terrified eyes lock with hers once again, his mouth open in a silent scream as the cool metal sinks home, stopping only when it hits the dull resistance of the mast at his back. He issues a sound like suffocation as she tears the blade from him in one swift, twisting movement, he falling against the deck as a crimson stain spread swiftly around him. Anne looks about to continue when Jack stops her, his hand on her arm, his voice soft.

'That's enough.'

She steps back, wiping the blade, with great show, upon the coat of Captain Spenlow, who now lies bleeding and prone on the deck of his ship. She breathes hard, a feeling of triumph coursing through her. She has shown them all that she will not be looked down upon by any man. All eyes are upon them – with the exception of Mary, who has turned her back on the spectacle, for she cannot watch an unarmed man hurt. It is not right. And at Anne's hands? It is all the more unsettling for it.

The defeated ship has been released at last, and the crew relieved of all useful possessions. The pirates have no clue how to divide up a parrot between them, but they have taken him anyway. He is a handsome beast, blue and yellow with an unmistakable Scottish accent.

'I'll gie ye a skelpit lug!' he threatens loudly to no-one in particular, the voice shrill.

He shuffles from one end of his perch to the other, cocking his head at these strangers, his feathers standing upright in fright as he sees something else.

The cat is all eyes, black as night, as she crouches down to stalk this strange thing that squawks obscenities at her. It flies back and forth around its cage in increasing agitation, its beak rattling at the bars, but they stand firm.

'Keep yer heid! Keep yer heid!'

The bird ignores his own warning for he has no way out. The cat sees this and settles herself for the long game, ears twitching as she reaches a paw through the bars, claws out sharp as knives, the parrot flapping and shrieking against the cage as blue and yellow feathers detach and float down on the deck below. Mr Dobbins smiles at his girl at play, and turns away, leaving the bird to its fate. His squawking high drama will be his undoing.

Meanwhile, the men count out the coins, and tobacco, and rum and other trifles between them, one share each, but for the captain, who gets two. They are happy enough – more is always better, but something is better than nothing and they will fill their bellies and drink their fill later to a job well done.

Mary watches silently and she tries to push from her mind the image of Anne's sword sinking into the stomach of the defeated ship's captain. She looks as sick as a dog.

Chapter 32

Late into the night, Mr Corner and Mr Bourn are still celebrating the effect of their rum ration with a rousing sea shanty. It has been a good day, and they have earned their share of loot, so why not? Inroads have been made into the fifty rolls of tobacco taken from Spenlow's ship, and the men have developed thick coughs to prove it.

Tam Weir has settled himself, very drunk, on top of a wine barrel. Swaying, he is determinedly enjoying a pipe, awkwardly filling the bowl before lighting it. He has barely begun to make it glow, the rich fumes of it filling the air around him, when a sharp voice sounds.

'There's gunpowder behind you, you damn fool – douse the pipe!'

Tam is clumsy with drink and unable to respond quickly. The quartermaster reaches him first, knocking the pipe clean out of his hand, the glowing embers scattering onto the floor, where the older man stamps them out with his bare foot. The shattered pipe and trampled tobacco make a sorry sight, and the lad regards them sorrowfully as he sways still on top of his perch.

Mr Corner grabs him by the shirt, and Tam regards him with unfocused eyes.

'Whasssa marrer?'

Mary and Mr Earl, disturbed mid-affection, join them dishevelled as the quartermaster speaks to Tam.

'Will you have us dead? There's no fire below decks, man.'

Tam looks at Mr Corner, puzzled, as he continues.

'You know this well enough from your last ship and from the Articles. We have your mark upon the document.'

He continues to look uncertain.

'Ar—arrrticles?'

Mary speaks up, irritation clear in her voice.

'You'll get no sense out of him tonight. Let him sleep it off. You can deal with him tomorrow.'

Mr Corner shakes his head, his face somewhere between anger and sadness.

'You stupid lad. There's nothing else for it.'

He lets go of the boy's collar and his voice softens slightly.

'Get some sleep and sober yourself up. You'll have to answer to Mr Fetherstone for this tomorrow. And you have only yourself to blame for it, you bloody fool.'

He leaves Tam where he is, none the wiser, as Mary turns to Mr Earl for an explanation.

'What does he mean? What will happen to him?'

He winces and won't meet her eyes.

'You'll find out soon enough. It will be morning before you know it.'

Tam lies prone and snoring – the effects of the previous evening's rum still very much in evidence. The stink of alcohol and more base things emanates from him, but he is not to be left to sleep it off.

A silent party of grim-faced men, with Mr Corner at their head, approaches and surrounds him, still unconscious in his bunk. There is to be no gentle treatment for him this morning.

'Get up! D'you hear me? Get up, I say!'

The quartermaster shakes him roughly until the lad half opens his eyes and does his best to focus on the face before him.

'Och – leave me be, man. Ma heid is killing!'

'You're to answer for your actions to the captain. It won't go well for you, you may as well know it.'

Tam's face changes as the events of the previous night begin to dawn on him, his eyes growing wider. For the first time, he seems to notice the men waiting ominously behind the quartermaster and his face turns fearful.

'Oh Christ – the pipe … But I dinnae—'

Mr Corner looks sternly.

'Get up and make yourself presentable. Or we'll drag you to the captain ourselves.'

Tam tries to do as he is bid, though it is obvious to all watching that drink still has a strong hold on him. His hands shake as he pulls on his breeches, as do his legs as he attempts to stand before his fellow crewmen. He is a sorry sight, and a frightened one at that – his eyes now wide and bloodshot in a pale and rum-sick face.

'Oh God – it wis a accident. I didnae mean anything by it.'

His words are becoming increasingly fast and garbled as he looks from face to face, searching for some understanding, or compassion.

'Wha' will he do? Wha' will the captain do tae me?'

The quartermaster shakes his head and directs the two men to take the lad's arms. He begins to panic in earnest now, and cries out.

'Wait – wait! Ah cin explain it – ah cin explain!'

But he is not given the opportunity, for a kick behind the knees brings him crashing forward onto the floor, before he is part carried, part dragged above. His eyes meet Mary's as he goes, pleading, but she stands there mute. Tom has laid a gentle hand upon her arm; she knows all too well there's nothing she can do to stop what must happen next.

As his cries become fainter in the open air, the quartermaster turns and addresses the remaining crew, every last man now awake and watching.

'Upstairs all of you. A man has breached the Articles, and we all know what that means. We could have been killed last night and he is due justice for it. You remember that Henry Morgan lost a ship in just such a way.'

There are murmurs of agreement from the assembled men.

At the far end of the deck, the remainder of the crew has gathered, forming an audience around the mast. The captain stands, resplendent in red frock coat and hat, with Anne at his side. Tam Weir is dragged to the front of the crowd, who part before him, watching silently as he comes to a stop, standing before Jack, who addresses the crowd.

'We are here to punish an act of foul negligence this morning, and it is something I do with a heavy heart. Every one of the men on board this ship is a friend and a comrade. We rely on each other for our survival and our prosperity. When someone puts his fellows in danger, there is no question that he must suffer for the good of the crew. By witnessing this suffering, we are all reminded of our responsibilities to our fellow crewmen and to *Revenge*. Mr Weir has put us all in danger, and must be punished for it.'

He nods towards Tam, who faces him uncertainly.

'Remove your shirt, Mr Weir.'

Tam wordlessly begins to remove his shirt and it is only as he fumbles that Mary realises that his hands are shaking. He is ghost white, his terror clamming up his mouth, but he manages to continue. Soon he stands before them all naked from the waist up. Two of the men step forward and bind his hands hard to the mast, his bare back exposed to the assembled crew. He is no more than a boy, the bones standing out from his scrawny back. Mary is not sure such a body can withstand what is to come.

The captain's gaze does not waver as he gives the order.

'Mr Fetherstone – if you will.'

Mr Fetherstone steps forward and unravels a snake-like whip. His face is impassive as he tests the weight, shaking it loose to slither and unravel itself, making a cruel sound against the deck as it does so. He takes a moment or two to familiarise himself with its heft. Then, readying himself, he draws back his arm and brings the end of the thing down hard across Tam Weir's back, drawing a scream from the depths of the poor boy's lungs, a deep red welt opening wide across the clammy flesh as Mary clamps her eyes shut and turns into Tom's shoulder. It is a pity that she cannot drive out the image of the first blow.

Mr Fetherstone returns to his task over and over, the noise of it hideous. The men wince and draw back with each blow as if the pain were their own, the boy's screams echoing around the deck for perhaps a dozen or more strokes until his voice becomes still.

Thirty lashes in all. A small mercy that he does not remain conscious for more than half of them.

George Fetherstone, now red and sweating from his exertions, lets the whip drop to the deck, leaving bloody trails as he does so. Tam is slumped against the mast, his knees buckled beneath him and all fight gone from his bloodied body. As two men move forward to untie him, the deck is host to a sullen and accusing horde. Tam is dragged away by the two kind souls, his back raw and bleeding, as Mary watches.

Anne is suddenly beside her, but Mary recoils as if from a flame. She is angry and Anne is the nearest thing she has to show it.

'This may as well be the Navy, for they have no truck with dignity either.'

Anne is about to reply, but Mary has already turned her back and walked away. Anne is left alone, her heart lurching.

So the capacity for cruelty is here too, unleashed on a boy. Mary has never understood the need to give it audience, men forced to watch the pain and debasement of one of their own. She turns away from it, eyes damp, hot anger rising in her. There is no need for it.

The boy is striped with open wounds, and refuses to speak. He does acknowledge Mary, for she tries to be kind, and brings him food and drink. At first, he is not sure he wants any of it if it keeps him alive in this godforsaken place, but it would take a braver man (or a mad one) to deliberately starve himself to death, and it would be ungrateful to Mary.

'He's just like the other captain, isn't he? Jack.'

Tam's voice is low and sullen.

Mary lowers her eyes.

'He is.'

Nothing more needs to be said as he sets about the miserable food. Mary wonders how she could have blinded herself to Jack.

It will not happen again, she will make sure of it, and she leaves young Tam to his supper, troubled thoughts crowding her mind.

Mary stays close to Tam over the following days. She whispers to him, soothes him, brings him food and stories. He softens to her, but not to the others, and particularly not to Jack.

'He'll need to get back to work soon,' Anne warns.

'Then perhaps tearing his flesh from him was not the best thing to do.'

Anne is not as sympathetic as Mary had expected.

'He brought it on himself. We might all have been blown to kingdom come – it was luck and nothing more that we weren't.'

'He is only a boy, and we can both find some compassion for him.'

'He needs to learn to look after himself. There won't always be someone like you to mother him – and there are captains that would have done more than was done.'

Anne is making excuses, they both know it. Mary feels Anne's need, the olive branch she holds out to her, but will not acknowledge it. Anne is a grown woman, and Tam is no more than a boy. He had followed Mary onto this ship, he had trusted her. And she has not done enough to protect him. From himself or from the others.

Anne feels herself pushed away by her friend, as if what has happened is somehow her fault. She is just a member of this crew, she wants to say. But she doesn't. She feels a new unease as she realises she does not know what to say to Mary. Mary glowers at her like a stranger and it pierces her heart. The words that come to her seem clumsy in her mind, would be clumsier in her mouth she knows, and so she stays silent.

Anne has watched as Mary has spoken to Tam quietly and gently. He had not moved at first, but soon he had turned to her, wincing in pain, tears streaming down his face. She had wiped them away with a hand, and Anne had found herself sick with jealousy at the sight. She had made herself stay only long enough to see Mary offering Tam ship's biscuit to eat under the silent gaze of the other pirates. Although they had offered him no help themselves, they had not stopped Mary from doing so.

Mary is angry at Anne, a burning thing that overwhelms her. She had hoped – expected – that Anne would do more, would have stopped it. It gnaws at her that Anne stood mutely by, a guilty bystander like the rest of them. Mary pauses, for an unexpected thought occurs to her. Perhaps Anne's influence is less than she would like. That her hold on Jack only takes her so far. Perhaps, Mary thinks, Anne's hands are as tied as her own.

Her brow knits in concern. Mary now sees clearly that Anne's position on ship is more precarious than her own. In Jack's eyes, Anne was brought aboard as part of the cabin furniture, and it is only her will that has made her a sailor and kept her here. Anne could be cast aside and returned to James Bonny should Jack's whim will it, and the law will see to the rest. A cold trickle of fear runs down her spine.

Mary thinks back to Breda, of her gilded time there with Arno. The freedom of making her own living to her own rules, now that was the thing. And she resolves to do it again, to be beholden to no one, and to do what she must in the meantime to come out of this well.

What Anne will do for herself she cannot tell, but that cannot be wholly Mary's concern. Mary must think of herself first, for she has learned all too well that no one else will do it for her, and circumstances have changed. She and her Tom must make plans.

Chapter 33

Life returns to an uneasy normality following the flogging. Tam Weir has not yet returned to active duty and instead lies immobile in his bunk, refusing to speak, his bare back still clearly showing the raw aftermath of his punishment. His face is a mix of pain and stubbornness when he meets the gaze of any of the men. He is an unsettling presence in the midst of the crew's quarters, the memory of his screams difficult to drive from anyone's mind.

Anne is concerned about Mary. She has been looking pale and tired, and has taken to keeping her own counsel where before she might have sought out Anne. She sees her lost in low discussions with Tom, night after night. Anne has chosen not to pry, for she has no desire to know the detail of their intimacy. But when she finds Mary alone, staring out to sea, she finds that her concern is too great.

'Is everything all right, Mary? You haven't said much for days.'

Anne feels the relief of being able to speak to her, here and alone.

Mary blinks, not having heard Anne there. Anne sees that Mary has become distracted, her face softening. Anne follows her gaze to see Mr Earl wielding a hammer at an unwieldy plank.

'We are going to marry when we settle. We can't be at sea for-ever, and we have almost enough money to be honest soon.'

Anne cannot speak, but Mary still has more to share.

'I have an eye on buying an inn, much as I had in Breda. And Tom will make his living as a carpenter, just as he does now – though honestly. We will make a family.'

Anne cannot breathe. She had never imagined that Mary might ever leave her. She had assumed they would always be together, never apart. She looks at her in dismay and struggles to find her voice.

'But you can't leave the ship. You are needed here. Your life is here.'

There is a desperation in her voice that she hardly recognises as herself.

'You are too good a sailor, and the ship needs Tom. A ship cannot be without a carpenter.'

'I am here by accident, Anne. Do you think that if Jack had known I was a woman he'd have invited me to join the crew?'

'He did not stop you.'

'He did not want to lose face in front of the men.'

'But he brought me aboard.'

Mary pauses, for she knows Anne cannot see it.

'I think you'll find that was quite a different circumstance …'

Anne stiffens.

'I have earned my place on this crew, just as you have. It doesn't matter that we are women.'

Mary smiles gently.

'You are not listening, Anne.'

Mary takes her hand and places it on her belly.

'I am pregnant. I am going to have a baby.'

Anne should have seen it, she knows, but she has been lost in her own thoughts of late. And Mary and her Tom, well, it was bound to happen. But she knows instinctively that this cannot end well. It is the greatest betrayal her body could make.

'I am glad for you,' says Anne, leadenly.

She leaves quickly, her limbs carrying her awkwardly. She cannot show Mary the horror that has lodged in her, the anger too. This is no place for a child. What this means she tries to push from her mind, but it is all bad news. She can only imagine what Jack will say, what it means for Mary. And when her time comes …?

Anne shudders for she knows that when it is Mary's time, she needs to be far away from it. She has seen enough in the past to know she cannot be there. Has seen glimpses of women on her father's plantation sweat, heave and bleed children into the world, with pain that can barely be endured.

Suddenly Mary is there beside her, her face a question.

Anne grasps her hand in her own.

'I'm sorry, Mary. I don't want you to leave. It's not what I wanted – not what I ever wanted. And I am frightened.'

She had not known she was going to say it, but knows it is right.

Mary squeezes Anne's hand.

'I'm frightened too. But it will be all right. I promise.'

Anne feels tears flood her eyes and spill down her cheeks. She does nothing to stop them.

'It will be all right, Anne. A new life will come into the world. And Tom and me will love him and keep him safe.'

Safe. With Mary at his side, he will always be safe.

Mary holds Anne's hand, warm and enclosed. They fall into silence, for nothing more can be said. They look up, watching the slow progress of clouds across the bluest of skies and sit side by side, a thousand miles away from one another.

Chapter 34

Mary can barely believe her own news. She and Arno had tried for a child for so long, and nothing had happened. She had begun to worry that there was something wrong with her, that she would never have a child of her own. But it seems it was only a matter of time – and perhaps the added prayers had helped.

She had hesitated to tell Tom her news at first. She told herself that it was because she wanted to be certain, to wait another month, but she had known it was more than that. She had seen enough men want nothing to do with the trouble they had brought when it came down to children, had seen enough abandoned women with babies they had no way to feed. Tom is everything to her now, and she is frightened what he will think. That he might not want her now that it is more than just her.

But he is a good man. It is why she loves him as she does. She had reminded herself of this as she had sought him out, quieting her nerves before taking his hand and leading him to a remote part of the deck to whisper the news. Tom had cried, and grasped her to him, said that they were blessed. And he had kissed her, her face shining with love, and gratitude, and relief.

But there are practicalities to consider, they both know it. What this will mean Mary is not sure, but she knows that she will not be allowed to stay aboard once the baby comes. And to take Tom with her? – well that is another problem altogether, though she has set her mind to find a solution.

And now that Mary has shared her secret with Anne, a new, fragile comfort has established itself between them.

'I don't think I ever heard a tale of a retired pirate. Perhaps I will be the first.'

Anne tries to imagine it.

'You – sat in a rocking chair with your knitting? I cannot see it.'

'Oh, but I can. Paid for by plunder, with a dozen grandchildren around my knees.'

Anne pauses, trying not to feel stung by her absence in Mary's mind.

'It is not what I see for myself.'

'Then what do you see?'

Anne has no answer yet, for the future swirls unknown and unseen behind the dark clouds of her mind's eye.

Mary considers her for a moment.

'Then what *did* you think? – when you started this? With Jack and the ship?'

'I wanted a different kind of world to the one I knew.'

'Well you have that. But that is never the end of things. What is it that you want now?'

She has Mary, and had thought that was enough. But Mary is on a different path now.

Mary's voice becomes gentler.

'We make our own way, you and me. But there are no markers. We have to forge our own, and the more courage you've shown, the more you need to find.'

Anne feels cold uncertainty in her throat and swallows it down.

'But what if I cannot?'

Mary considers it.

'I cannot do it for you. You have to find your own answer to that, Anne.'

She is suddenly adrift, her mind tumbling thought over thought. She feels Mary's hand upon her shoulder.

'You will make a discovery of yourself. It will be a great adventure.'

Anne shakes her head and makes to leave, but Mary tries again.

'If you had your own ship?'

It makes her pause. Anne does not want to be captain of what she already has. But the possibilities of a ship and where it might take her? The world opens up before her, the map of oceans vast and unknown. She had not seen it for what it was before, but now it sits before her, shining, a jewel hiding in plain sight.

'We have a ship and yet we only know the trade routes. I think I should like to sail east to see what is out there for myself.'

Mary sees a shift in Anne as she contemplates this unthought future, and it makes her heart swell.

'So what is stopping you?'

Anne has no answer for this, and Mary continues.

'You have followed Jack so far. Do you trust him with your life?'

Anne knows without a doubt that she does not, and Mary sees it.

'Then you had better start trusting yourself and start planning. You cannot live only in the present forever.'

Chapter 35

Life on the ship continues as the baby grows. Decks are scrubbed, sails mended, money is lost at cards and dice, men curse, fight and sleep. And Mary too begins to grow.

Jack sees it at last with a jolt, but takes his time to react, for it is not a situation he has dealt with before. Why would it be? He is naturally appalled, if not a little proud of Thomas Earl. He had not realised the man had it in him. It makes him wonder for a moment why Anne has not fallen too, for he believes he is a better man by far than his carpenter. But no matter. It is, he supposes, the natural consequence of some women's nature, but it does not make for the smooth running of his ship. Mary is still capable, but for how much longer?

But in the end, there is really only one course of action and Jack must be the man to enforce it.

Mary is with Anne, a dismantled cannon between them, but it's not this that he points at when he finally speaks but at Mary's swelling belly.

'So this will be Mr Earl's doing, then.'

Mary nods, awkward for once.

'A ship is not a place for a child, and a pirate ship less so, that is clear enough. You cannot continue as part of this crew for much longer, I am sure you understand. We must put you ashore when the time comes, Mary.'

Things are moving faster than she wanted, and Anne does not like it.

'I could look after her, and the baby too.'

Jack shakes his head.

'It is out of the question. And besides, I do not see you as the caring type, Anne.'

Her fists bunch as anger burns in her face.

Jack steps back, his voice mocking.

'Perhaps Anne can go with you, Mary, since she is so concerned about your welfare. Particularly since she did not think to mention this to me.'

It stings, for the words come fully formed. Anne's cheeks are flushed as she answers.

'My place is here. As is Mary's, as you well know.'

If Anne goes, she will choose her time. She will not let him offload her so easily.

'Perhaps, but it is no longer Mary's since she has been so careless.'

Mary has caught Anne's temper and steps towards Jack.

'Careless? There was nothing careless—'

But Jack has tired of this particular game and holds up a hand wearily.

'There is nothing more to be said. The only consideration now is when you will leave us, Mary. My mind is made up.'

He turns and walks away, Anne's eyes boring into the back of his retreating figure. Words sound angrily in her head.

You are not the captain of me.

But it is too soon. Anne does not yet know what her next step should be, her decision not yet made.

Mary speaks urgently to her.

'Perhaps it would not be so bad if you came with me. That you don't want Jack—'

'I do not know what I will do.' There are too many thoughts, too much to think about.

Anne is caught.

Jack limits her. She has outgrown him, she finally sees it. There is a wider world out there that Mary has painted for her, and she cannot let herself be limited by a man or a ship. But that is not all. There is a deeper concern troubling Anne.

She does not want to lose Mary, but she cannot know what Mary will become once the child is here. She knows that they cannot drink, and talk, and fight as they do now, for that is not what mothers so. Mary's time and attention will be for the child, and Anne cannot bear the thought of sharing that.

But if Anne leaves this ship and is no longer a pirate, then what is she? That thought most of all catches in her throat. And now that she has tasted it, it will not go away.

Chapter 36

Mary does not sleep easy, thoughts of the baby and Jack's recent judgement keeping her wide awake into the early hours. It leaves her ill-tempered, so it is no surprise when less than an hour into the day angry voices draw all attention to the far side of the ship, where Mary stands her ground against Titus Oates, her Tom prone on the ground.

'You raise a hand to Tom and you raise a hand to me, Titus.'

The man's hammer fist is still raised, itching to finish the job it has started. His eyes glitter.

'He looked at me without respect, and I defended my honour.'

Mary splutters at this.

'Your *honour*?! You don't have any, man, and you're due no respect from what I've seen.'

This is too much for him to process.

'Just get out of my way, woman!'

Anne has pushed her way through the crowd and had intended to hold Mary back from doing the man further harm, though Titus suddenly changes her mind. Mr Oates tries to fling Mary aside but, much as expected, she ducks under the clumsy arm and launches herself at him. He falls to the deck with a resounding thud as Mary sets about him with her fists.

Anne sees that Jack is making his way towards them in ill humour, and decides it would be sensible to resume her previous plan as if she had intended it all along. She steps in and grabs at Mary's arms, trying to drag her off the prone and battered Mr Oates. But Mary is slippery and seems to have more than four limbs as she wriggles and turns, kicking out at the prostrate gunner while her arms are briefly incapacitated.

Jack steps in to take an arm and soon Mary is restrained, red and panting, as is Anne.

'Well?'

Jack spits the word out. They let Mary go, and she brushes herself down. Her temper is still up, and she looks towards Tom. He is now sat upright, though he holds his head and groans. She turns to Jack and speaks.

'He punched Tom. So I punched him.'

Jack groans inwardly.

'It is just a fight. Let them finish it.'

Mr Oates struggles to get back to his feet.

'She got in the way, Captain. You know I don't fight women.'

Mary moves quickly and, before he knows what is happening, Jack's sword is in Mary's hand and Mr Oates's chin is perched on the sharp tip of it.

Titus moves his wide eyes to meet Mary's and speaks urgently through the tiny gap that prevents him being skewered.

'My beef isn't with you, Mary, it's with Tom.'

She snarls closer, the blade not moving.

'I choose to deputise for him.'

He would like to strike her, but the balance of flesh and blade is too delicate, so he swallows instead, trying to make his eyes talk.

Jack steps forward, sighs and shakes his head.

'Really, Mary? Must we do this? I run a harmonious ship – or at least I should like to. There's time to step back from this and we can forget the whole thing if you will both shake hands.'

Mary has not shifted her murderous gaze from the man before her, who seems equally fired.

'I choose not to.'

Jack's shoulders drop.

'Then we must change course for the nearest cay, and you can fight it out like men.'

He does not correct himself, but holds out his hand.

'But in the meantime – my sword, if you would be so kind.'

The perfect spot for a duel has been sighted. It is barely an island, just a spit of sand wide and long enough for a sword fight, they are told. Mr Earl continues to try to talk Mary out of her decision, but he is wasting his breath for Mary has made her mind up and will not be swayed.

'Let me fight him, Mary. It is what he wanted, after all.'

She shakes her head and Tom continues.

'I must have upset him. I don't know what I did, but—'

'He is too hard for you. I must do it – it's obvious. He won't get past me. Besides, you have me a crib to build.'

Tom drops his voice.

'But what about the baby?'

She sees the concern in his face, and softens for a moment.

'The baby can fight his own battles when the time comes. In the meantime, he has me.'

Mr Oates knows all too well that this is not how things should be. He is already regretting choosing Tom to take out his bad temper on, an easier target for his frustrations about Mary and her way with the guns that were so recently his. He would not have chosen her direct, and with good reason. He has not yet fully understood that an indignant woman, and a pregnant one at that, is not someone to be trifled with, though he is beginning to suspect it. His own wife, bless her soul, went into the next life mutely, after all, at the bidding of his own hands, but he does not expect that Mary shall be so obliging. He cracks the knuckles of his great mallet hands and smiles in satisfaction. Well perhaps it's time Mary was taught a lesson. She has been getting ahead of herself since she came aboard, and he doesn't like it at all. He is just the man to knock some sense into that head of hers.

Anne is worried for Mary. Titus Oates is little better than a snarling bear; all teeth, claws and instinct. He is brutal and efficient, a hulking hammer blow of a man. He does not play by the rules. Anne has no doubt that Mary is good, but her mouth dries when she thinks of it. When she looks at them in the boats ahead, his bulk blots Mary out.

The first boat nudges against the island as Mary steps into the shallows, knee-deep in swirling sand and water, dragging the boat forward to steady its purchase on the beach. Her adversary is sullen as he makes his way onto this suggestion of dry land, followed close behind by the quartermaster. Their crewmates bear witness from the longboats, waiting for the entertainment to come.

Mr Fetherstone takes position between the two pirates as they square up to one another, their eyes narrowing in murderous concentration.

'According to the Articles, you have a right to resolve your quarrel here, and then it goes no further. Do you understand?'

They nod their assent, neither taking their eyes from the other for a moment.

'Then may the best man win. Take your marks.'

Titus Oates draws his cutlass slowly. His eyes widen. But there is no time to respond as Mary takes out a pistol and calmly shoots him in the leg, the explosion echoing around the cay. He falls to the ground bellowing, writhing in the sand.

As if sensing that the captain might admonish her for her actions, she turns to him coolly.

'That is the way we fight in the Army – quick and clean. You have to remember that I never was a naval man before now. And besides, it is hardly right that a man should fight a woman, is it? Especially when she is to have a baby?'

The captain is clearly at a loss for words as Mary strides across the short space to her wounded crewmate, his face leaching colour as unconsciousness beckons. She puts her face close to his.

'Mr Oates – do you concede?'

He answers in curses and whimpers and a small nod as he wraps his fingers tightly around the injured limb, blood flowing thickly between them.

And so the matter is resolved.

Anne rocks in silent laughter, Mary acknowledging her with a conspiratorial wink.

'Beaten – and beaten by a woman at that,' says Mary lightly.

Samuel Teague and Joshua Hands stagger ashore through the shallows to help the injured man.

'The doctor will need to sew him back together.'

The men don't look happy as one takes his shoulders, the other his wriggling feet and try to lift him.

'Christ, man – when did you get so fat?' grumbles Samuel Teague as the gunner continues to whimper and squirm.

'Stay still or you can stay here and bleed out,' says Joshua Hands. Mr Oates pushes his lips together in brave forbearance as his dead weight is manhandled and dropped into the boat with a loud thud, his crewmates climbing in after him, wet and ill tempered.

Mary makes her way to a third boat where Mr Earl is waiting.

'I told you not to worry.'

She climbs into the boat with some difficulty, it tilting alarmingly as she manages to haul herself in with Tom's help.

'I don't know why I ever did,' and he takes her hand, smiling and thanking his lucky stars he is on the right side of her.

The journey back to the ship is more difficult than the one out. Mary's honour is intact, which is more than can be said for Mr Oates's leg. He is left under no illusion that he is anything but a bloody inconvenience to his crewmates, who tread on him, exasperated, only some of it accidental, as he lies lumpen and bleeding at their feet.

The doctor is waiting as they return, eyeing his new patient glumly and refilling his tankard before gesturing for the injured man to be brought below decks.

'A gunshot? Unexpected,' he murmurs, poking a finger into the wound and prompting his patient to squeal like a pig. 'No rest for the wicked,' he says to no one in particular and steels himself for the coming struggle against bone, skin and sinew that seems to become more difficult each day.

'I had hoped you'd go easy on him.' Jack is tetchy now that he has Mary on her own.

'And why would I do that?'

His eyes glitter in annoyance.

'A pistol is hardly sporting.'

'Sporting, no, but it was effective, was it not?'

He prickles at the words.

'And who will do his work now?'

'Ask any of this lot. They seem to have precious little to do but torment each other.'

Jack smarts, aware that the crew are listening, waiting for his response.

'I'll remind you I'm your captain, and you'll speak to me as such.'

Her expression is neutral as she answers.

'Yes. Captain.'

He feels the pause, a beat too long.

Chapter 37

Mr Oates is slow to forget the incident, the humiliation burning at him. For several weeks, he walks stiffly, his heavily bandaged leg still giving him gyp, as he has bored the men in telling.

'Teach you to upset Mary,' he is told more than once.

The wince he meets this with is not only one of pain.

Mary, however, is fine, her belly growing prouder by the day. She talks happily away to her baby boy within – for she is certain it is a 'he' – and tells him about her duties, the men, his father – for Tom is proud too.

'And what's Mr Bourn doing? He is fixing the sails with a needle. And what is this? It's a cannon and we must keep it clean and working in case the Navy come calling.'

If this baby emerges less than a sailor, it is not for want of trying, for Mary has taken to teaching him knots when the day is done too. Her ankles have begun to swell, and it's good to take the weight off her feet, for he's a good weight to be carrying around.

She might seem mad to some as she chatters away to herself.

But the men do not mind. Some had children once, and they look on her with a fondness for the lost things they once had.

Mr Teague has told her about his own children, left behind in England and assuming him dead.

'I don't think I will see them again, more's the pity.'

He insists on helping her now with the cannon, for she has become slower, though no less able.

'Be careful there, mother.'

And she glows at the word, for she knows it is hers alone.

Tom sits with her, working at a piece of timber that will become a bowl for the baby. He has made it smooth as a pebble, for no child of his will suffer even a splinter. This child shall never know discomfort – the thought of it drives him to distraction – and the bowl will be proof of it.

He has started a menagerie for him in wood, and has a ship in mind too – a miniature of *Revenge* – for his son. Mary seems sure it is a boy, and who is he to doubt her? Mary will like the toys, though he has not yet told her his plan. He would like to surprise her with it, if he can think how to make the thing without her knowing.

'What shall we call him, Tom?'

He does not look up from his work, though his face lights up.

'Let's meet him first. We shouldn't decide before we see what will suit. Our son will have a name soon enough.'

And so the baby is unnamed – out loud at least. Mary had thought once that she would call her child Arno, but that was a lifetime ago, clouded in sadness. This is new, and good. Mary has always liked the name 'Jem', though she keeps it tucked away. 'Jem' will suit him, she knows it.

She wraps her arms around her belly and rests her head on the chest of her Tom, the blood beat of his heart soothing her.

Still here. Still here. Still here.

Chapter 38

Days pass before a ship is spotted. They are to take it. The preparations are routine now, and they are ready when they draw near the enemy vessel, their death's head flag flying above them. There is less panic from the other ship than they have come to expect, but perhaps it is their lucky day.

They pull alongside the ship ready to start their hellcat charge, tensing to spill onto the deck of the enemy, but there is something wrong. Mary and Jack feel it first. It is too quiet – where are the men on the deck of the other ship?

Anne sees that Mary is unsettled and grasps her sword closer as she breathes in, out, in, as she tries to make sense of what she is seeing. Then suddenly there is a voice from the other ship shouting out to 'Fire!' and the world begins to burn.

The explosion of fire from the enemy cannon blows Titus Oates backwards, leaving him tattered and bloody. His good remaining leg gapes down to blood and sinew as he screams out in pain, prone on the deck, his eyes rolling back into his head.

Anne stands stock-still, sword wavering in her hand, unable to tear her eyes from him. So this is what combat can be, an unfurling horror.

Mary sees her, veers back and shakes her until she is looking into her eyes.

'Stay here and help the doctor. Mr Mayhew needs you. I will do the other work for both of us. They will regret fighting back.'

And Mary is gone – leaping over the side of the ship, sword held high, roaring as she takes her demons to her enemies.

Anne is faint and sick, but determines to put her leaden limbs to use. If Mary can do this when carrying a child, then so can she. She shouts across to the doctor, who gazes on his first patient with resignation.

'Let's get this man below decks.'

He has to shout to be heard above the noise of cannon fire. The smell of newly burnt flesh assaults her as they descend to the doctor's workroom, their heavy burden screaming between them. Every jolt, every knock causes him new agony, and there are many of them before they deposit him, groaning and sweating, on the butcher's table. The smell is new to Anne, the smell of fear and decay. Nothing good comes from this table, and the patient is all too aware of it.

The doctor passes Titus Oates a bottle and a thick piece of rope.

'Drink what you can of the rum, for it will help. And when you've done, keep the rope between your teeth and bite down. I will be as quick as I can.'

His bedside manner is lacking, but he has seen this all too often, and knows the odds are slim whatever he does.

Mr Oates sets to screaming again as he sees the saw, tries to get off the table to run, but the doctor shakes his head sadly.

'And where will you go, Titus? I know it is butchery, but you will have a chance. You will be dead of gangrene in the week if we don't do this.'

The man slumps back, defeated by the horrible logic.

The doctor turns to Anne.

'Hold him. You will need all your strength to do it.'

Mr Mayhew is a man of few words, and has already turned away to his array of vicious instruments, leaving Anne with no choice but to grip Titus's shoulders with all her strength. The stink of the slaughterhouse is about the place and the animal sounds of the injured man fill her with terror. There is a wildness in the surgeon's bloodshot eyes, and a strong smell of drink on his breath.

He ties off the injured limb swiftly before he brings the saw down with a thud. It cuts into the flesh above the gaping wound and the doctor glumly goes about his business to the sound of a barely muffled scream that will not end. He wields the instrument, bone and flesh no match for his determination and Mr Oates's screams and bulging eyes attest. Anne looks away, but cannot unhear the saw gnawing through bone, feel the warmth of thick blood spattering her hands.

Soon, the leg submits below the knee and thuds dumbly to the floor, sawdust doing its best to stem the flow of blood and its owner groans and screams through the gag until, mercifully, he passes out and is still.

Anne still holds his shoulders, white-knuckled, until the doctor, in an unlikely show of gentleness, unpicks her fingers from the flesh and forces a bottle into her hands.

'And now you know why I stay drunk.'

His breath attests to it as he sways, watching her drink the rum back, eyes tight closed as she wills it to take her to where Mr Oates has gone, the burning liquor a road she hopes will carry her to oblivion, and quickly.

But there is no such luck. The fight continues to thunder above, and before she has finished drinking, Richard Corner is half dragged in by Mr Dobbins, who throws him at the doctor in a panic. Mr Corner is lucky not to have lost his eyes to the shrapnel, though half his face is a mess of raw meat, wood and metal fragments that Mr Mayhew must unravel as best he can.

Mr Dobbins turns his face away from the new patient before he is stopped by the sight of Titus Oates, lying bleeding on the operating table. He turns to Anne in anguish, but there is nothing to be said; he leaves as quickly as he can, stumbling in his haste to do so. He is thankful that he can play no further part in the horror show, his skin crawling through his clothes as he escapes back to the madness above. It is a better place than here.

But there is no such escape for Anne. The doctor blinks at his new patient, removing his spectacles to take a closer look at the wound. Expectations of success are low, but the doctor takes his handkerchief, wipes his nose, before taking the rag to the tattered hole, the injured man's teeth grinning yellow and red through it, and he meets the terrified eyes of Mr Corner.

'Merely a flesh wound, though this will undoubtedly hurt.'

He is as good as his word, the man's howling reaching up and through the deck as Anne bears down with all her strength again, this time closing her eyes and ears to the horror of it. She wishes briefly for her own piece of rope to bite down on as the doctor begins the grim work of slow and agonising pain, and she is in hell.

Day gives way to night. A hole the size of a man's head has been torn in the side of the ship, the flash of pistols and cannon lighting up the dark. As Anne throws open the hatch to get some air, flames from the burning ship alongside light up the sky a sickly red.

The strange light illuminates the injuries below – the white bone of Titus Oates's leg reaching through his torn flesh as he hangs onto it in agony, Richard Corner screaming hideously as he covers his eyes, blood flowing freely between his fingers as he tries to cover up God knows what miserable hurt.

Sprawled on the deck, Joshua Hands lies wide-eyed and still, his shirt generous with blood around a large fragment of the shattered hull which hangs from him at a horrible angle. Samuel Teague sits alone, his back against the main mast, holding his stomach as a bloom of blood fans out from a gunshot wound. There is no hope for them and will be sent overboard before the day is done.

Tam Weir is hard at work with a sack of sawdust, scattering it about the deck in thick handfuls, the worst of the gore soaking into it and preventing the remaining men slipping in their shipmate's blood as they work. She sees another of the boys struggling under the weight of powder for the magazines that he carries to the men working at their posts and Anne is soon carrying the same, thankful to be of help to anyone but the doctor. She seems to pay no heed to the terrifying turmoil around her, the screeching sounds of battle and pain, until some time later it is finished.

The enemy ship has been taken at last, and everything is still but for the crackling of burning wood, woodsmoke catching in the eyes and throat.

Mary and the other men return after a time, weary and silent, their faces fixed. The spoils are few, but hard won. Their treatment of the defeated crew has been less than kind, stabbings and beatings handed out in multiples for those they have taken themselves. They have taught the men a lesson, but they have learned a few themselves. They are bruised, leaden, and only a little better off than they were before. Today has not gone well, though they are still alive. It barely seems enough.

Anne's heart sinks as she watches her crewmates return. She is ashamed of her lack of action, ashamed that she has shared the doctor's work with only numbness and horror, but he and his patients are now sleeping off the efforts of the day.

She sees Jack, who quickly averts his eyes, causing her cheeks to burn. She is surprised to find that she cares what he thinks of her, and that it is not good. And then she feels Mary's hand on her back.

When she turns, Mary presses a small bag of coins into her trembling hands.

'Your share of not very much. And how is Titus?'

'Alive.'

She cannot meet Mary's eyes, and she speaks to her gently.

'You did your best for them, and no one can ask for more than that.'

She shakes her head, fights the nausea that rises in her.

'I was a coward.'

'What you did is not the work of a coward. Lie down a while and gather your strength.'

Anne cannot help but feel her own inadequacies drowning her.

'You proved yourself again today, as I should have done.'

Mary looks at her, a cloud passes overhead. She squeezes her hand, nothing more needing to be said.

Next time, Anne thinks, she is determined to be ready. She will not let herself or Mary down again.

Mr Oates's leg is sent to a watery grave by the doctor, now drunk as a lord – and yet still not as drunk as he hoped to be. His one-legged patient is left with only fever dreams for company, in which he tries to run but falls, over and over again, until – no matter how much he struggles to stay above it – he is swallowed by the ground.

Chapter 39

It is late October, and the unrelenting heat and blazing sunshine of what passes for a Caribbean autumn has made the crew lethargic and irritable. It has been almost two weeks since the last raid, and the men's wounds are healing, but the discomfort of it still weighs heavy on them. There has not been a breath of wind for days, and the sails hang as listless as the men below. Not even an increase in the rum ration has lightened the mood.

The captain's usual joviality is strained, for he has seen that the men are quieter than usual, and quiet is never a good sign on a pirate ship. He remembers such a silence just before he accused his former captain – Captain Vane – of cowardice and cast him adrift. He had been untouchable then, carried to the ranks of captain by popular vote.

But now? Jack's dreams become increasingly uneasy, his sleep poor, as sneaking men with cutlasses haunt the far reaches of his thoughts, just waiting for their chance to pounce as he falls into restless sleep.

Despite the efforts of Mr Fetherstone on the captain's behalf to lift the spirits of the men, the stubborn silence continues, and the sun continues to beat down relentlessly, day after day.

But change is coming, as it always does. It begins with a shift in the air.

Anne watches from the crow's nest as a seagull soars above the ocean, the first movement in days. And then a breeze caresses her cheek, so unexpectedly that she raises her fingers to it, as if it had been a kiss. The breeze is sharp and is followed by a gentle but definite further breath of cool air.

From her post, she can see a huddle of crewmen at the stern of the ship, tight-lipped as they watch the ocean as it closes in behind them. It has become unreadable. The familiar blue translucence is gone, replaced by an obstinate lead grey that might have been slate for all it gives away.

What lurks beneath is a matter for the darkest reaches of the mind to conjure with, superstition summoning forth strange monsters from the clay of fear and the unknown.

The breeze has gathered itself, steady and cool, beginning to pick at their clothing.

'Storm coming, then?'

Mr Bourn is matter-of-fact, sombre.

John Fenwick answers.

'Strange type of storm, if you ask me. It's something worse than bad luck that's following this ship and we're going to be seeing it soon enough.'

He continues.

'I saw the sea take my last ship and her crew during a storm. The men who sailed with her are nothing but ghosts.'

'God has them now.'

Noah Harwood offers this up, his voice unconvinced, as John Fenwick adds to the gloom he has created.

'They're not with God – the air is thick here with the spirits of the dead. Something bad is coming this way, you mark my words. Every last one of us needs to make his peace with the devil, the fairies, or whatever else they believe in, because it will not leave us in peace until it has finished with us.'

But Mr Bourn is having none of it.

'Keep your tales of misery to yourself, John Fenwick, we don't need your superstitious rubbish. A storm is coming is all.'

He bristles, but the men begin to murmur nervously among themselves as the captain appears. The dark circles beneath his eyes are apparent, and his smile takes some effort to conjure up.

'What is it, lads? Not scaring yourselves for a little storm, are you?'

John Fenwick answers.

'No, Captain. It's not a storm we're scared of.'

They will not meet his eyes, he sees it plainly.

'Have I ever let you down, lads? Do you think there's anything I would do to let this –' he waves his arm expansively '– go wrong for us? I will make it right. Trust me, I have plans more powerful than superstition and magic.'

As if to prove him wrong, the sky darkens, heavy clouds heading straight for them. The men glance up at one another silently as they disperse.

Soon a cold, cutting wind whips itself out of thin air and gains strength by the minute. Jack is relieved to have orders to give at last, ordering that the cannons and cargo are secured while the boatswain and his men turn their attention to the sails. Anne descends quickly to the relative safety of the deck, lending her efforts to securing the rigging.

The mast and cannon are secured for the storm, which is now inevitable. Hatches are battened, sails furled and tied. The clouds multiply and close in upon one another, and the sky quickly darkens. There is a low grumble, a flash, and the prickle of first rain. Then a patter, a thrum, and the deluge begins.

The ship rocks gently at first, but the storm has only just begun. The men who can be spared are sent below decks to wait out the next hours, taking to their hammocks with prayers or lucky charms, depending on their beliefs. For the rest, there are eyes clenched closed and hands that hold on for dear life to the rough ropework of their bunks as they begin to sway together like pendulums.

Above them, the waves grow in size and power as the rain pours down from thunderous skies, and soon the swell of the slate-grey ocean is rocking the ship like a cork. The wind howls loud, the *Revenge* tipping wildly in the maddened sea, her crew rattling around like dice in a cup below decks. The crew left on deck to battle the elements are already soaked to their skins, eyes salt-red facing into the world turned upside down, walls of black water looming ahead of them.

The ship creaks and lurches her way through the squall, the wind shrieking around the masts and making the sails billow like ghosts despite their restraints. Lightning tears open the sky, the heavy thrum of driving rain sending the few remaining men who do not have duties to fulfil scurrying below decks.

Anne stands firm on deck, gazing across the rolling black ocean. Sea spray reaches out with salty fingers as the rain assaults her from above, the drumming weight having soaked her already.

Mary tries to make her way to Anne, but a lurch of her guts and a hasty rush to the side of the ship to unburden herself interrupts her progress. The captain approaches, a little unsteady due to the increasing tilt of the deck.

'Get below decks, Mary, you need sea legs for this.'

A cannon breaks free of its tackle and rolls dumbly across the deck, while the remaining men stumble to and fro, lurching in time with the ship. Jack is headed for the helm, where the first mate struggles to hold the ship's course, and Mary needs no further telling.

She feels her nausea subside as she heads towards the hatch and places her hand on the cold wet metal with relief. This at least is solid and real. The ship has taken on a strange life of its own. The hatch door swings itself open violently out of her grasp, showing the men below an unwelcome vista of black drenching rain and a sea leached of all natural colour, great walls of water of immense heights and force. Fear lodges itself in her chest as she stands there stock-still.

Noah Harwood's bunk below is closest and he yells out to her from the yellow darkness.

'For God's sake, close the bloody thing – none of us needs to see this.'

Mary snaps to and slides down the steps, dragging the hatch closed behind her. There is some comfort to the thickness of wood and metal between her and what lies outside, and she crosses their quarters below like a drunken man, staggering side to side as she makes her way back to her bunk that sways before her. Her crewmates have fared little better than her, their groans, prayers and sickness hardly making for a comfortable retreat.

She is glad to reach the sanctuary of her hammock without incident, climbing in with some effort before closing her eyes tight and curling up like a child in its mother's lap, telling herself over and over that it will be finished soon enough like a bad dream if only she wills it hard enough. Tom reaches out his hand to hers, and they hold onto one another in the darkness.

But the storm will be heard. The timbers of the ship creak and groan, as do the crew, as they are flung, rocked and unsettled in body and mind. A wine barrel has broken free and rolls around like a drunkard, though none of the crew try to stop it.

Mary tries to lose herself in unconsciousness for some time, until she cannot stand it and gives up on the idea of sleep. She looks for Anne but cannot see her anywhere; surely she cannot still be above decks?

Fear presses in on her once again and it makes up her mind. She will look for Anne, and if anything is coming for her, she will meet it eye to eye.

Mary emerges once again from the hatch into the world above. The rain lashes down relentlessly, the primeval howl of the storm filling her senses, until she sees a lone figure at the side of the ship. It takes a moment for her eyes, stung by salt, to focus before she realises the figure is Anne. She grips the rail, her feet planted firmly on the deck, her clothes hanging drenched around her, her face raised up to the onslaught.

Mary is transfixed by her, at one with the storm and fury around her. She has the urge to move closer, but the treacherous conditions prevent it; that and the fact that Anne considers herself quite alone. After a few moments, Mary, unseen, takes herself below decks, the vision of Anne fixed in her head as she navigates the groaning, vomiting mass of humanity that surrounds her.

Back in her bunk, by some small miracle, Mary finds herself shortly asleep, drifting away from the foul reality, holding on to the single thought of Anne, stood alone.

Chapter 40

By the next morning, the storm has blown itself out, and a soft cool has taken its place. One of the sails hangs limp like a dislocated arm, the wheel and thump as it hits, useless, against the mast beating out a maddening rhythm.

As she blinks cautiously into the reality of the new day, Mary is greatly relieved to see a return to calm, and the absence of drumming rain. The morning has brought with it the promise of clear skies ahead. After the storm comes good weather, and there are reasons to be cautiously hopeful.

All men are safe, thank God, but they have lost a good portion of their provisions, the barrels thrown overboard in the night to lighten their load. Noah Harwood's heart breaks for the lost salted pork, dried beef and biscuit now feeding the fishes. There will be hell to pay when they next meet another ship, for they will need all the provisions they have, but for now they are alive.

In worse news, Titus Oates wakes to find that his missing leg is the least of his problems. To Mr Mayhew's concern, though not his surprise, he sees that the wound will not heal, red fingers of infection reaching from the stump and further up into the leg. The doctor takes a good quantity of rum and continues to tend his patient, who becomes more feverish and wild-eyed as the hours pass until the inevitable happens and Mr Oates dies, screaming that a chariot that only he can see has come to take him to Hell.

But as he breathes his fevered last, his mind takes him to a happier place than he deserves. As life leaves his mangled body, he imagines himself back home in Cornwall, the hills soft, and he sees his childhood home ahead of him. To his joy, his mother is waiting for him and waves, her cheeks rosy, smiling in a way that she never did in life. She wipes floury hands on her apron as she asks if he would like a slice of pie. He runs – for he can run again now – and gathers her tight in his arms in a swell of gratitude and love and he is home.

For lack of a chariot, however, the earthly remains of Mr Oates are wrapped in sailcloth, the ends sewn together as a shroud by his apprentice, Patrick Carty. The boy sheds a few tears for him (the only man who does), falling and dampening the cloth that contains the dead man. Once the boy is done, the captain says a few tired words about bravery and a life well lived to the assembled crew before four of the men tip their dead comrade over the side of the ship without further cere-mony. The waiting sea swallows him whole with a gulp and he is gone forever, following the salted pork and dried beef that will be missed more than he.

But a whisper has begun that will not be stopped. A whisper that says Mr Oates would not have died as he did were he able to move faster. That he could have moved faster were it not for an injury that had slowed him down. That Mary Read was the cause of the injury, and that perhaps it makes her in some way responsi-ble for Mr Oates's death. It gives the men pause for thought. They may not have liked the man, but he did not deserve to die like this. Opinion fragments, and not in Mary's favour.

Meanwhile, Jack does his duty and asks the doctor for details for his log.

'What was the cause of Mr Oates's death?'

Mr Mayhew looks up at him with watery eyes, concentrating hard to bring the man in the red coat into focus.

'In my professional opinion, bad luck. Stopping breathing most likely a factor in it too.'

The doctor takes a long swig from a bottle and slumps back down against his makeshift bed.

For a moment, Jack considers remonstrating, but – really – what is the use? Instead he sighs, clipped and impatient.

'Just so,' he says, wondering if the world will ever behave itself as he has every right to expect as captain of this ship.

But there is a reason why Mr Mayhew is as he is today. As a man of learning, he knows, to his misfortune, that he will follow Mr Oates within a day or two. Only days before the storm, he had stumbled and found himself impaled in the left thigh by one of his own knives. It had not been a deep cut, but deep enough for the filth accumulated from his daily work to pollute his blood.

Pestilence is easily passed from one man to the next aboard ship, and it is perhaps fitting that his knives will become the instruments of his own death. Tiredness and nausea he is familiar enough with, and he has drunk his way through it as normal over the previous days, but the swelling and heat where the wound will not heal have made him realise the worst.

The doctor is a pragmatic man, and has made his peace with the inevitable long ago. He does not mention it to anyone, but takes to his bottle with more than usual devotion, and watches with detached professional interest as the wound turns gangrenous, his leg becoming black as coal. He keeps his predicament private, for any intervention now will be both painful and useless.

But in this fog of infection, his mind will not rest. The things he has seen …

He shuts his eyes against the images that rise up and drinks back more rum, the reassuring fire of it beating a path to his guts. What did they expect of him? He is a mere man, in a world filled with pain and sickness. What did he ever think that he could do about it? He has always been just one man shouting into the storm. He has never done more than patch them together to delay the inevitable.

A tear releases itself and rolls slowly down his cheek, and he raises a hand to feel its warm salty wetness. When was the last time he cried? He cannot remember. It seems that he only has enough pity left for himself. Not much of a doctor, then, and never much of a man.

He suddenly remembers a woman with green eyes, long ago, and his heart contracts. He hears her even now.

'I don't understand. Why must you drink like this?'

He had been puzzled that she could not see for herself, the world being as it is.

'Why would I not?'

She had cried then. But that was a lifetime ago, and the heart is just a muscle, is it not?

He sees things all too clearly now. He has been a coward. He did not want to think, did not want to feel. He had surrendered himself gladly to the embrace of drink, which has been, in the end, his greatest love.

It has done its work once again, and he welcomes the familiar numbing warmth. He raises the bottle unsteadily to an invisible gathering before taking another long swig, wiping the tears from his face as he does so.

Here's to life and to leaving it – rotten bastard that it is.

Chapter 41

They find the good doctor dead the next morning, empty bottle in hand.

Just as Mr Oates had been, the doctor is wrapped in sailcloth and heaved overboard, where fish will burrow through the shroud to feast on his pickled flesh.

Jack draws a second skull in the logbook against the names of the dead men. He has never become accustomed to recording deaths of his crew, but it is something he has had to learn. He has failed them, as captain, to see them sent to the depths, weighed down with shot, part of the sea for evermore. There have been no prayers, for what good has ever come of prayer? But he will think of them. When he is alone and there is a silence.

There are more silences than before, he notes over the coming days and weeks. No good can come of thinking and silences. But what has led to this strange turn of affairs? This run of bad luck, for it is certainly that.

And it comes to him suddenly, a thought fully formed. And once thought it cannot be unthought.

Women are bad luck. And his ship is overrun by them.

They are in his rigging. At his guns. Eating his food. Distracting his men, or at least his carpenter. Conspiring together in corners. Refusing his advances where once they were welcomed. What he not long ago considered an act of outrageous bravery on his part – taking two women onto his ship – has grown old very quickly.

Of Anne he had expected sweetness and compliance, and he has been sorely disappointed for she has been neither. And as for Mary …

He shakes his head in disbelief at his own naivete. They are like men, only more trouble. The sudden clarity of it sours his mood. He now realises why he has become suspicious of their laughter, their sword practice, of their easy proximity.

To counter this over the coming days, for he has made it a resolution, he begins to drink more, sulks, and showily seeks out his officers on matters of great importance when either of the women approach. He becomes cold to Anne, not that she minds. It makes him more angry than before.

And Mary sees it.

'Why is he acting like an arsehole?' she asks Anne.

'Because he is,' Anne replies, and they collapse in shared laughter.

Jack pretends not to notice, but he thinks back on his recent tally of prizes. A schooner near Port Maria. Two merchant sloops off Hispaniola. Seven fishing boats. He winces at the latter, but his men must eat, and it saves them a great deal of trouble to take what they need rather than to find it themselves. He would like to think it is common sense rather than a lack of ambition for more. But if he is to be hanged for little more than a few paltry fishing boats?

Jack was once a man who shared a table with Blackbeard as a comrade, singing and drinking with him as a friend. He was a man who mutinied when he found his captain wanting. The crew had chosen him, Jack Rackham, as their captain in his place. But that seems so long ago. He is older, and, by God, he feels it. Blackbeard is dead at the hands of the Navy, and Charles Vane is hanged, the last of the old pirates to be brought to justice.

Jack ponders the weights and measures of plunder taken since he took the *Revenge*. He counts his share of the spoils, and where it has left him. It is modest at best, and hardly worth a man's life. He has been a pirate for years. He is a good captain, and an experienced sailor. He knows every creek, every inlet of this vast area, but where has it got him?

On consideration, he realises that it has got him precisely nowhere. And it is Anne's fault.

Chapter 42

The tensions that predated the storm have brewed and darkened.

The captain watches his crew more closely than ever, the weapons he carries displayed more prominently than usual. The men watch back, whispered conversations and meaningful glances exchanged amongst themselves in a way that, in the captain's eyes, hint at mutiny. After all, he should know better than most.

To add to his problems, the death of Mr Mayhew has left Jack with a vacancy, for a doctor is an essential part of any crew. They have Tom Earl, of course, if it is only limbs to be removed, but a carpenter cannot fill these shoes indefinitely. What they need now is a scholarly man who can attend to other ailments. If Jack needed an excuse to return to land to avail himself of such a man, now is the time. That he can present it to the men as an act of beneficence from their captain, even better, for the mood of the crew will not be changed.

He has been told repeatedly by the ship's master that shore leave is needed, and has repeatedly said that they cannot risk the Navy catching up with them. It is true enough, but there is a reluctance too; to go ashore is to admit that things have not worked out as the captain would have liked and he has not been ready for that. And so still he tarries.

It is Tom Earl who provides the final reason. He has tried his best, but Mr Earl cannot reverse the rot that has set into *Revenge*. They have sailed her hard for months without being able to take her ashore and tend her wounds. The recent weeks have taken their toll. He is only one man, after all, and the lady, though magnificent still, has seen better days.

Her sails are patched following their run-in with the merchant ship, and the storm has added insult to injury. Her hull and deck are pockmarked by shot and shrapnel. Her paint is peeling. Shipworm and barnacles layer themselves thickly under her waterline, their growing bulk dragging against the ocean she once cut through like a knife.

The indignities inflicted upon her have been soothed as best they can, but there is an unmistakable truth: *Revenge* is in poor health and her convalescence cannot happen at sea. Mr Earl speaks quietly to Mr Fetherstone, his brow furrowed as he is forced to admit that it is beyond his abilities. He cannot continue to patch her up.

The master approaches the captain warily, but knows he must say what he has come to say. The man in charge of the men and the ship has concerns about both, and the captain must solve it, whatever his temper.

'The men are in poor spirits, Jack, and need a change. And the ship needs her rest – you can see it for yourself. No good can come of things as they are.'

Jack looks about him at the state of his once pristine ship and winces. *Revenge*, he sees, bears the scars of his failure. It is in the mood of the crew too.

'I can see how she is, and I know my men too. You're right – there's no more delaying it. You can assemble the crew and I will speak to them.'

Whatever has changed the captain's mind is of little consequence. Mr Fetherstone is greatly relieved and goes about his task – a pleasant one at last – assembling the men who eye the captain suspiciously.

Jack takes to the helm, where he can better command his audience, and to remind them who is their captain.

'We are to have ourselves some shore leave, lads. What say you?'

His words puncture the silence as if he had lanced a boil, claps and cheers greeting the news. He feels a sense of relief and descends the stairs to find Anne, a smile on her face for once.

'The men will be happier now they know they can expect a little freedom.'

He looks at her wearily.

'Well, things couldn't continue as they were. A change will do us all some good – and I have business I need to attend to.'

'And what business is that?'

He could tell her it is none of her business, but realises he cannot find the strength.

'Now that I have taken care of the business of not being thrown off my own ship by fractious men, there is a man I need to see …'

He does not elaborate. He cannot admit even to himself that he has been forced here to ask for help.

Chapter 43

The ladies of the island will earn their money tonight. The men of *Revenge* begin their preparations in earnest for they have ladies to impress. The late Mr Mayhew had readied himself for the inevitable. As any considerate naval doctor would do, he has assembled mercury enough for all of them, his legacy to the crew, who will drink or administer the poison direct to their syphilis sores they will earn tonight, to their individual preference.

The men are already waiting impatiently on deck, eyes straining toward the island that must be out there somewhere. It is unusual for so many men to be milling about at this hour, but there is a yearning for the sight of civilisation after the confinement of the ship.

And then, the first glimpse of land – a rocky cliff face topped with an abundance of strange trees, gulls spilling from the heights, and golden sand leading into the shallows. The island is a welcome sight after so much time at sea, an uncharacteristic cheerfulness overcoming the crew.

Other ships already sit at anchor in the harbour, their masts waving welcome to the rhythm of the sea, and soon *Revenge* will join them. But there are still duties to be fulfilled and hidden dangers to be navigated as they approach land. Water sucks and swirls at the rocks, a reminder that they are not clear of trouble yet.

The water peaks and ripples; the sea translucent and impenetrable in turn as they approach the shallows. Mary is transfixed: she can see sand, deep below the water, its surface littered with the bones and shells of long dead things, rotten timbers and coins, some sunk for luck and some through misadventure.

The turquoise water above is alive with darting shapes of fish. Iridescent, sleek, striped and colourful, big and small, as they flash and slow, dart and dive in their element, bodies distorted by the prism of the water.

Mary has never seen anything like it – has never seen colours like these – and stands transfixed by the jewel dance below as the fish play in the shadows of the rigging, while Tom Earl shudders and crosses himself at the sight of such unnatural things, a reflex from long ago, and leaves Mary to her wide-mouthed rapture, taking himself below decks where it is dark and the air stinks, as nature intended.

They cast anchor some distance from the island. It is enough to bring out the natural poetry in the crew, the men talking amongst themselves of strange and wonderful flora, birds the colour of gemstones, and of the buxom attributes of the women of the town who will soon enjoy their dubious company.

Mr Fetherstone has split the crew into two groups, one to take shore leave while the other guards the ship, with the second group to enjoy their time ashore when their crewmates return. It is still true that there is no honour amongst thieves, and the captain knows better than to trust to luck. Anne cannot understand it until he makes himself clear.

'We're going to a den of villains and cut-throats. There's not one of them wouldn't take my ship if I let them.'

'But don't you worry about the men left behind?'

He looks at her strangely.

'They are my crew and have my trust.'

He does not sound convinced.

The men consigned to the second group are hardly delighted, but are mollified by the knowledge that their time will come. Their dreams will raise eyebrows tonight as they imagine what – and who – they will do when they take their turn ashore.

Two rowboats are lowered to meet the waves beneath them, and with not a little difficulty on Mary's part due to her belly, she makes her way clumsily into the boat to the sound of mock cheers and laughter from the assembled men. She does not seem to mind, the relief of being off ship and headed towards dry land obvious. Tom has been left behind as there are jobs that must be done that only he can do, but she has Anne with her at least. Tam Weir is left behind too, and waves at Mary uncertainly and she waves back, smiling, now that she is safely seated.

John Howell and John Davies man the oars, their barely contained hostility of previous days forgotten as they power the first cargo of crew towards land. Flying fish follow the rowboats, strange creatures that span the elements, their mouths sucking at air while black unblinking eyes observe the men. Another marvel for Mary to wonder at and to tell her son.

'Are they mermaids?' Tam says worried, seeing the same fish.

His crewmates snort at him in derision, so he assumes not. He worries for Mary, and for himself. His heart has been breaking for weeks, knowing that she must soon be set ashore for good, to bring her baby into the world. She will leave him behind, he knows it must happen, and he looks around him to see what will be left for him.

These men are not his friends. Had it not been for Mary, he would not have been here at all. He does not belong here, and not for the first time, he worries what will become of him without Mary's protection. He has been thinking about this long and hard, and has come to a conclusion all of his own. He knows what he must do and now, an unfamiliar surge of certainty floods through him.

Tam is one of the few men aboard who can swim, for most sailors know that a swift death by drowning is kinder if the ship goes down. It's the way of the sea.

Tam watches until Mary becomes nothing but a speck in the distant rowboat, tears blinked back and unshed, before he heaves himself into the lower reaches of the rigging, glances behind to check that he is unobserved, and jumps overboard. He has not been seen for he is of little interest to anyone.

The sea welcomes him with warm salt arms, pulling him towards the depths before he kicks his feet and surges to the surface with a pop. He shakes his head to clear the water from his ears and bobs where he is for a moment, cresting the waves clumsily. The angry welts on his back begin to smart at the salt water as if to remind him why he is here, and he starts to move his arms and legs uncertainly, awkwardly propelling himself towards the closest of the anchored ships. He has had his fill of this ship, and will leave it to Fate to find him a new one. Whatever he finds next cannot be as bad as life on *Revenge*.

The further they row away from *Revenge*, the lighter the mood becomes, the cooling spray from the waves a welcome novelty. There is an anticipation of firm ground beneath their feet, and even more the prospect of a good meal or two which does not rely on the remaining paltry rations on board.

Noah Harwood is in the first landing party and, smiling broadly, can barely contain himself at the thought of the edible riches that he will have to pick from to replenish his pantry. He giggles to himself like a schoolgirl and Mary cannot help but smile at the unlikely sound.

It does not take long for the second boat to reach land, the smell of warm ground reaching them long before the boat is moored. With just a few more pulls on the oars, they overcome the waves and are all but landborne again.

The captain plunges out of the boat first into two or so feet of water, hauling himself onto dry land, smiling broadly as if he had delivered the place to them personally.

'Here at last, lads! Make as merry as you like, for life is short and shore leave even shorter. We'll meet back here before the last tide changes tomorrow.'

Mary steps clumsily from the second rowboat and into the shallows that still separate them from land, wincing at the expected cold to find it warm. She looks puzzled until her attention is distracted by sweat trickling down her forehead into her eyes.

'Christ – you didn't warn me it was hot as hell!'

She quickly turns red in the face, her hair already sodden as she drags herself ashore, where, to her horror, she finds it hotter still. She had not realised that it was sea breezes cooling her on board ship, and now she finds herself all at sea without them. She is used to England and Holland, where weather is cold, wet and honest, and this place is clearly unnatural. This sun does nothing but shine hard in a blue sky, the palm trees with their wagging fingers are too green, the strange white sand sucks at her feet and whispers as she tries to walk on it.

The ground underfoot is scorched, and bites at the soles of her feet like demons of hell, the hopping gait she has adopted causing Anne great amusement that she resents mightily. If she wasn't dying in the heat of this hellhole, she'd bear a grudge, but right now she can't think to carry any more than she must, so the half-formed resentment is cast aside as Mary makes her way, miserable and undignified, towards the town.

The air is thick with the heavy sweetness of strange flowers, while jewel-coloured birds shriek and call from trees she does not recognise. Her skin prickles and shrinks as she walks, the Caribbean sun amused by this too-white Englishwoman in its sights.

Anne cannot help but smile, trying and failing to hide it.

'You will have to get used to it if you have your sights set on the mainland.'

Mary looks like she is ready to be put out of her misery.

'There must be somewhere in the whole wide place that has the imagination not to be so bloody hot as this. Somewhere with cold and rain – snow even. God, I miss snow.'

Anne leaves her to it and keeps on walking, the smirk still alive on her face. She thinks with great satisfaction that she is finally better at something than Mary.

Chapter 44

If Mary had thought the heat crushing on shore, it is nothing compared to that of the place itself. The strange air presses against her face, red hot and heavy with moisture. The heat wraps itself around her like a sickbed blanket. Sweat thickens around her eyes and nose, runs freely down her back.

A swarm of buzzing flies descend and travels with her like a black cloud so she seems to carry her bad temper with her. Her clothes have become heavy and awkward with sweat as if they have changed their purpose to become impediments to normal movement. They swaddle her legs and arms, walking becoming like a bad dream as she struggles against the things that fight against her, strangling her all over, their very nature altered.

'Even the air burns! It doesn't want to be breathed!'

Mary has a sudden vision of herself as a roasted pig on a spit and wishes for nothing less than death.

When it occurs to Anne to check again on Mary's flagging progress, she is greatly amused by this red, sweating creature.

'Keep up, Mary – tell your legs that the end of the journey is worth it. And besides, if you don't keep up with us, the heat looks like it will finish you.'

Mary does not doubt it for a moment as the bloody sun continues to beat down mercilessly on her hide, as her nostrils are violently assaulted by a smog of human stench and stale beer. The port has suddenly given way to a narrow, ramshackle street that leads into the town itself, a place that seems thrown together more by accident than design.

The earthquakes through the years have not helped, with the latest having almost finished them for good. But not quite. Buildings lurch and teeter as if drunk, tipping in towards one another as though the roofs are whispering secrets, balconies and windows hanging stupefied and open-mouthed towards the ground below.

The pirates make their way into the noisy fray, the press of humanity closing in on them. The place swarms with strange foreigners and escaped slaves, impenetrable languages being spoken all around them. The clothes too are a sight for sore eyes – grown men in excesses of silks and satin, ruffles and scarves, gaudy jewellery and silver-buckled shoes – every whim of fashion piled on with contempt for restraint. Visible skin of every shade is adorned with pictures of mermaids, ships, or the names of lost loves.

The stench of people, the squalor of the place, with all manner of livestock moving shambolically with the crowds create a heady scent. Mary is dazed by it all, but her gaze is drawn upward by a number of harshly cooing voices, only to see a group of raucous women leaning out precariously from the windows above as they pass, engaged in jiggling displays of naked flesh. The sudden keening of a baby crying from somewhere within is quickly shushed – for this is no place for innocence.

In such a teeming place, it is not possible to look upwards for long, for fear of running into someone or something, so Mary returns her gaze to the street and the strange sights before her. The bawdy houses and taverns have blocked out the breeze so that the powerful heat presses down upon her further, causing her sweat to form waterfalls.

Mary forces herself to push on to keep pace with her crewmates, wishing herself most fervently back in Plymouth.

Chapter 45

They arrive at The Black Pig Tavern, an establishment whose reputation precedes it – such as it is. It is a ramshackle sort of place, shot through by decay. The windows of the tavern sit skew-whiff, while lizards, no bigger than a thumb, scurry across the wall by the open door, green fingers spread wide.

Anne pushes the door open and steps inside, her crewmates following close behind. The crewmen jangle as they walk, their bags of coins held close. The contents will be spent in search of oblivion of whatever kind they choose – wine, rum and beer, dice and cards, and of course the women. They will be lucky to come out penniless, shirts still on their backs.

Jack smiles fondly at the clientele of pirates, outcasts, whores and others who have reached the limit of their options. He and his companions are obviously known here – cheers and whistles meet their appearance as the alarming crowd stop what they are doing and turn to watch the spectacle. Mock bows and curtseys are dropped to their new audience. Mary, who is finally free to catch her scattered breath, notes that it is all very jolly, for now at least.

The landlord, a rough-looking bearded man in an apron, makes his way through the crowd with some difficulty.

'Captain Rackham – you are, as always, most welcome. I apologise we aren't more prepared for you coming – we expected you later.'

The man is nervous despite his bulk and rubs at his hands as he speaks.

Jack smiles magnanimously.

'Not to worry, my dear Alastair. We thought it best to come straight here and enjoy the best hospitality the island has to offer.'

Alastair leans in close and lowers his voice to a whisper.

'There is a gentleman here to see you. An important gentleman.'

He nods with great meaning before he continues.

'I have put him in the back room and seen to his requirements – I hope that's acceptable?'

Jack nods, and he is ushered, along with Anne and Mary, towards the back of the tavern, where a bear of a man stands between them and a curtained-off room, his arms folded, his skin a tapestry of blue and black ink. His muscled arms bear maps, sea monsters and patterns that wind around and through one another, intricate as mazes. They are arms to get lost in.

Mary stares at him, mouth agape.

'Does that hurt?'

He glances at her, then back into the middle distance, his face unmoving.

'It did. Now it does not.'

Mary continues to stare as the man drops his illustrated arms and parts the heavy curtain for them, urging them through with only a jut of his chin.

Anne has to nudge Mary to remember herself.

'You're staring.'

'I've never seen anything like it.'

Anne shakes her head, smiling, as a short man in a crimson waistcoat and breeches, a feathered hat and heavy jewellery stands to greet them. He looks greatly amused by the women that he takes no pains to hide, before he addresses Jack.

'I did not trust the gossip, but it seems that our Captain Rackham does indeed crew his ship with women.'

The voice has a Welsh lilt.

Jack tries, and fails, to smile.

'Two women amongst many men.'

'Though they have forgotten to come dressed as women, I see.'

Mary takes the opportunity to clear phlegm from her throat onto the floor by the man's feet.

'Just as you forgot to come dressed as a man,' she adds.

His smile fades.

'But I at least am forgetting my manners – I am Captain Bartholomew Roberts, and you should be well advised to remember it.'

'You will be difficult to forget, dressed like that.'

Jack smiles now, all teeth.

Anne is shocked to hear the name, for she knows it, and the reputation behind it, all too well. So this is Bart Roberts, a pirate famed for his bloodthirst and cruelty, happy to turn on his crew as well as his captives. The story she remembers most vividly is that of a captured sailor, his guts nailed to the mast, forced to dance to the prompting of burning torches as his innards unravelled before him.

Roberts has chosen to ignore Mary and continues, addressing Jack only.

'And this ...' he gestures towards the end of the table, where a thin man in wire spectacles has stopped shovelling chicken into his mouth to stare, '... is Captain Johnson, who is here to write about me – isn't that right, man?'

Johnson nods, gulping to clear his mouth of food, and hastily wipes his hands on his coat before he stands and moves from the shadows. He removes the hat and bows with a flourish, the feather dancing as he does so.

'Charmed, I'm sure,' says Anne drily.

Johnson returns to an upright position, replacing his hat.

'This is indeed a marvellous surprise. I am writing an account of the pirates, and I should be very remiss indeed if I did not include you ladies in it, as well as our good Captain Rackham of course. Three for the price of one.'

He rubs his hands together and smiles, sure of the impact he has had.

'I can tell you we are no ladies, be sure of that.'

Anne challenges Johnson to speak with her stare as Mary stands behind her, amplifying her glare. He looks confused, before trying another tack.

'Ah – of course – I misspoke. And what exactly do you do on board Captain Rackham's ship?'

'Exactly what the men do – only better.' Mary's hand rests on her cutlass, the fingers closing slow around it as she holds his gaze.

His hands are up, the colour draining from him as he shrinks back towards the corner of the room.

'I meant no disrespect – my apologies.'

To his relief, more chicken, bread and a plate of strange fruit arrives, Mary forgets her temper and falls on it hungrily. Whatever privations she has learned to live with, a lack of good food is not one of them. Especially in her current state.

Bart Roberts puts his hand on Jack's back and steers him to the far end of the table.

'Perhaps we should take this opportunity to talk more privately, Jack. I had heard that you had taken command of Captain Vane's ship – it shows a stout heart. I am sorry to find you in such straitened circumstances – for you will certainly need your courage now with your choice of crew.'

Anne bristles but does not respond, sitting down by Mary and joining her in the food.

Jack pulls a chair closer to Roberts.

'Your reputation precedes you, Captain Roberts, and I have a proposal for you. My ship is in need of repair, and there is safety in numbers, as Blackbeard taught us all. I should like to propose an alliance, an agreement between gentlemen, to protect each other's business.'

Bart Roberts dabs at his mouth with a handkerchief, his face giving nothing away.

'That is certainly a strategy that has worked before. Though we do not exactly meet on equal terms, do we? I think that your ship is in need of far greater protection than my own.'

It is true, of course, but the words clearly smart.

Jack tries again.

'As you say, but once my ship is repaired and we are back to full strength …'

Roberts raises a hand to indicate he should stop.

'What do you mean, "full strength"?'

Jack has given more away than he intended to and so there is nothing for it. He digs his nails into the palms of his hands before he continues in what he hopes is a nonchalant way.

'We lost our doctor and a crewman – we must find ourselves another doctor before we can be on our way.'

Roberts tuts and shakes his head sadly.

'I am afraid that doctors are few and far between. There are no spares here, and you are hardly in a position to steal one …'

Jack suddenly sees how hopeless a case he must seem, the certainty he had of a successful meeting disappearing in a heartbeat.

Roberts' attention has switched and he is now studying Anne and Mary at the end of the table, where they are setting about refreshment with enthusiasm.

'I have to say that it's an unusual choice you made, Jack, to let women aboard. I have it written in my Articles that any man bringing a woman aboard my ship will be put to death. I hang the guilty crewmen from the rigging and use them as target practice – it discourages the crew from any similar thoughts of their own. What an instrument of division and quarrel you have brought into the midst of your crew.'

Christ, the women again. There is more to him and his crew than mere women.

'I don't care what they are as long as they work and keep the peace doing it. There have been no problems with Anne and Mary aboard, save what we'd have from any man.'

This is clearly a lie, but he prefers not to let Roberts know the truth. The Welshman raises his eyebrows quizzically.

'Then you are a lucky man indeed, to have your men so tame. My own experience tells me that men are weak in flesh and spirit – and that only a firm hand and prayer will bring them to heel.'

'I make my own luck. And besides, I've always considered prayer as a refuge for weaker men.'

Roberts's crucifix should have told Jack of the man's supposed piety, but it is too late. There is an immediate shift in the mood of the room and the Welshman's demeanour changes.

'A man who can admit his own weaknesses and draw on the strength of the Almighty is a stronger one for it. Perhaps if you had been more of a godly persuasion your recent history should not have been quite so chequered, shall we call it?'

'A run of bad luck is all …'

'Bad luck? My services are very much in demand, and I only ally myself with successful men if the need arises. I have no such need, as you are no doubt aware. I hear that your most recent encounter was a little more – tricky – than you might have expected. Do you think you might be losing your touch, Jack?'

Jack's eyes blaze and it is with some effort that he controls his temper.

'The last engagement had an unfortunate outcome, it's true, but I am more interested to know how you might have come by this information?'

That smarm of a smile again.

'You know how men talk. And you are not the only member of your crew who has tried to better themselves by association with me. I have found the flow of information about your recent successes – and otherwise – fairly free.'

'I pride myself on the loyalty of every man of my crew – so whoever has been talking is a liar.'

There is a pause before Roberts speaks again with great satisfaction.

'Perhaps not the loyalty of *every* man.'

Jack's humiliation burns hot in his face, though the writer's ears have pricked up, Johnson licking the nib of his quill with growing excitement as his eyes dart between the two pirate captains.

Bart Roberts shakes his head in an approximation of sadness.

'All I will say is that I have offered a place on my ship to your young Scotsman, who no longer wishes to sail with you. We plucked him out of the ocean, so keen was he to escape from your ship. He appears to have taken the stripes you gave him very personally.'

Mary stops eating as she realises with a shock they are talking about Tam. Anne looks on anxiously as Jack's face runs from white to scarlet in only seconds. But Bart Roberts continues, as if oblivious.

'I consider myself a good judge of men, Jack, and it is unfortunate that I find I cannot bring myself to ally with you. Women aboard ship – why, any man knows that cannot stand. Men become no better than a rabble in the presence of women. No wonder your crew deserts you. However, as you can see, you have an excellent choice of new crew out in the tavern and I hope we shall part as friends on this point.'

Jack's face is now twisted in anger, and Anne speaks quickly, trying to appease him.

'Tam is no loss, Jack – we can take our pick of ten men here who will do a better job.'

The voice is pleading, an attempt to save face for him, but he is having none of it. His voice when it comes is low and cold, and he sees only Captain Roberts.

'So there is to be no alliance? Then I have come here for nothing.'

Roberts unfurls himself, no longer making any attempt at friendliness.

'I have considered your offer, Jack. I am pleased to have met you, of course, but I hear that you have made a personal enemy of Governor Rogers – and I am in no particular hurry to swing from his gallows. He is outraged, I understand, that you have led Miss Bonny astray. I have always found it wise to draw a distinct line between business and pleasure, but you appear to have crossed that line some time back. You have made yourself a personal enemy of the governor. You have put yourself top of the list for capture, and that's the kind of attention I can do without.'

Roberts spreads out his hands, as if it were out of his control.

'I am a modest man, Jack, and my affairs work best out of the glare of your notoriety. In the circumstances, I understand that increasing your firepower is advisable, but I have a crew to consider, and I should hate to commit them to a suicide mission. Let's shake on it, and I will wish you well. I know that Johnson here has been pleased to meet with you and your charming ladies.'

The smile on Roberts's face is tight and unpleasant, and Jack stiffens in silent fury.

'So you will not help me – to join forces, our crews together?'

Roberts holds up a hand.

'Although I am not a gambling man, I do not like the odds I see before me. I have the livelihood of my crew to think of, and it would be … unwise – for me to align with someone who seems to me a dead man walking.'

Jack flares at this, his hand flying to his sword, as the tattooed hulk appears, his pistol drawn.

Captain Roberts holds up his hands as if in surrender.

'Let us part as friends, Jack. Friends who have been honest with one another and wish the other only the best. For I am sure I need not remind you, some of us have more friends than others.'

Jack puts a lid on his temper for now, his hand moving slowly from the sword as he watches the tattooed man do the same. He understands diplomacy when he must, and manages to control his tone as he speaks.

'I had hoped for more than this, as you know. But my future successes will be your disappointment that you did not trust me more. You will hear a great deal more of Jack Rackham.'

Roberts smiles thinly.

'Of that, I have no doubt.'

Chapter 46

Anne and Mary follow Jack as he leaves the room in a thunderous temper. None of them speak until the velvet curtain has dropped and they are back in the tavern.

It is Anne who speaks first, an urgency in her voice.

'He is only one man, Jack, and we are doing quite well on our own.'

His face is dark as he turns on her.

'As you have so often told me, "quite well" is not good enough. So shall we return to just getting by, and wait for the Navy to catch us?'

'You know that's not what I meant.' Anne's face is flushed and she speaks as quietly as she can to avoid drawing attention to them. But Jack will not hear her.

'What a marvellous surprise that you have made me famous in the wrong way – the most wanted man in the Caribbean, no less! Well, I intend to celebrate this bit of news by getting heroically drunk, and I intend to do it alone. You and Mary may as well go to Bart Roberts's pet writer – I should hate to see the bastard go empty-handed. Besides, it seems that the world is only interested in the female company I keep, so let's not disappoint your public.'

Petulance does not sit well with him, and if he anticipates the reassurance and ministrations of his woman Jack is to go wanting. Her voice loses its sugar-coating and she matches his bitterness.

'We had agreed that we should spend this time together.'

Anne has told herself that she must at least try with Jack, but he seems to have frustrated her even in this.

'Then that's one more thing that I have disappointed you in.'

They glare at one another, unspeaking, as Mary watches on, uncomfortable.

'Drink yourself stupid then – though you hardly need my permission for that.'

He sneers at her.

'Indeed I don't.'

And with that he is gone, a full-blown fury asserting itself as he does so, his shore leave lurching ahead of him, an unwelcome thing.

Anne knows his temper. Let him simmer, and let him drink it off.

She turns to Mary to find that Captain Johnson is suddenly with them.

'I should very much like it if you should join me for wine – and more food, if you will have it. There is plenty of it and you did not have time earlier to enjoy it. I have certainly eaten worse. And I am sure you have stories to tell.'

He swallows hard, hopefully, as Mary looks across to a table in the corner of the tavern and sees a wonderful sight. A temptation of food has been laid out for them, a roast hog joining a host of other dead and roasted creatures at the table. Her condition has made her ravenous, her appetite insatiable. With Jack gone who knows where and the other men dispersed for their leisure, they have nothing else to keep them from it.

Anne sees Mary all but carried across the room by the aromas of cooked meat, and sighs.

'We have tales sure enough, and it seems I have nothing better to do. And as Mary is eating for two, let's to it.'

Chapter 47

The women have filled their bellies as much as they are able, as the scattered carcases will attest. Mary sighs with pleasure, patting at her stomach, grease still running down her chin. The writer has finished his scribbling and has left them to it with his profuse thanks. Pirates will sell a book, he is certain, but women pirates? He had not expected that. He rubs his hands with glee.

Anne has surprised herself. In her speaking of their voyages and adventures, the sand of her discomfort has quietly become a pearl. She has not seen Ireland, or the Orient, though she has heard stories of them both, and realises she is curious to see for herself. She has seen only a fraction of the Caribbean trade routes as part of someone else's journey, and has begun to think that she should like to see more. Perhaps this is what she has wanted all along, was the reason that she had started on this path. To set out with the purpose of a known destination, with the next discovery just out of reach. She will need to think more on it.

Anne drains the last of her wine before wiping her mouth on her sleeve. It is good claret, but they cannot stay here at this table forever. She turns and looks around the tavern.

'Where has Jack got himself to?'

Mary takes a swig from a tankard before she replies.

'He'll be with the crew and up to no good, I'll bet. We should get up to some no good of our own.'

Anne shakes her head.

'I'd better find him first. He went off in a temper, and that never ends well.'

His absence concerns her. At least if she can see him she knows what he is doing. An absent Jack could be up to anything. Before them are men laid waste by the power of self-indulgence. Insensible bodies lie draped dramatically across tables, the detritus of food scattered about them – half-eaten carcases of uncertain species, loaves of bread torn open, tankards and bottles tipped over, broken and dripping. Half-dressed women drape themselves over the few men who remain upright, the spilling flesh and painted faces showing that they at least are still open for business.

Anne stands and staggers, the wine being stronger than she realised, and she stumbles towards the nearest table occupied by some of the working girls and their clients. Anne taps one of the women on the shoulder. She looks up and unwinds herself from a crewman, who promptly slides to the floor. Her bright yellow hair sets off the unnatural pink of her cheeks, and she smiles, displaying a mouth of black stumps.

'You after a jump?'

Anne shakes her head and frowns, for she has more pressing matters to attend to.

'I am not here for that. I am looking for Captain Rackham.'

The woman slowly looks her up and down.

'Shame, but there are other paying clients waiting, and sadly they will not fuck themselves.'

She makes her way over to the next table with an exaggerated sway of her hips, and rubs the groin of one of the men there affectionately.

They have been overheard and an orange-haired woman nearby tears herself away from the amorous advances of a bald man, extracting her tongue wetly from his mouth.

'Belle should just have told you. He's upstairs with Tilly and Flo. Been up there a good amount of time, too.'

Mary puts her hand on Anne's arm. 'I'm sure it's not what you think. I'm sure that Jack—'

But Mary does not get to finish, for Anne is already running towards the stairs, quite sure that she'll find Jack exactly where she thinks, leaping over drunken, half-naked bodies, hearing them complain and rouse themselves as she passes. They had not quite made it as far as a bedroom, for this is no church, but she suspects that Jack has. She won't be made to look a fool by him or anyone else.

Anne reaches the landing and is faced with four doors, but only one of them is closed. She flings the heavy door open, its recoil like a clap of thunder. And there is Jack, red-faced in his exertions and naked but for a red-headed Poll attached to him by her arse, while another smacks his backside at every thrust.

Jack freezes as Anne enters the room, before the smacker looks up and calls out cheerfully.

'If you want to join us, it'll cost you a guinea.'

But Jack has hastily undocked himself, retreating from this shrew who has drawn her sword and advances on him as he leaps from the bed, cupping his embarrassment.

Anne roars, the girls shriek shrilly and flee, naked and screaming for their lives for a madwoman is upon them. They vacate the room at a rate of knots, holding discarded underthings to protect what little modesty they have left.

The door slams shut, and Jack is left alone with Anne. She watches as he shrivels miserably in the corner he has retreated to.

'You hen-hearted fucker. This is what you do when I leave you alone?'

'I wasn't alone – I had company.'

His attitude is not helping and she steps forward, stopping as she sees him wince again.

'I hope for your sake it was worth it, for that is the last time I will call you my lover. Christ, that I ever thought—'

But she does not get to finish. There is a hammering of fists at the door, and she reaches for her cutlass, thinking that the girls have returned with help. But it is only Mary, and she looks flushed, her face troubled.

'The Navy are coming – we have to leave. Now.'

Anne's voice is tight and controlled as she speaks to Jack.

'You will meet us back at the port. I will wake your drink-sodden crew and tell them to drag their sorry arses back.'

She barges her way out of the room, down the stairs and out of the tavern as Mary watches. She turns back to Jack, doing her best to keep her eyes above his waist.

'Best drag your own sorry arse there yourself, for she's in no mood to do it for you.'

Mary turns her back on him and heads for the stairs as Jack scrabbles for his clothes.

Chapter 48

Low black clouds obscure the blue skies of earlier, there are rumbling threats of rain. It starts out of nowhere, hot wet drops that spatter onto the world far below, in no time soaking the sullen crew and turning the ground beneath them to sludge, filth splashing onto their clothes as they head back towards *Revenge*.

They are a sorry sight. The men stumble and grimace at the harsh light of day which fights with their impending hangovers. But they are quick. This town must keep its secrets, and their lookouts, ever alert, have done their job. The unwelcome news of a Navy ship nearby is enough to keep them focused.

Anne and Jack, both thunderous, refuse to look at one other, while Mary does her best to keep up, watching and troubled as sobriety creeps up on her again.

She hears the sharp sound of a baby crying from an upstairs window, the noise quickly shushed and muffled. Mary stops and cranes her neck but she cannot see where the cries came from, but the silencing of it unsettles her greatly. She waits, but there are no further sounds, no evidence the baby was there at all, and when she remembers herself, she has to hurry to catch up her crewmates.

Anne's temper has wrapped itself around her, a maelstrom of emotions as she walks quickly towards the shore, trying to outpace her writhing thoughts. The baby's cry has made her stomach lurch for she has realised that her monthly bleed is late. And she is never late.

It does not take long for them to reach the shoreline, where they stumble silently into the rowboats. The men had been promised more freedom than this and a sour atmosphere clouds the boats as the men pick up the oars once again, attacking the waves in temper as they make their painful way back towards the ship.

They are watched by their delighted crewmates on board, thinking their own taste of freedom has come early, but not knowing why. They call out to the men below, a carnival atmosphere brewing that will soon be ruined.

Mr Fetherstone stands by the bow of the ship and shouts out cheerfully.

'Back already, Captain? The boys are keen to have a taste of shore leave themselves.'

Jack is clearly determined to take out his frustrations on someone or other as he clambers aboard and strides towards the luckless man.

'And which of you bloody fools allowed our young Scotsman to get away?'

The volume is unnecessary, and the mood is set. His glower is shared suspiciously with the rest of the men, ready to pounce on any guilty look.

Mr Fetherstone takes a step back and stammers.

'By the time we saw him swimming, he was out of range for our pistols, Captain. We did think to give chase, but we thought the sharks would have him first.'

Jack puts his face very close to Mr Fetherstone's, snarling.

'It wasn't the sharks but Bart Roberts got him. You have made me look like an idiot. What do you say to that?'

Mr Fetherstone stumbles over an apology as the captain turns from him and roars.

'The ship will sail without further delay – we are not safe here, and I'm not about to take any further chances. I am in no mood to listen to complaints, but I shall see you right, as always.'

Mary's earlier drunkenness is giving way to unwelcome sobriety. She stands swaying slightly as Anne takes her arm to steady her, concern showing on her face.

'But I haven't seen a midwife yet. You said I'd have enough time ashore.'

Jack hears and turns to her coldly.

'You had time enough, and now it will have to wait. Anne will help you if it comes to it, but let's hope for your sake that you can hold on.'

He turns his back on them both, breathing deeply, his anger barely contained. He makes great efforts to control his voice as he speaks.

'I will be in my cabin. If anyone comes looking for me, there had better be a damn good reason for it.'

He begins to walk towards the cabin as the crew stays silent.

Anne falters on her feet. The sour juices of her own insides force their way into her mouth. She suddenly sees her mother's face, waxen from laudanum, her hair drenched in sweat. She turns pale as she rushes to the side of the ship, where she begins to vomit, a yellow cloud that blooms and disperses in the bluest of seas below her.

Anne feels Mary's hand on her back as she wipes at her mouth, shaking. Mary is whispering soothing things to her, but all she can see is Jack, his face as white as hers, his mouth set.

Chapter 49

'But a baby?!' Anne's eyes are red from crying. They are at sea again, but she cannot think of that. Her mind has become a whirligig, she has not wanted to believe that her body could betray her like this, but there is no denying it now. This is something she cannot ignore, cannot outrun. Her world has come crashing down upon her because of her own carelessness.

Mary holds her hand, patting it, but is far more cheerful at the news than her crewmate.

'We shall nurse them together. Imagine the terrors they'll be!'

Anne collapses on the deck in a heap.

'I'm done for. How could this have happened?'

Mary knows better than to answer, but understands all too well. Too much rum and a moment of weakness was all it took to end up like this. She knows that for Anne to fall pregnant has never been part of the plan, though, in truth, she suspects that there was never much in the way of a plan.

Anne's face is swollen by tears, her eyes nothing more than slits.

'Children ruin a woman's life. My mother said so.'

Mary sighs, exasperated.

'I suspect she just meant you.'

Anne streaks a shining trail across her cheek as she wipes her nose with her sleeve, hiccupping at the brief abatement of tears.

'But why? I may as well have stayed at home.'

Self pity doesn't suit her, but she is wallowing in it now.

'Now that is a crock. You know full well there's too much mercury in you. That's why we're both here.'

Mary finishes speaking, dredging her mind for something to appease her when the levee breaks and Anne sets to wailing loudly.

Mary sighs deeply to herself, sits down alongside her as the men do their best to ignore them both. It is surprisingly easy when a woman is crying. Mary pats Anne's hand, in for the long haul until she stops. It is going to be a long night.

Sleep finally takes Anne; there is only so much time a storm can last before calm takes its place. She is dead to the world, her cares forgotten for a while, and Mary watches over her. Mary has Tom to help her with this new life she is bringing to the world, but what does Anne have? She sighs deeply, feeling the weight of the predicament. Anne has given herself a great deal of trouble for a man she barely likes. And despite herself, Mary knows that as her friend, she must help her. Quite what that will entail she does not know, but Anne is a complication she had not reckoned with.

It is a while later that Anne stirs, night fallen black and silent, and she has a tankard of beer placed in her hand. She drinks it greedily, for she has leached herself of water, as Mary speaks.

'Feeling better?'

Anne pauses for a moment, drinks the dregs of the beer, before she answers, miserably.

'I suppose I must get used to it.'

Mary nods. 'That you must. Not wanting it does not stop children, after all. There would be a lot less children in the world if that were so. We'll just have to make the best of things.'

'I suppose I must talk to Jack.'

He is suddenly stood before them, his shadow blocking out the moonlight.

'So it's true then. Another baby on its way.'

His voice is dull, and when they look up, they cannot see his face in the darkness.

Their silence speaks volumes, and when he sighs, it is with his whole body.

'Then we will put you both ashore, as I told you. A ship is no place for women and children.'

He is already gone. And in the returning moonlight, the two women look at one another with something like fear in their eyes.

Anne quickly follows Jack to his cabin, though it is clear it is the last thing he wants.

'Jack – we must talk.'

She closes the door behind her as he sits down heavily at the table, looking at her with accusing eyes.

'How could you let it happen?'

She had not expected that. She laughs leadenly.

'I seem to remember your having a part in it. The part you like best to think with.'

This was not in his plan. Jack has never wanted the permanence of ties. A dalliance with Anne whilst it suited was how it began. It had surprised him when he had begun to feel more for her, but he had made peace with that long ago. But a child?

He had never intended to be remembered in this world for anything other than his daring. The legend of Jack Rackham. The stuff of ballads and nightmares. He has no wish to be remembered as a father, would never become an open purse for some woman and her mewling brat.

Jack is responsible for his crew, and Anne is one of them. But when he puts her ashore, the child is her responsibility and he wants no part of it. When she is off his ship, she will become just another woman. She will become needy, grow fat no doubt, beholden first and always to a small new life. And he refuses to imagine a world where he will not be Anne's main concern.

He shakes his head.

'The sea is no place for children.'

Her voice is bitter.

'It was not what I wanted either.'

He has not seen her look like this before. Vulnerable. Frightened, even.

'Then what is it that you want?'

She has an answer, but how can she share it with him now? A child is not something she had considered in her dreams of far-off lands. But she had not seen Jack there either.

'For now we have the baby to consider. I will need a place to go, as will Mary.'

He considers it for a moment.

'There is a place I know in Havana ...'

Jack already feels his resolve falter. He knows people in Cuba, they would ensure a good life for a child. But things would not be the same. He was thinking of asking her to come back. But would she leave the child behind and sail with him again? Is he even sure that this is what he still wants?

'It was not supposed to be like this, Anne. It was supposed to be about adventure, the sea ... And about love.'

The word hangs queasily in the air. He sees her face, and his falls. His voice loses its certainty.

'So not even that. That at least I had assumed …'

This stops her dead.

'I found that I could not.'

He is lost. She flushes at the sight of it. It is true, but she understands the cruelty of what she has said. They should have left quietly, as Mary had suggested. So many things could have been left unsaid. But it is too late now.

Jack gathers himself and gets to his feet, speaking as gruffly as he is able.

'So you see that I am right, and it is best we part. For the sake of the child, let us say.'

He seems about to step towards her but thinks better of it.

'When we next reach port, both you and Mary will leave us. Perhaps we will even shake hands on it.'

He smiles at her, stiff and wooden, but she cannot bring herself to reciprocate.

Chapter 50

'We need a plan. I had not thought it would come to this so quickly, but it has.'

Anne is pacing and agitated, but Mary is lost in her own thoughts.

'Tom will be expected to stay. I cannot go without Tom – we have set our hearts on a place together.'

'We'll need somewhere to stay. And food. And a midwife – we must both have a midwife.'

Mary looks at her.

'I have some money put aside. Enough for a down payment. Perhaps an inn might suit us both. We can work together, until Tom can join us.'

It is as if Anne has been slapped.

'Work?'

Mary would laugh, if their situation were not so dire.

'It is what people do when they have no money. You have been a blind woman, Anne – you are to fend for yourself now. Unless, of course, you have money put aside?'

Mary looks at her, briefly hopeful, but Anne shakes her head.

'I lost it at dice.'

'All of it?'

'All of it.'

There has always been so much money. There has always been more to come, and it came so easy. Anne had not stopped to think ...

Uncertainty swallows her. She thinks of the money that has slipped through her fingers, of what it could now mean for her. She has always treated money with contempt, for she has always associated it with her father. But the coins and notes represent something else; she has realised too late. A place to live. Food on the table. Time to think. She has never been familiar with lack and want, but their shadows loom large now. She has allowed it to happen through her own thoughtlessness.

Jack is his own man. He is fond of her – more than that – but she had always known that she would tire of him first. As one adventure had begun to pall, she would leap feet first into another. But that has not happened. She has leapt into a new adventure – motherhood – just this was not of her own volition. She had never considered that she would need to think beyond the here and now, but she is learning.

She has realised too late, though, that reality hits harder the less money there is. She sees the sense now in Mary, counting her coins into a sea chest, stowing them away like the treasure they undoubtedly are. Mary has bought herself time and some peace of mind with those coins, while Anne has squandered away that much and so much more again. A simple shift in her luck and she is only just out of reach of the dripping jaws of Fate.

Mary has not given up yet.

'Perhaps Jack will help you?'

'I don't want his money.'

Anne's answer is immediate, bursting from her, but Mary persists.

'Says the woman who has never done without it. Do not dismiss it out of hand. He is responsible for your condition, after all.'

And doesn't she know it.

Anne snarls her answer.

'I would rather starve.'

'Spoken like someone who has never done such a thing. There is no romance in poverty, let me tell you.'

Mary would continue but sees tears threaten in Anne's eyes.

'I have been careful and have enough money set aside to see us both fine for a while. Jack can't risk putting us ashore with the Navy after us. I need to think about what I do about Tom. In the meantime, we both need to get some rest.'

Mary will do everything she can to keep her future dream alive, for she feels it slipping through her fingers. She had planned to work her way out of this life into one she has chosen for herself, but there has not been enough time. There were choices before. Not as many as she would have liked, but choices nonetheless. Mary had not noticed so many doors closing silently on her until she has reached this point. Her options have narrowed to one, and she does not like it at all.

Chapter 51

A sensible man would set sail in the dead of night to hide his ship's course, but a sensible man would not be caught with his pants down by his wife and the Navy. So the pirate crew set off in haste the same way they came, giving the spies everything they need.

News of *Revenge* and her whereabouts has been passed by word of mouth, from sailor to sailor, from ship to ship, and finally from ship to port. The news has made its way up the hill, and into the ear of a certain Captain Barnet through a whispering servant, nervous about waking his master at such a strange hour, though he immediately springs from his sleep to naval readiness as His Majesty has every right to expect of his officers.

Captain Barnet has a commission to hunt pirates, and hunt them he will. If they knew better, the crew of *Revenge* would quake at his name. He is dogged, bears each slight against King and Country as if it is a personal thing, hardens his very being to any softer feeling. He will have them, and they will hang. He allows himself a flush of pride at the thought of it and continues the preparation of his person.

It is his God-given duty to bring Rackham and his crew to justice. There are wild rumours of women pirates aboard, but he has dismissed this as poppycock, naturally. Too much rum too easily consumed by the men these days, he notes wryly.

He leans in to his looking glass, frowning, and smoothes down his eyebrows so that they return to their intended place in an orderly fashion. He steps back to admire himself. This, he thinks, is the face of a British naval hero. Perhaps his portrait will be painted by royal appointment some day, with his dogs, his servants, his wife even, should the composition allow it. In it, he will point purposefully out to sea, his face stern. A fine figure he'd make too, framed in ornate gilt.

Satisfied with what he sees, he demands tea, for even heroes must have their sustenance. He is known to expect this at inconvenient hours, this same servant has often grumbled about it, but a kettle is put on to boil at once to prepare the captain for this momentous day. A sloop with twelve guns and fifty-four men awaits his command in the harbour below.

He will join them shortly, once he has partaken of tea. History has been made of less.

Chapter 52

The Navy is still in pursuit, they know it. The crew is unsettled and fractious. Their captain paces the deck, lost in thought. He has no refuge now, and the eyes of the men follow him, questioning, anticipating what their next move may be.

They are sailing along the north shore of Jamaica, its green lushness mocking the trapped crew. The temperature and humidity of the day rise and things must come to a head one way or another.

It is late afternoon when Mr Fetherstone feels safe enough to join the captain at the helm, he looking gloomy. The ship's master puts on a show of good spirits.

'Join us for a drink, Captain. It will cheer you.'

'It will take more than a drink to cheer me.'

'This is not like you, Jack. Yesterday is gone, and you still have your ship. And Anne.'

'Oh let us not forget about Anne. I am growing tired, Mr Fetherstone. We had the governor's pardon and she persuaded me back to sea. Look where it has got us.'

Jack is not the only one to have been totalling up a disappointing haul, and Mr Fetherstone does not need to be reminded of it. But there is always tomorrow, and the next week, and their luck has held thus far. They have evaded capture again. Someone is looking down on them, as he has always known it in his soul. But the men are tired, and that is his immediate concern.

'When a man is this low, there is only one answer. It is what rum exists for. Has it ever let you down? I would say this is the perfect time to get powerfully drunk.'

Jack lifts his head and smiles despite himself.

'I've heard worse ideas, George. You are right, as always. If we can walk or talk within the hour, then we have done something wrong. Call the men together and we will make a night of it.'

The master turns to the huddle of gloomy crew.

'Captain Rackham has said we are to finish our work and get very drunk. Will you join your captain in this fine endeavour?'

Mr Fenwick brightens.

'Why the hell not? If it's drink you're offering, I'm your man.'

Mary and Anne stand together and watch uneasy.

'What is he doing? With the Navy so close?'

Anne shakes her head.

'He is pretending it's not happening.'

Jack smiles broadly, the master of his domain once again.

'And why not? Lads – let's get one of those casks open and bring out the cards. There's been work enough for one day!'

A murmur of approval greets his words and the captain breathes a small sigh of relief. It is short-lived, as Anne closes in on him.

'This isn't a good idea. You know they'll be looking for us – we should keep moving.'

The eyes of the crew are on them, for Anne has not kept her voice low.

Jack is clearly irritated by her challenge, and prickles under the waiting gaze of his men.

'The crew have a right to their leisure, and this is as good a time as any to do it. Their captain will not see them disappointed.'

The rising colour of her face shows that she is less than convinced.

'We are not clear of danger yet, and you know it. It makes no sense to let the crew drink themselves senseless when they need their wits about them.'

His eyes are cold as he replies.

'As the captain of this ship, I have made a decision for my crew, and as a member of my crew you will accept it. I will not hear any more from you. Is that understood?'

She is about to speak again when his face becomes fierce, daring her to reply. She holds his eyes, her defiance not cowed, until the loud thud of the hatch makes them both turn quickly, breaking the tension of the moment. A barrel of rum has appeared and is caught and rolled down the deck to the vocal satisfaction of the men.

The captain speaks loudly, his performance resumed.

'Here we go, lads, your captain promised you a party, and a party is what you shall have. Let us have some music!'

He turns back to Anne.

'I think we are done, are we not?'

Mary feels the sting of his words keenly, for herself and for Anne.

Anne sees clearly for the first time that they have no place here. They have no place anywhere, and their time is running out.

Chapter 53

It is night-time when Mary comes to. The rigging and latticed wood of the ship cast a cobweb of shadows across the rippling water. The ship is silent, her crew asleep. Or mostly so.

She opens groggy eyes to take in a dark expanse of clear sky, silver stars blinking back startled. Her mouth is filthy with a thick taste. She tries to sit up, but the sudden lurch threatens not only her beating head but the swilling contents of her stomach. She has been drinking, then. It is only through sheer will and gulped breaths of cool sea air that she keeps the turtle stew down where it was intended to be.

As the world begins to settle before her eyes, she becomes aware of a scene of carnage. The deck of the ship is strewn with the drunken crew, unconscious, with snores, belches, and drowsy mutterings. Bodies lie prone and sprawled all over, their faces dead white in the moonlight, empty bottles rolling hypnotically around them as if some strange spirit stirs them.

A lone figure appears by the main mast. It seems a spectre from some supernatural realm, roaming silent across the deck, casting long shadows over the bodies in the cold moonlight. But as the strange light illuminates the face, Mary sees that it is Anne.

Anne does not see Mary as she steps between the prone men, greeting each with a sharp kick as she does so. The shapes let out low groans at her attentions, but none of them wake. As she moves across the deck, she kicks each man harder than the last, her temper blackening with each muffled blow.

She kicks hard at the stomach of Mr Dobbins, the most serene of the sleepers, who grunts and turns over to stay where he is, lost in a dream of naked girls that he is reluctant to leave.

Mary watches her quiet at first, but the baby begins to squirm, awkward and kicking, until she cannot ignore it and sighs, giving up on the thought of sleep. Anne is startled at first by the moving figure but relaxes her grip on her cutlass when she sees that it is Mary.

'Can't sleep?'

Mary rubs at her back and belly as Anne shakes her head. She cannot sleep, for dark thoughts about Jack are loud and insistent in her head and will not let her rest. Jack has become sloppy, and she is partly to blame. He has let his feelings for her cloud his judgement, and that puts them all in danger.

Mary places a hand on Anne's arm.

'What's the matter?'

Anne lifts her eyes to Mary's. Her voice is all but a whisper.

'He will kill us all.'

Mary realises that she has half expected it, but cannot bring herself to dismiss it. It is as likely an outcome as any, and they are soon to be cast aside.

'Then let's not let him.'

The women lapse into silence together as the ship rocks gently to the waves beneath.

Then suddenly there is a distant but unmistakable sound of a voice floating across the blackness of the night, breaking the stillness like the snap of a dry stick. The voice is sharply stifled by a second, urgent and vicious.

'Be quiet, damn you!'

Mary's hackles rise at once, and she is on her feet, with Anne beside her. The voices should not be there, that much is clear, and what they must mean is obvious. Every sinew of her strains at the direction of the voices.

One minute, two pass. There is the slow trickle of fear, every sense heightened. There are no more voices to be heard against the rise and fall of the ocean, but they now knew they are there in the darkness.

Mary moves like a cat across to the side of the ship despite her size, still and silent as her eyes narrow into the darkness beyond, Anne by her side, who tries to speak.

She shushes her quickly, eyes briefly blazing a warning into hers before she turns her gaze back towards the blank dark beyond. Anne's eyes follow hers, scanning the blackness ahead for anything that might explain away the voices. The stillness has taken on a different quality now, the sound of their own heartbeats threatening to drown out any further clues beyond.

Anne strains to hear or see something, as Mary starts and draws her sword. Something is out there, something that is coming their way.

A sea of wigs. Rolling waves, bobbing boats, and a brace of wigs inside. Sliding almost silently through the darkened ocean towards the ship before it, joined by other small boats, each with their cargo of soldiers. Edging closer until the men in the boats – dozens of them – are near enough to hear the groan of the ancient timbers, and the rumble and slap of waves against the hull of the ship.

The rowboats draw closer still to the ship, the soldiers sweating beneath their horsehair and wool, the Caribbean climate wrapping itself thickly around them even at this time of the night. They hear Anne clearly, for there is no time left for subtlety or games as she shouts, tries to rally the crew.

'Get up and fight – there are soldiers here!'

The pirates react slowly, as if unsure what is real and what a dream, their movements thick and groggy as they struggle to sit up, sleep pulled cruelly out from beneath them.

'What is it? What do you say?'

The men begin to stagger slowly to their feet, looking around them as if they had not seen the ship before, their responses thick and dull.

'To your stations – the Navy are here!'

Anne is frantic, Mary calm as she checks her pistols, and the activity stirs the men, their faces finally registering the danger they and the *Revenge* are in. Within minutes, the deck is a hive of halting activity, the drunken stupor of most of the hands a sorry sight at such a moment.

Mary glances at them, shaking her head, and hands Anne a dagger.

'I hope luck is with us tonight. We're going to need it.'

The captain has appeared from his cabin, squinting and holding himself upright in an unconvincing show of sobriety just as the clouds part, moonlight revealing the full extent of the enemy soldiers they face. They are outnumbered, convincingly so, and Jack's face shows it all too well.

The boats are so close now that the faces of the soldiers can be seen, fright and determination in equal measure, night air carrying the sounds of the efforts of the men who pull at the oars to bring their boats nearer. There is a scraping sound as they draw alongside, though there is barely time to acknowledge it before the fighting starts.

Mary fires the first shot off the tiller of the ship. The explosion of gunfire is startling, and then all hell breaks loose.

'They have jammed the tiller. We haven't much time!'

It is already hopeless. The roar of cannon fire tears the darkness open, the cannonball hurtling through the boom and sending it smashing down hard onto the deck. The first of two dozen or so grappling hooks land inches to her right, the tautening rope and the scrambling sounds just feet away suggesting the weight of a soldier at the end of each rope.

There are six of the crew now at the sides of the ship, raining down pistol fire and random missiles on the approaching soldiers below. Their screams and the sounds of falling bodies tell them that they have been at least partly successful, but more ropes join the original number and it soon becomes hopeless as perhaps five, then ten, then twenty-five soldiers are upon the deck and engaging directly with the drink-encumbered crew. But there is little fight in the men, and first Richard Corner, then John Davies lay down their weapons and submit to the enemy.

Mary fires a swivel gun at the deck of the enemy ship, all darkness until the devil retaliates with a broadside of cannon fire, scorching the air between them before it hits the *Revenge* side on, and she staggers under the weight of it, the blast carrying away the boom and disabling her where she sits.

Captain Barnet has their full attention now.

Barnet brings his ship alongside, a volley of small shot announcing this new proximity as his men prepare to board the pirate vessel, expecting success in their sheer weight of numbers. And they have the element of surprise, for as they board, weapons readied, the thunder of unfamiliar feet sounding across the boards of the *Revenge*, the men are groggy and unprepared.

Grappling hooks and boarding axes are brought to play, but the grenadoes are an unexpected addition to their arsenal. The grenadoes – and Barnet – have done their job.

'To your work, lads,' shouts Mary, but there is no response.

Anne and Mary turn to look at one another, an unspoken accord passing between them. They must do this alone, without the help of the crew. Everything has led to this. There is an inevitability to it, and they are ready. They have always been ready. They breathe, the beat of passing seconds sounded by their hearts. Their swords are drawn, their pistols cocked and they turn together to face the enemy.

Before them is a sight the soldiers will never forget. Anne and Mary stand side by side, planted to the deck, cutlasses and pistols waving, seeming together like the goddess Kali, multi-armed and reeking of death.

There is a frightened hesitation from the men, but it ends quickly, for Mary raises a pistol and shoots the nearest man square in the chest, he falling and toppling the men behind him like dominoes. Her bullet spent, she strides forward, turns the pistol to use as a club on the next man standing, he crumpling to the deck with a howl as Anne quickly follows Mary's lead with her sword.

They fly at Barnet's men wielding cutlasses and axes, hurling obscenities.

The scattered soldiers have remembered themselves now and fall forward with an angry roar, boots thudding against timber, the clash of swords, shouts and bellows all around.

The women fight like Furies, screaming as they try to repel the advance. Anne slices at a soldier, who falls backwards into his comrades, clutching at his eye with a scream and knocking three men over in his wake. She takes the chance to throw open the hatch to encourage more crew to the deck, but to their shame they stay where they are.

'Is there not a man among you? You can die up here or die down there – it is your choice!'

She fires into the hold without pause and returns to the battle above with new fury. But it is already too late – the soldiers have overwhelmed the men on deck, the red uniformed figures stood over the cowering crew, the onslaught merciless as sword, pistol butts, fist and boot are used to subdue any last attempts at resistance.

A look of madness is in the eyes of the women as they roar and respond still. They snarl and spit, slicing and shooting into the wall of men before them, but there is only so much time the advancing tide can be held back. As the soldiers fight on, the sheer weight of numbers – perhaps eleven or twelve – begin to overpower them.

In the confusion, a rifle butt catches Anne in the face and breaks her nose, blood rushing from the startled wound as she slumps to her knees, and then falls to the deck. Dazed, she looks towards Mary, who is horribly outnumbered.

Mary does her best to hold back the horde, but suddenly her legs weaken beneath her. She crumples and falls, and the world tilts and tips on its side. The advancing mob make their move and she disappears behind a press of men.

Tom calls out to her 'Mary!' in anguish as he receives a fist to the face for his trouble, and he too falls, still and silent.

There is a storm of noise, but a clear voice can be heard through it. 'Enough. We surrender.'

Chapter 54

Anne can barely believe what she has heard. It is Jack's voice.
And he has called quarter. This man who spat when talking of the
cowardice of other captains, of blowing his ship up rather than
have it captured, has surrendered and damned them all to hell.
And he has been listened to, for the remaining pirates lay down
their weapons, hands raised in surrender as the soldiers, unable to
believe their luck at first, begin to push the defeated men towards
the far end of the ship, penning them in like cattle.

'You too – get over there with your lot.'

But Anne will not leave Mary, has cradled her head in her
arms as she lies prone on the deck, panting heavily.

It lasts for only a moment. The women are dragged to their
feet, Anne writhing and kicking at her two captors. It breaks her
heart to see that Mary does not.

The women have become the cause of consternation and hilarity, the soldiers staring, nudging one another, and speaking about
them lewdly and loudly. Anne is vocal for them both, but, to their
shame, none of the men adds his voice to hers.

The soldiers are cocksure and self-congratulatory, just as the
pirates had been when the fight had gone their way. But good luck
has deserted them, and they must face the consequences. One of

the soldiers, his wig skew-whiff, climbs the mast and tears down the black flag, draping it around himself like a cape as he lumpenly descends, the others cheering and laughing at him, the fabric skull misshapen around his shoulders.

The crew of the *Revenge* are manacled together at the ankles and wrists, the shackles holding them together in one miserable row. The black iron is cold and heavy, the noise of it jarring as they struggle to move when they are prodded, or hit with the butts of guns, some clumsy beast with dozens of legs. The pirates are sullen, bloody and defeated, a sight to delight Captain Barnet, who struts up and down before them, his hands held tightly together behind his back, unwilling to hide his satisfaction.

He falters when he sees Anne and Mary; he had thought of them as nothing more than a fiction, but here they are. Flesh and blood. He manages to tear himself away and approaches Jack, whose right eye is bruised and swollen in his bloodied face.

'You are now prisoners of His Majesty. I have the pleasure of delivering you to justice. You have dishonoured your men in surrender, I am sure you know that. I will mark it in my account of the proceedings.'

Jack does not need to be reminded of what he has done. His miserable rum-soaked crew will die for it, for his failing.

'Kill me now then – it will be something to remember in your dotage.'

Barnet smiles and shakes his head.

'I am an honourable man, and as such I shall not deprive the hangman of his living. You will be made an example of, and may God help you for that.'

They sit now dumbly chained together, the mood one of heart-sinking defeat.

A familiar black shape slips through the legs of one of the soldiers. He is startled, but his face softens as he bends to stroke the cat. She in turn is grateful for his attentions, responding with enthusiasm as he scratches behind her ears.

Mr Dobbins calls out to her, part panic, part indignity.

'Alice! Come here to me, my girl! Come to me!'

Alice pauses, looking towards Mr Dobbins for a moment. Perhaps her conscience is pricked, perhaps she might have been about to approach her friend. But at that moment the soldier begins to scratch under her chin and her attention is all his.

Mr Dobbins watches helplessly as she enjoys the fussing of this other man before she loses interest and runs off at pace towards the Navy ship alongside. There is a tension as she plans her jump, a flash of black and she is gone, allegiances switched in a moment.

'They're going to take her? My little girl?'

His voice breaks alongside the indignity of tears.

Mr Fetherstone is chained to his left and speaks to him gruffly.

'It's for the best, man. She's a fine mouser and they will take care of her. That is what you would want for her, is it not?'

He nods miserably, his face wet from tears. But he does not have time to dwell on his Alice's casual betrayal – the captured crew have orders barked at them before they are pushed and man-handled into standing. Soon, the prisoners are loaded onto the Navy ship, the Union Jack now raised and flying from the mast of the *Revenge*. She is a pirate ship no more, but a prize of war. It is a final insult, a reminder, if it were needed, that the world has spun off-kilter and will never be the same again.

They are forced below decks of the Navy ship and stowed like cargo, the mood dark and silent. Anne cannot look at Jack, not that he notices, for his gaze is a thousand miles away. He has used up all the words he has, and has nothing more to say.

The Navy ship turns her bow towards Jamaica and heads into the coming dawn. In the darkness of the lower deck, Anne holds Mary to her as she shivers uncontrollably, her face leached of colour, her Tom too far away to see or to help.

Chapter 55

The sun rises blood red, rippling across the sea as the victors and their prisoners put ashore at Davis's Cove. Major Richard James is already waiting with his guard, news having spread fast of this glorious victory in the fight against the pirates, his chest puffed at the honour of escorting the scum to Spanish Town jail.

His men are unnecessarily rough, their bayonets coming into play in reluctant backsides and stomachs where they must, the pirates surly and unhelpful, their language ripe and foul, much as expected. He recognises Rackham from his red coat, of course, though he is much the worse for wear from the beating he has endured, his cuffs torn and hanging from him like rags.

He is startled to see the two women at first, though they are hardly dressed as women. They wear the long trousers and jackets of the other pirates, handkerchiefs around their hair with hats on top. So the rumour is true! No wonder, then, that Rackham has come to this sorry pass if he will man his ship with women. Nothing but bad luck, and Rackham has two of the buggers. They glare back at him, and his smirk fades fast.

He is about to share some witty comment, but stops as he sees Captain Barnet's face. This man does not care who or what these villains are, they are prisoners of the Crown.

'Major James. Good to see you as always, sir. The prisoners are ready – I wish you an easy time of it. And your men should expect an extra shilling or two for their troubles.'

He beams broadly, for this is an unexpected boon.

'I shall consider it an honour to deliver them to justice.'

'I should expect no less.'

And Jonathan Barnet is gone, striding out to his next bit of business, for this is the way a reputation is built, in successes such as these.

Armed guards lead the pirates through town, muskets at the ready. It has been raining, and the mud mires under them, the muck of the place grasping at their feet, making them slip every few steps and weighing them down like a bad dream. They are cowed and miserable, stumbling and dragging chains through the streets as they are heckled by a delighted crowd who had not expected such a spectacle to be brought before them so early in the day.

A carnival develops around the prisoners as word spreads quickly that not only pirates, but women pirates, have been captured. The crowds jeer, hoot and hiss, pushing one another aside to get a better look, until irritation leads to flying fists and some of the soldiers are ordered to break up the brawl, goddammit, and restore some semblance of order as twenty or so men and women try to kill one another in the procession's wake, the pirates all but forgotten.

Jack has seen former shipmates endure such a thing, but he never expected to see it for himself. It is bloody miserable, and he thinks mournfully of the King's pardon so casually thrown away. And for what?

For a woman, a loud voice in his head scolds him.

And it is right. He was bored, no more than that, and she showed him a way out. A pity that the destination will be the gallows.

The prisoners struggle to keep their footing, their ankles dragged down by the weight of their restraints, a shuffling gait the only possible way to make progress. Heavy chains grate back and forth through the shackles of the man in front as their legs have no option but to keep pace or stumble and be beaten for it.

Anne still wears a look of grim fury, her left eye almost swollen shut now in her bruised face. Mary is ahead of her, limping painfully, but jutting out her chin as if daring the crowd to act. They call out, throw rubbish if they have any to hand, but the soldiers keep the crowd at bay.

The sun rises overhead and daylight breaks to show their journey's end. The prison is a great edifice of stone, a monument to the permanence of law and order. The sturdy doors creak open to greet them, the cool air of the dark interior offering some solace from the rising heat of the outside world. It is the last natural warmth they will know.

The prisoners are pushed down the steep incline of a long corridor into the depths of the prison. Anne and Mary's shackles are unlocked, freeing them from the rest of the crew before they are prodded with bayonets and led away on their own, further into the bowels of the prison. Although less shackled than before, Mary struggles with the guards to turn her head to shout back.

'Stay strong, Tom. Me and the baby will be fine.'

He tries to answer, but the words die in his throat as Mary disappears into the darkness. He is almost knocked on his backside as the jailors jostle him out of the way as Jack is unshackled too and the captain led off to a separate cell, just as the women have been.

Jack disappears into the gloom before another door is opened before them and the remaining crew are ushered into the foulest and darkest of cells. Their stomachs rebel at the stench of it as they become aware of an undulating mass around their feet.

'What the hell is it?' asks John Fenwick, scrambling at whatever it is with his heel, one of the shapes slithering over his bare foot like an eel, causing him to scream out, unsettling the men even further. They recoil from it, their shackles still holding tight as they try to scurry away from the mass, horrified by the unknown.

As their eyes became accustomed to the gloom, the mass reveals itself as a scuttling pack of rats, their coats matted, black eyes glittering at their new cellmates. One of the creatures creeps closer to Richard Corner, sniffing at his boot as if curious about the contents. He is allowed a brief moment before the quartermaster raises his other foot and smashes the rat's brains into the floor of the cell, its friends shrieking and running back to their hiding places.

As panic retreats for now and breathing becomes steadier, an unwelcome coldness settles damply onto their flesh, one that will seep into their bones over the coming days. But it is not only cold that will plague them.

Fear has its own smell, and it pervades every inch of the prison.

'It is worse than Newgate, and that is saying something,' says John Howell, and there is a murmur of agreement as the men take stock.

The cell is miserable, as it is meant to be. The walls run green with slime, the thick air used too many times by too many men, the smell of human waste. Now that the rats have retreated for a time, the floor seethes with insects, the tic tic of scuttling legs, the uneven glimmer of moving carapaces.

The men find the wall and settle down as best they can, the damp of the floor and walls creeping into their clothes, their skin wet with the filth. This is the last place they will see and they know it too well. There is only a glimpse of sky possible through the tiny barred window, cruelly high, just enough to lend twilight to the gloom during daylight. Just enough for them to see one another, secured by pinions and shackles, beaten and waiting for death.

The door reopens after a time, a physician sent to attend to the wounds of Mr Davies. He is in a bad way, drifting on the edges of consciousness. The wound to his stomach is open and raw, and the doctor wastes no time in niceties.

'Does this hurt?'

He pushes a finger into the wound as Mr Davies curses and swears, writhing under the probing finger.

'Yes – it would do. Nasty business. We'll dig out the bullet and patch you up – don't want you dying before you can be hanged now, do we?'

Mr Davies lies pale and panting, staring wide-eyed at the torturer who stands before him.

'If you think that hurt, just wait until you receive my treatment!'

His crewmates turn away as brusque medical attentions are administered, his screams a precursor to what is to come.

In the grim silence that follows, once the doctor has left and Mr Davies has passed out from his pain, it is only Tom Earl who speaks.

'I suppose I shall never see the baby, then.'

He keeps his gaze ahead of him as tears fall from his eyes.

A large supportive arm of James Dobbins snakes around his fallen shoulders and pulls him in as dry sobs begin to heave through him. Both men, after all, have lost their loves today and can at least offer one another a little comfort.

It is perhaps an hour later, when Tom has cried himself out and silence descends once again, that George Fetherstone clears his throat before speaking, his voice strained.

'I should like to say a prayer for our poor souls, for if God is listening, he will perhaps offer mercy for us sinners.'

And he begins, the men tolerant for once of such a display of religion. They may not believe in it, or Him, but they have nothing to lose now. The words fall thick in the darkness as Mr Earl sets to weeping again, but this time there is no help or reassurance left in Mr Dobbins.

It is John Howell who breaks the silence left by the finished prayer.

'Stay strong, man. We will die together, and not alone.'

Tom Earl will spend every one of his remaining hours awake, thinking of Mary, and knowing what is coming for him, sleep having now forsaken him for good.

Chapter 56

Jack's cell is similar to that of his crew, though a larger window allows more light to enter. This is less about status than it is about practicalities, for his captors have plans for him. They are plans he will want no part of, but it is out of his hands.

There are few perks to the job of jailor, but to be able to tell their friends that they broke the bones of a pirate captain? Well, that is something to amuse their grandchildren as they dandle them on their knees. They cannot have their fun before he has stood trial of course, but after? Well, after the trial, he is theirs until the hangman takes him. They have precious little else to do but wait.

Jack is all too aware of his position, captured and imprisoned. He hears nothing but the slow drip, drip of water, reminding him, if it were needed, that the place runs with damp. Cold has already begun to creep into his bones as if he were back in the long dark winters of Bristol, a place he had sought to escape forever, and the slabs of the cell walls prevent any sounds of comfort. He does not expect good cheer from his men, but he would like to hear their voices once again. Without them he is stripped bare. As of the women ... well, he tries not to think of the women. He has troubles enough of his own.

In the coming hours, he finds himself unable to sleep so much as doze on his nerves, jolts of panic bringing him sharply back to his sorry predicament. He dreams of home, but it is not the home he would choose to remember. Instead, his dreams are filled with the memories of dead pirates, hanging lifeless and bloated in their chains at Execution Dock. No matter how much he tries to discourage his mind from the image of gibbeted corpses garlanding the Thames, it will return him to this darkest of places.

He tortures himself. It will make what is to come easier in a way.

Mary and Anne's cell is a little better than those of their crewmates, and only the two of them are in it. The walls still run wet with slime, the floors awash with insects, but the cell is slightly more comfortable, furnished as it has been with two makeshift beds. These women may be pirates, but they are women nonetheless and must be shown a modicum of civility. Until their trial, of course, when they will be hanged with the rest of them. The law is, after all, still the law, whoever you are.

Anne paces as if she might find a way out, locked in her own thoughts. Mary watches her briefly, but feels a black fog descending that she has not felt for some time. She realises she is exhausted and takes to the bed, for there is nothing more to be done. Mary lies with her face turned to the wall, her eyes closed, cradling her belly.

Chapter 57

The courtroom is a hot and stinking place, curious onlookers packed into the heaving room ready for the sport to come. Humanity in all shapes and sizes hang from the upper gallery of the room, holding on for dear life as they strain to look at the prisoners like animals in an exhibit. They call out, overfamiliar and provocative, goading the men for a response that does not come. The audience shout and holler to one another too so that the rolling wave of chatter is entirely disconcerting.

The pirates to a man hold themselves upright, facing determinedly forward and unseeing, as they wait for the proceedings to begin. There is no sign of Anne and Mary.

They do not have long to wait for an attendant to bring the court to order.

'All rise for Sir Nicholas Lawes, Governor of Jamaica and appointed judge of this court!'

It is the Admiralty Court, no less, for British Justice must show its displeasure with as much pomp and noise as it can. Sir Nicholas has had the last ten days to prepare himself for such an enterprise and he is more than ready. The witnesses have taken time to round up, but he will not allow these villains to evade justice.

Sir Nicholas makes a slow and stately way to his desk at the head of the room, his gait marred by signs of gout. As he takes his rightful place, wincing as he lowers himself into the chair, all eyes are upon him.

He is a fat, elderly man, red in the face, sweat running in thick ribbons from his wig and down into his collar so that he steams where he sits. His face carries a heavy air of ill temper, and he shoots venomous glances at the prisoners over the top of his pince-nez while he waits for the charges to be read.

The same attendant, puffed up with his own importance, clears his throat unnecessarily. The crowd see that the sport is about to begin, and they hush one another, beginning to quiet themselves so that the clerk can be heard. He loosens the ribbon that holds the scroll in place before he unfurls it with a long-practised flourish.

'These articles shall be read at this High Court of Admiralty. Held at the town of St Jago de la Vega, Jamaica, on the twenty-eighth day of November, in the seventh year of the reign of our sovereign lord George, by the grace of God, of Great Britain, France and Ireland, King, and of Jamaica, Lord, Defender of the Faith.'

He pauses for breath, the verbiage delivered without incident.

'We are here by virtue of a commission from his Majesty, issued under the Act of Parliament entitled "An Act for the more effectual suppression of Piracy", for the trying, hearing, determining and adjudging, of all piracies, felonies and robberies committed in or upon the sea, or in any haven, river or creek where the Admirals have power, authority or jurisdiction before His Excellency, Sir Nicholas Lawes.'

The clerk allows himself a small bow towards Sir Nicholas, who inclines his head graciously to acknowledge his authority, and connection to His Majesty.

'The charge is: that in the seventh year of the reign of our said Lord the King, upon the high sea, in a certain sloop, the following did feloniously and wickedly consult and agree together, to rob, plunder and to take, all that they should meet with on the high seas. And in the execution of their evil designs, with force and arms, did piratically, feloniously and in a hostile manner, attack, engage and take several vessels which they did plunder.'

He pauses for effect before he turns to the prisoners.

'The accused are the men that stand now before you. I name them as Jack Rackham, George Fetherstone, Richard Corner, John Davies, John Howell, John Fenwick, Thomas Bourn, James Dobbins, Patrick Carty, Thomas Earl and Noah Harwood.'

As each name is read out, the men stare at the ground before them as if refusing to acknowledge their own names. Only Jack keeps his gaze steady on the man who judges them all.

As no response comes from the accused, Sir Nicholas prompts the clerk.

'Mr Norris, if you will?'

'You are here to face charges that on the first day of September that said accused, alongside Mary Read and Anne Bonny, spinsters, upon the high seas, in a certain sloop did conspire to rob and plunder and take persons and subjects of our said Lord the King ...'

It takes a moment or two to register with the crowd, but mention of women brings a rising wave of catcalls, foot stamping and an increase in excitement and volume that leads to another temporary halt to the proceedings. The room ripples, the crowd craning their necks further to see these strange creatures who remain tantalisingly below ground, locked in their cells for now.

Sir Nicholas is outraged.

'Silence! Silence, I say! You shall treat this courtroom with respect or I shall clear you from it like vermin, and what sport will there be for you then, eh?'

Relative calm once again achieved, the judge indicates to the clerk that proceedings should resume.

He clears his throat loudly once again, reasserting his authority and directs his comments to the dock.

'How do you plead to the charges?'

Jack speaks first, breaking into a familiar smile.

'Not guilty, Your Honour. Naturally.'

One by one, the ragbag of men in the dock repeats the same surly response in unconvincing denial.

'Not guilty.'

All eyes are on Sir Nicholas as he opens his mouth as if to speak, but he merely raises a hand to stifle a yawn.

'Very well then. Let's at it, shall we.'

The clerk of court takes his cue.

'If you will allow it, we shall call our first witness. For the prosecution, we call Thomas Spenlow'.

A uniformed officer, hat held in hand, takes to the witness stand. He is all too familiar to the men, and Jack acknowledges him with a small bow. Captain Spenlow is in better shape than when they left him speared and bleeding on the deck of his ransacked ship, but he still blanches as his gaze rises to face the pirate crew.

His testimony takes almost an hour, no detail spared as the clerk prompts him to retell the painful experience. He is tentative at first, but soon finds his voice to tell them of violence, torture and robbery. He is encouraged to show his wound, and complies to reveal a large puckered tear across his abdomen, to the horror and delight of the gallery.

The courtroom is spellbound, with even the mob in the galleries reduced to silence as they revel in every word uttered by the witness before them. When his testimony is ended, no one is left in any doubt of its effect.

Sir Nicholas speaks to his witness.

'It is clear that you were put in corporeal fear for your lives, Captain.'

'That we were, Your Honour. All of them here, the women included, were very ready and willing to join the fight, as well as swearing and cursing.'

There is some laughter from the gallery at this, but Sir Nicholas is not quite finished yet. He raises his gavel and brings it down sharply as if he wished certain fingers had been beneath it. His jowls wobble as he barks.

'I shall bring this court to order!'

He glowers at the gallery and sees them suitably subdue themselves for now. Satisfied, he turns back to his witness.

'And I shall see to it that your bravery in coming here today shall not be in vain, Mr Spenlow.'

As the captain leaves the platform with obvious relief, excited chatter amongst the upper gallery breaks out. Sir Nicholas looks at the prisoners sternly, though none respond as he would like.

It is then that a voice from the dock unexpectedly raises itself.

'Your Honour, there has been a mistake – I should not be here!'

Shouts and mocking laughter fill the room, the gargoyles in the gallery animated and vocal again, drowning out the voice as Sir Nicholas turns on him.

'You, sir, are a prisoner of the Crown and shall treat this court with the respect it is due. You will stay quiet unless expressly spoken to.'

John Fenwick, for it is he, seems hurt by the rebuke and is spurred on by some sense of injustice that determines to be out. The judge's face has turned a deep purple as he continues, much to the disgust of his crewmates. 'But, Your Honour!'

'Quiet! Or you shall be punished severely for your impertinence. What is your name?'

He is about to answer, when Jack steps forward, glaring sideways at Mr Fenwick in warning as he does so.

'The prisoner's name is John Fenwick, Your Honour. He is a member of my crew, more's the pity, though an abject coward, as you can see.'

The crowd jeers from the gallery and the eyes of his crewmates bore into John Fenwick with contempt, pity and amusement. Sir Nicholas is less than happy.

'If you speak out of turn once again, Mr Fenwick, I shall have you flogged. Now, I shall not hear from you again until I specifically require it. Do you understand me, sir.'

It is not a question but Mr Fenwick nods at him dumbly as the judge continues.

Mr Spenlow is not the only witness, and there is a great deal of evidence to be shared with the court, for a great many transgressions have been committed. The evidence is irrefutable.

It is some hours later, and Sir Nicholas peruses his notes leisurely, for justice should not be served lightly.

An air of expectation buzzes around the room like the droning of bees. Finally, Sir Nicholas adjusts his wig, confides with his clerk and reaches below his desk to pull out a small square of black fabric. It continues its journey past his forehead being placed atop his wig before he clears his throat and pronounces:

'This Court has found you guilty of the piracies, robberies and felonies charged against you. Do you have anything to say, or offer, why sentences of death should not pass upon you, for these said offences?'

The air is thick with expectation, but the prisoners stay silent.

'Very well. Jack Rackham, George Fetherstone, Richard Corner, John Davies, John Howell, John Fenwick, Thomas Bourn, James Dobbins, Patrick Carty, Thomas Earl and Noah Harwood… You shall go hence from whence you came, and from thence to the place of execution, where you shall be hanged by the neck until you are dead.'

For the first time, there is a glimmer of humanity in the man's eyes.

'May God in his infinite mercy be merciful to your souls.'

Chapter 58

The trial of the women has not yet begun, but the mob is in fine spirits and fine voice too. They have already seen pirates condemned to death, and now there are more to follow. Who would have thought it of women? They settle in for the entertainment to come.

The anticipation is palpable as the women are finally brought up from their cell, hands and feet chained. They jut out their chins defiantly, as the court descends into a storm of catcalls, jeers and whistles that all but drown out the frantic efforts of the clerk to maintain order.

Anne and Mary are bruised and tattered, but defiant and unbowed too. They have not been given a chance to wash or change out of their old clothes, their bloodstained shirts likely to prejudice a fair hearing, their trousers and general men's garb even more so.

Sir Nicholas, purple with the effort of making himself heard, finally manages to bring the overflowing gallery to something approaching silence. Scowling at the crowd malevolently, he finally turns his attention to Anne and Mary, adjusting his spectacles on the end of his nose to do so. He stares at them for a few moments as they return his gaze, unflinching.

'Good Lord ...'

He seems to remember himself and, clearing his throat, instructs the clerk to begin reading the charges.

'The accused are Mary Read and Anne Bonny, late of the island of Providence, spinsters ...'

At this, Mary breaks her silence and objects most strongly.

'I am married just as surely as if it had happened in Church!'

The gallery erupts in laughter, with apparently every one of them keen to share their opinion loudly with the court. Wearily, the judge bangs his gavel until the row subsides enough for him to be heard.

'I have no intention of this taking all day. Treat this court with respect or I shall throw every last one of you out.'

'Does that include us?'

Mary's insolence draws a further roar of approval from the gallery, now wholly on the side of this strange woman before them.

Greatly flustered, Sir Nicholas attempts to wrestle back control of his court.

'Silence, goddammit!'

Whether this is intended for the gallery or Mary, it is difficult to tell, but it does its job. As the racket subsides to a more manageable level, he readjusts his spectacles and resumes, his face a rictus of control.

'You are accused of having taken an active part in the piracies carried out by the captain and crew of the sloop *Revenge*. We have received testimony that you do not seem to have been kept by force, but remained by your own free will. Is that correct?'

He watches aghast as they answer 'yes' in turn. The gallery expresses their surprise and approval at volume.

'Well, it is not my place here to find you unnatural, but I shall leave it to the conscience of every man and woman here to judge you so. And one of your victims whom was run through with a sword – Captain Thomas Spenlow of His Majesty's ship *Starling* – reports that you were both "very profligate, cursing and swearing much, and very ready and willing to do most anything on board". Can this also be right?'

'We were not there for the fun of it but to earn our share.'

Anne is hardly helping her cause or Mary's, and the court erupts once again, a great deal of foot stamping accompanying her words. She too has the popular vote.

Sir Nicholas has by now clearly run to the end of his patience as he waves his gavel like a weapon at this gathering of his fellow citizens.

'Enough, do you understand me? Enough!'

Their animal enthusiasm is briefly calmed to civilised levels once again as he speaks to Anne and Mary directly.

'You admit your guilt then. You are clearly beyond all decency, and I shall soon come to my judgement. You know what is to happen to your crew? What do you say to their hanging?'

There is a brief silence as every man and woman in the court strains to hear the answer. They are not disappointed as Mary speaks, clear and practised.

'If hanging were not the case, every coward would turn pirate and men of greater courage starve. Our boys are ready for death, though it is a shame they must give away their lives to someone like you.'

Sir Nicholas is temporarily lost for words, though the gallery is less circumspect, with boos and hissing clearly heard amongst the other uncalled-for commentary. When he finally speaks, the judge is all business again, the familiar black cap appearing on his head.

'Then you shall share the fate of your fellow crew. You shall both be hanged by the neck until you are dead. And may God be merciful to your souls.'

A small smile crosses Anne's face as Mary stands by her, head held high.

'We should like to inform the court that we are both quick with child, and pray that execution of the sentence may be stayed.'

Mary adds her own footnote.

'You asked what I thought of your hanging our crew? You have taken my baby's father from him, and from me.'

Sir Nicholas's outrage shows itself in his now purple face as he tries and fails to compose himself. The crowd in the court erupts loudly – jeering, indignation, hilarity – as he struggles to be heard.

'So you plead your bellies? Very well then. As the law dictates, the sentence of death shall be respited while an inspection be made. I trust for both your sakes that you have been honest on this point at least.'

The struggling women are dragged from the court by the soldiers, their shouts drowned out as chaos descends on the courtroom. For once, Sir Nicholas allows it to happen, for he is suddenly feeling his age. Every last year of it. He permits himself a small tot of whisky from the hip flask he keeps about his person for just such occasions, though, thank God, there have been few occasions as bad as this. He smacks his lips and congratulates himself on his excellent taste in whisky, and makes a note to himself that he must order more. It takes so long for ships to reach them here, so it is best to plan ahead.

The crowd is growing impatient as the minutes pass, and are just becoming a little too fractious as he sees that the prisoners are returning. The women are returned to the dock by the same soldiers that took them down, and he takes a moment to tuck away his hip flask once again. The defiance is still there, but the women appear hot and dishevelled. Anne's mood has visibly darkened, Mary's even more so.

His Honour is handed a piece of paper before addressing them again.

'Well, Miss Read, it seems that you are indeed with child.'

She glares at him with undisguised savagery as she pulls up her shirt to show the undisputed truth of the statement.

'Any idiot could have seen that for himself if he took the time to look. Shame on you and that dirty bastard of a sergeant!'

Sir Nicholas looks rather nauseated as the gallery erupts in jeers and boos.

'You will cover yourself up, madam. Your shame has no place in this courtroom. And you – Miss Bonny – I understand that you have also been found to be with child?'

She glares at him.

'I am. That a life unborn should save us from death is a strange thing indeed.'

Sir Nicholas removes his glasses.

'You are mistaken, madam. This is merely a temporary stay of execution until your baby is born. You will have time enough to repent before we meet again.'

He turns to the nearest soldier.

'Take these women back to their cell. The case is adjourned for now.'

Chapter 59

The day has been a trying one, and Sir Nicholas is glad to be home. That the women are pregnant leaves him in a quandary. He cannot hang them, more's the pity. He should dearly like to do so, but the law is quite clear on this particular set of circumstances. Unlikely that two of them should be with child, never mind just one. He shakes his head. But, of course, for what else would women of their kind do when left with savages?

He must punish them, naturally, and most surely will, but he must be able to justify (to the law, of course, but most of all to his wife, who has become very vocal on the matter in the short time he has returned to his own house) that he is mindful of their condition. He is their reluctant protector until he can resume in his role of their judge and executioner.

Once he had adjourned the court and processed this farce that has constituted his day, he issues begrudging instructions that the women are to receive blankets. Their rations are to be increased, and furthermore shall be supplemented with meat. Not meat that would grace his own table, of course, but meat nonetheless. His wife will be satisfied with that for now, he is sure. For what else these women have done ... He shudders and closes his eyes to it.

The children these women bear (his wife has reminded him forcefully) will come into the world washed clean of sin. No doubt if he allowed the babes to stay with their mothers they would turn villain themselves, but the sentence of execution prevents that from happening, thank God.

That said, he has not yet decided on what his course of action should be. If he is to save their mortal souls, then the right thing would be to remove the babies at the earliest opportunity and hand them over to a barren woman, perhaps. They will be grateful, and his obligation fulfilled. It is no more than it is to take kittens from a cat.

He chuckles to himself to think of his own humanity. What would His Majesty think if he knew his faithful servant harboured such tender thoughts? He shakes his head at the thought, and reminds himself with satisfaction that at least the men will swing for what they have done. For now he will content himself with that.

Chapter 60

Jack has been granted a final wish to see Anne and to say good-bye to her. She is, after all, the mother of his future child and the court must respect the rights of the unborn. The material fact is that he has given away his gold tooth to his jailor in return for the visit. It was to be his pension, but he has no use for that – or his tooth – now. At least this way he can say his goodbyes to Anne.

He has not been as fair to her as he might have been. The baby will be just as much his. He grimaces for a moment, for what a thing it would have been to meet his own child. That it cannot ever happen now makes him feel something close to regret.

Anne is taken from her cell as Mary sleeps, uncertain about what is happening, for she is shushed and instructed to follow, and she is in no position to refuse. Mary sleeps like the dead or she would no doubt have requests of her own.

Anne follows the jailor, who leads her like a dog on a chain, his lantern shedding unwelcome light on slimed walls and darting rats as they follow the rough corridors further underground.

At last, they reach a cell door, one of many, the criss-cross lattice of bars masking whatever is inside.

'He's in there.'

She looks at the jailor in confusion as he turns the key and the door creaks open.

'I'll leave you for now.'

Anne stumbles forward into the cell to find the interior faintly lit by another torch, a figure sat shackled to the wall. She cannot see the face at first but she recognises the voice.

'And here she is. The cause of it all.'

It is Jack. She does not step any further forward but instead waits for her eyes to adapt to the novelty of lamplight.

She blinks at the figure as he slowly slips into focus, the features sharper. He has been brutalised, left limp like a rag doll. He stands with some difficulty and smiles. She is shocked by the sight of him but stays tight-lipped.

He has been the focus of animal boredom, his jailors imaginative in their infliction of pain. Sinews stretched to breaking point, soft tissues bruised and burned, fingers and toes splintered. He is a wreck of the man he once was, and urges her with sunken eyes to acknowledge it.

'I have asked them to bring you so that I can say goodbye. I had kept myself from the hangman quite well until now, but it seems that you have brought me to my knees.'

She looks at him coldly. He gazes back at her intently, half smiling awkwardly as if trying to fix something long broken.

'I am glad to see you, Anne.'

His tone is soft, a surprise to them both. Her gaze flits from his to review the cell. It is far worse than she and Mary have, she notes, but she still not does trust her voice.

'Have you nothing to say to me now? No last kind words?'

His voice has a quiet desperation, and she answers him at last, her voice quite clear.

'I wish you a speedy death, Jack. I am sorry for you.'

He replies with a hollow, unbelieving laugh.

'After everything we have been through, that is all you can say to me? You have nothing more tender? No words of comfort for your love?'

Her eyes flash as the words spill out of her like snakes.

'If you'd have fought like a man, you needn't have died like a dog. Your cowardice has killed us all. There is nothing more to be said.'

He laughs, shocked, but regains himself.

'Well, not quite all. It is my child that you carry, after all. What a picture of a family we'd have made.'

He looks at her sadly.

'So it seems our little love affair is at an end. As am I.'

He bows his head, as Anne's voice softens.

'Die well, Jack. I promise you that I will keep our daughter safe from men like you.'

He laughs quietly as he looks at her one last time, an unexpected softness in his eyes.

'As well you should.'

He seems about to speak again but finds himself out of words.

Anne turns to her guard.

'I am done here.'

She allows herself to be led away by the jailor, her hands shaking. Her eyes glitter, though with anger or unshed tears it is hard to say.

Chapter 61

Lost in her own thoughts, Anne is oblivious to the muffled screams from other cells, hidden in the darkness of corridors that wind off into blackness, their inhabitants never seen, for they are nothing to do with her. They are adrift in the urgent misery of their own business.

Elsewhere in the prison, the crew are sleeping, or mostly so. They are visited by spectres of the long-departed, of children who would never see another birthday, of long-dead mothers, hard-lived and joyless, of men killed by their hands, staring empty-eyed and dispassionate at these wretches who will soon join them.

There are half-remembered loves, glimpses of childish things long gone, the lost smiles of wives and sisters, the memory of full stomachs and warm beds. Faces emerge crystal clear from the fog of forgotten memories and in their dreams they weep with joy and relief that they are here with them now.

Love is spoken of, often for the first time, dear ones held tight now they have been found again after so, so long. Favourite dogs play and scamper around them, delighted their masters are home at last, all wagging tails and pink tongues. Mr Dobbins dreams happily of Alice, all his again with her soft fur and rumbling purr. They talk, drink and laugh, or take wives or lovers to more private places, all lightness and gratitude long into the night of their dreams.

It is a brief kind of heaven, a blessing that they have been given whatever they have been and done before. Softer feelings make themselves remembered, buried so long under want and need and anger, they blossom like flowers in spring. Their hearts thaw and once again they are able to feel for more than just themselves, a strange and wonderful thing that transports them from the squalor of the waking world.

But all too soon dawn breaks. These whisps of memory begin to lose their shape, step back into the shadows, become ghosts again, dissolving into day as the men are woken by the guards as a lone cock crows harshly outside the walls.

The wrench of it is almost too much to bear, too cruel, as they come to, eyes rubbed and heads shaken, and remember with black horror where they are and what today will be.

Chapter 62

They come for them early morning before the sun is fully over-head, out of consideration for the citizens of the place, who have turned up to see justice done. Grim silence sits on them like a physical weight, the men facing their inevitable end alone in their own heads with their fears and misery.

Today is the day they will die.

Their jailor enters the stinking room. His face and voice are empty of emotion as only the truly stupid can be.

'Get up. You need to follow me.'

He looks at them with dead eyes, as if they are already beyond the help of ordinary men.

'I said get up.'

Their legs obey him, stunned into action.

The soldiers waiting outside the cell door avert their eyes and remain silent, perhaps some last vestiges of human decency preventing them from goading the pirate crew in their last precious minutes of life.

Dragging their chains behind them, they follow their jailors, dumb acquiescence making their feet respond, though they do not do it quietly.

The sun stares down on them unblinking, its light blinding them as they emerge from the darkness of the prison. They stagger, lifting chained hands to their eyes to blot it out, yet the warmth of sunshine on cold skin is a wonderful thing, the simple joy of it raising a smile from Thomas Earl at least. Their eyes adjust after a time, and their faces look up into a perfect azure sky, the like of which they are sure they have never seen before. They try to forget that they will never see it again.

'Such a beautiful day ...'

And then they see it, the end of them. The gallows stands before them, black and heavy against the morning sky.

A large crowd has gathered for the entertainment, the noise of shouting and jeering rising as the prisoners come into view.

The baying becomes louder still as a lone figure is dragged past the crew by two soldiers in their parade-yard finery. The figure is smeared with filth, the face so broken that he is almost unrecognisable.

'Good God, it is the captain,' Noah Harwood says, and they realise in horror that he is right.

'God abandoned us long ago,' spits Mr Carty, who is prodded with a bayonet for his profanity.

Jack is dragged up the steps of the scaffold, his legs giving way beneath him as he is dropped onto the platform. He tries to raise himself up but is too weak to do so on his own, and so he is hauled to his feet by the soldiers.

A solemn priest with a Bible stands by the masked hangman, his head bowed and hands demurely crossed upon themselves. An official in a too-large frock coat steps forward, holding up a hand to quiet the thronging mass, who jostle to get a better view of the horrors to come.

The man clears his throat with great self-importance before unfurling a scroll and begins to read, his voice carrying across the now hushed crowd.

'On behalf of His Majesty, the King, His Excellency Sir Nicholas Lawes, Governor of Jamaica, has found these men guilty of acts of piracy. It has been decreed that they shall be brought to this place of execution, where they shall be hanged by the neck until they are dead. May God have mercy upon their souls.'

As he steps back, his black words spoken, the excitement of the crowd rises palpably as they begin to catcall and jeer again. And then something unexpected. Jack is pushed to one side and he realises with a jolt what they have planned. As Patrick Carty, the youngest by far of his crew, is pushed, terrified, up the stairs of the gallows, he understands that he will not go first. They will make Jack watch his crew die first.

Patrick – barely seventeen years old – is crying as if he had never left his mother, looking desperately to Jack for some kind of comfort that he cannot give, his eyes wide and terrified as he is hauled up the ladder to die.

He cries and struggles, pissing himself noisily as the noose is tightened around his neck, the sounds of his last pointless words choked out of him by the rough ministrations of the executioner.

There are delighted screams from the mob as the trap drops open beneath Mr Carty and he falls to the end of the rope. Thankfully the crew are spared the sounds of his death, swallowed as it is in a frenzied roar of approval from the crowd.

Patrick's limbs fight uncontrollably, but after a time, when the movements slow and they are sure the prisoner is dead, the soldiers cut down his body, it still twitching, the eyes fixed and bulging in knowledge of death. The crew watch it all in mute horror, all too aware they will follow. That they do not turn away is to lend strength to one another, for they have nothing else left to them now.

One by one, the men take their place on the platform, faces set in terrified resignation, or spitting rage, but however they face their tormentors, it is no matter, for they all meet their death the same. And so they dance, their legs jerking to the insistence of the drums as life is throttled from them. Most refuse to die contrite and penitent, but instead roaring at the world as they had lived.

Those unlucky men left behind are unable to tear their eyes from the scene before them, knowing that they could not be more human than they are now. The efficiency of it is relentless, the prayers, the last words if any, the drop, swing and jerk of them at the end of the rope a waking nightmare. And one after another they are dispatched and cut down as if they were nothing more than vermin, the next man taking the place of his dead friend, the rope still warm from his murdered skin.

When it is Tom Earl's turn, in his hand is a small piece of oak, a jagged thing, from the helm of *Revenge*, broken off by cannon fire as the ship protected him as well as she could, her last act of love. He thinks of the ship, of his Mary, of the baby he will never see, and he plunges the wood deep into the cushion of his palm, blood blooming red and precious. But whatever he had hoped for he barely feels as the platform is pulled away from beneath him, air rushes up and he is plunged into the void.

George Fetherstone is the last of the crew to die, and he does his best to do it bravely.

'An honour, Captain,' he says with a shaky salute, but Jack cannot speak, can barely look as his master is manoeuvred into place on the scaffold.

Mr Fetherstone looks down on the piled bodies of his dead comrades, before looking out in dumb horror at the crowd. Their voices are loud and insistent, upturned faces full of hate and excitement. He wants to speak, to make them understand what it is that they consider such entertainment, but black fear has his tongue and it is nothing now but a useless piece of flesh in his mouth.

He would cry out but finds he cannot before the noose does its work, the words exploding in his mind as death claims him, *God take me and save me!*

But there are no certainties here, God or otherwise, and it is done.

Jack's heart breaks. His boys are dead. He feels the torment of grief for every last one of them. He deserves to follow, for there is nothing left for him here. He has seen his crew swing, and has not been able to do them the kindness of a quicker death, of lending his weight to their legs as they fight against the rope and thin air. One after another, and they are gone, their wicked lives done. It is as it should be, but God knows he never thought it would come to this.

Jack casts his eyes to the sky – cloudless and perfect – and whispers something like a prayer for them all, and for himself. Anne can look after herself, as she has shown so often. She is the reason they are all here. But he stops himself short. He knows this is not the case. They are here today – their dying day – because he has allowed himself to become less than he was. He is the reason his boys are dead, and he is to follow. And so he smiles sadly to himself and nods to the hangman.

'Let's not keep the Devil waiting.'

The hangman is quick to throw the rope around Jack's neck, his hands still tied at his front. He thinks of his men, his ship, and of Anne. He has done more living than most men ever do, and has loved honestly. He has had, he thinks, a good life all told. The drums roll again, the crowd roars impatient, then a drop, a snap, and he is gone.

Chapter 63

It has been a restless night for Anne and Mary. The guards have told them when the men are to die, and how, for they want to wrest every last ounce of pain from their prisoners. The announcement has not left the bastards disappointed, for neither of the women can hide their anguish, though Anne does better at it.

They have heard their boys, chains dragging, as they are led out to die with not a little cursing and shouting. Mary had stood banging and screaming at the door of their cell, swearing at the guards to let her out, but what was the use of that? They did not come then, for they had their work cut out dragging the men out to be hanged. And besides, was it not more painful for the women to have to imagine the suffering of their crew?

They could hear too the excitement of the mob, the frantic drum roll and wild cheering of the crowd as each man was called to account, each one, one after another, sounding the same. The efficiency of it all, over and over. They could imagine it all too well for they had seen hangings before. But how different it is now that it is Tom, and Jack, and the rest of the boys.

It is some time before the drums stop, the silence heavy with the deaths of their men. That is when Mary falls to weeping, slumping down, the weight of it too much to bear, head buried in her hands. She makes no sound, there is just a silent flow of tears through knotted fingers, clear rivers leaving tracks in the dirt of her skin. It is not the first time Anne has seen her cry, but she has never seen such hopelessness before and it terrifies her.

How have they come to this? To see Mary diminished is almost too much to bear, and yet Anne cannot comfort her. She knows that she should go to her, reassure her that she is not alone, to give her hope. But she cannot. To her shame, Anne sees Mary's tears as a weakness, a luxury they can ill afford if they are to get through this. Perhaps she is afraid, too, that her own strength will be sapped if she offers herself up to Mary this way. Perhaps she is also aware, somewhere deep down, that she does not have the strength to do it, for this is a new thing that leaves her raw. And so Anne sits at the far side of the dank prison cell, her knees clasped to her chest, watching Mary's misery from a distance.

She tries not to think of Jack, but she cannot help it. She is angry at him, though she knows there is no use being angry at a dead man. There is part of her that needs to mourn him, but she knows that is a dangerous road to take. Grief will topple down upon her if she stays with her regrets too long, so she pushes them out with thoughts of his failings instead. If he had acted like a captain, the men would not be dead. And perhaps if he had been more of a man, she would not despise him as she is trying hard not to do so now.

And yet he drifts into her mind unbidden, his face smiling if she is lucky, his eyes soft, and her heart aches for him, stupidly, this memory, this thing of fragile remembrance. She thinks that their unborn child knows it too, that her father is gone so cruelly, that they are left alone. There is a gnawing sense of dread too, knowing that their baby will grow, and demand to be born. And what will happen then? Anne tries to block it out, but a voice still whispers at the back of my mind, *You are alone now. You are alone.*

The women know that the men will not be buried as the dead have every right to expect – not for a long time to come. They know all too well what will happen – the tarring of the bodies, the bone-breaking to make the gibbeting easier. Their corpses hauled through the town and hung like lanterns along the coast, a spectacle for months or even years to come. Their dead eyes made to look out on the ocean, mocking them even in death. It is too cruel. And Anne cannot help but think that she shares the blame for it.

Mary has not spoken for over a day, but she is no longer crying. She has exhausted herself with it, and lies dazed, staring dully into the space between them. Anne is equally mute. This is not the time for words.

Time passes, who knows how long.

Anne has found something in herself that was lacking before, for Mary's sake, and sits holding her. She does not speak often, but when she does, Mary's voice is small and brittle.

'I was going to call him Jem.'

Anne smiles.

'It is a pretty name.'

'He was going to be the happiest child who ever lived, and I was going to make him fat. And Tom and me would love him. And each other.'

Anne's heart lurches for Mary and her unborn son. But for herself and her daughter too, for she knows it will be a girl. A girl made of her spirit and Jack's.

'You would have made it perfect, Mary.'

Mary smiles sadly.

'I would.'

They sit in silence for a time.

'What about you?'

Anne is suddenly back in Charles Town in the chaos of her childhood. There is money of course, but that is not what she remembers. Instead it is her father's raging temper towards the world, and the look of fury on his face whenever his daughter appears. Her mother, never forgiving the man she married for forcing her to leave Ireland, her one true love. Her crying with great heaving sobs before the laudanum took hold and brought her peace for a while. The short-lived lapdogs her mother would grasp far too tightly, feeding them sugar until their teeth rotted out of their heads and they smelled like Hell. Anne tiptoeing into her mother's bedroom to sit and watch her as she slept, wondering why her mama was so sad, and wondering if she would ever hold Anne like she held those miserable dogs.

Anne squeezes Mary's hand tightly and rests her face against her hair, breathing in the scent of her.

'I had hoped the same as you.'

Chapter 64

Mary's eyes are sunken in their blackened hollows. The size of her belly says the child will come soon. Anne cannot imagine the guards will bring a midwife when the time comes, and that can only mean she will have to bring the baby into the world alone, for Mary's sake. It frightens her, for she now knows all too well that life is a slippery thing, and she cannot bear to think of holding it, so fragile, in her hands. God help them both when Mary's child arrives. A world of terrors opens itself up then.

One of the guards at least has shown a little kindness where he can, his own wife, as he has told them, being pregnant with their first child. He does not show it when his fellows are around – and who can blame him? – but he is kind enough when he is alone with the women. He ensures that they have enough beer, a small amount of extra bread, and news of life beyond these walls. This is more than they should expect, and they are grateful for it.

Mary in particular is hungry for news of the outside – how hot? Is it cloudy? How the sea looks today, and what flowers are blooming now? Anne is thankful that Mary takes some happiness from this, and contents herself with the bittersweet information of the world beyond. The guard has brought an old shawl for Mary's baby when it comes too, and they stow it away like the precious cargo it is.

'Do you remember when you met?'

It is so long since Mary has spoken that it takes a moment for Anne to gather herself. There is something not right in her voice – a weakening.

'Tell me about Jack. About when you first met. Tell me how he loved you.'

A wave of emotion from nowhere. Anne takes time to steady herself, takes deep breaths, blinks back against unexpected tears until she has mastered them. They are tears for Jack, and for Mary too. If she lets them out now, there will be too many to hold back and they will overwhelm her.

'I am tired, Mary. Maybe tomorrow.'

They are together, of course, when her time comes. Mary's belly is drum-tight, and her baby is ready to join them in the world and their miserable circumstance.

'Hold on,' Anne has said to her, 'hold on, for it will not be long until we are free of this place' (if only that were true), but Jem is impatient to be in the world.

As the pains come more quickly, Mary looks towards Anne for comfort and Anne tries to smile back, squeezing her hand with both of hers. She is the best hope Mary has.

There are prying eyes at the cell door that they do their best to ignore as Anne helps Mary to lie down on the filthy floor, covering her up as best she can, but there is no dignity in it. The baby has begun to force his slow way from her, and Anne steels herself for what is to come.

Pain cuts through Mary like a hot knife, caustic and burning. Her mind reels with it, lurching and nauseous. Anne can see the struggle as the baby tries to be born, but can sense too that there is not enough fight in him. This is only the beginning of it, this tiny thing that relies on Anne to help them both.

The baby has no idea of the struggle it will be once he is here, to keep going, to keep living, but perhaps he senses the truth of it now. As hours pass, he becomes reluctant to leave his safe place inside Mary, and Anne understands it all too well – but knows too that it is killing her friend.

Despite her best intentions Anne finds herself little more than a bystander as she watches life and death fighting for the upper hand, this miracle of birth turned tragedy in front of her. She cannot help but wonder if this will be her in a few short months, hanging on to hope and life until they are worn away to nothing, exposing the yawning maw of death below.

'You need to be strong, Mary, to hold on.'

Anne knows that she is torturing them both, for Mary is doing all she can. Anne cannot bear it, knowing that she is asking Mary for more than her poor self can take.

On and on. Mary writhing, trying not to cry out, trying not to give those prying eyes the satisfaction of it, but she is only human after all. She holds onto Anne's shirt with clenched fists as if she thinks Anne might tear herself away at any moment. Anne shushes her, smoothing her hair.

There is nothing left but the dumb horror of what they have become. Anne can only see the clammy white hands fixed to her like a vice, the pained, wild eyes searing her face as if Mary is trying to find some meaning that isn't there. She has no comfort to give her and the knowledge of it sits like a brick in her stomach.

New waves of pain throw Mary onto her side, screaming as she breaks the hold she has on Anne, delirium taking hold of her. And Anne goes to her at once, creeping forward on her knees, her hands reaching out. She must try to bring Mary and her baby through it. And she knows it is beyond her, that she would rather fight a hundred fights than be here on her own with Mary now. She knows that if she fails, both of them will slip away from her, and that it will be no fault but Anne's.

'Will they not send help? Please …'

Mary asks again, weaker now, but the guards continue to gawp. They refuse them a midwife, a doctor, or even water to help or to make her more comfortable, as if what is happening before them is merely some sideshow for their entertainment.

Anne pleads with them, such is her own rising panic.

'There is a baby being born – show the poor mite some mercy if you cannot show it to his mother!'

But there is no such thing as mercy here. And Mary hears Anne's words, being torn as she is, her brow burning with a fever that consumes her. She grasps Anne's hand and looks pained into her face.

'Do not let my baby die.'

The child has become still inside her, refusing to draw breath as if death were preferable to what he senses in the world beyond his mother's belly. And Mary knows that this small life she has carried inside her is passing on, for she cries out as if it is the end of the world itself, her strength falling away from her as she lies with this half-dead child half born.

Anne cries out 'For pity's sake! Bring a doctor.'

The jailor shakes his head, but he pushes something under the door.

'There will be no doctor, but this knife will help.'

Anne picks it up and looks at it dumbly. She has watched Mary grow weaker, her breath becoming shallower and her eyes flickering shut, before she can find her strength. Anne knows what she must do.

She speaks to Mary with all the sweetness she can muster, her heart breaking.

'I am sorry, Mary. I must get the baby out of you.'

Tears fall down Mary's face as she nods, miserably.

And so Anne goes about her work, for Mary's sake. She plunges the sharp blade into Mary to find that she is soft and yielding and it takes almost no time for her to remove the tiny, unmoving body that slithers out, leaving Anne's hands bloody.

She knows that the child should cry out, should grasp at life while it can, but it does nothing – just lies there limp and unmoving. She picks him up and pats his back as she has seen done, hoping not to hurt him.

There is the smell of warm coins. The baby, all grease and blood and stillness. His mouth is open to cry out at the world, but his eyes – impossibly small – are closed and will not open.

Mary's eyes open briefly and she smiles painfully, her face white, her hair matted, her breath rapid still.

'Is he beautiful, Anne? Is my baby beautiful?'

The tiny thing is bloodied and slimy from his recent struggles, but they are behind him now. He is beyond Anne's help. She wraps him in the shawl from their jailor, turning her face away from Mary to suppress a sob that has forced itself into her throat. She swallows hard before she trusts herself to speak again.

'He is very beautiful, Mary. Your little boy is beautiful.'

But when Anne turns back to place him against her heart, she sees that Mary has gone too.

Chapter 65

The world has spun off its axis and Anne is left behind.

She is bone-tired. The weight of what she has endured presses down on her like a physical thing.

Her bruises heal long before her mind, but madness will not take her. Her wits remain stubbornly present and functional, showing her flashes of the horrors she has so recently seen. Her mind seems determined to torture her. Sleep has abandoned her too, allowing memories of Jack and the crew to visit her, over and over again. And Mary. Always Mary, and her silent baby. She is raw with it.

Anne had not known before that she is two people. There is the body that wishes it were finished, that has known pleasure, and pain, and now grows a baby inside itself. But now that the noise around her has stopped and she is on her own, there is another Anne who has been hiding in her shadow.

This Anne is silent, anxious, confused by her own thoughts, questioning. She knows all too well what loss is. It makes her twist and fall inside her own head, a lurching feeling that appals her. She is not just a creature of flesh and blood after all, but one of mind. And it terrifies her.

She cannot break away from this new Anne, the unwelcome one that whispers and worries at her, pulling to the fore again and again what she would choose to forget – the suffering, the death. *And what of your baby?* it asks over and over. *And what of your baby?*

She has never been one for lessons, and she does her best to close her eyes and ears to this one, but it is useless. This Anne is determined to be heard.

The spirits of the dead are watching. They wait, dispassionate, for it is nothing to them if she comes with them now, or later. But they are curious, as they watch her keen and suffer, the fight of her lost in the filthy horror her life has become. So much loss, and so little left to live for, and yet here she still is. The animal part of her demands to keep breathing despite herself, an exhausted battle that plays out within her heart and head.

It has been weeks since Mary's death, though Anne would have to guess how many. The days have been interminable, day and night slithering and sliding over one another in the damp twilight of her cell, and she has had no reason to keep track of them. She has stopped walking the small distance she is allowed, knows that she should keep her strength up and her wits about her, but it is futile. She has slowly submitted to the whispering heat that tells her to lie down, sleep, let stillness have her. It is seductive and she is ready to be seduced by thoughts other than the loss of everything she had so recently, of Jack, her freedom, and of Mary. Of Mary most of all.

The memories and faces still flicker into focus as if a candle has been held beneath them, but they are less distinct, the images muddy, as a dark feeling of heaviness overtakes her, turns her limbs to lead, makes it a supreme effort to open her eyes or lift herself from her bunk, until after a little while she does not try to resist it anymore. She waits for the darkness to come and claim her, held back by this mortal frame with sweat-slicked hair and thinning face, though her belly stays determinedly taut and full.

This security in her belly that keeps her safe until it frees itself into the living world. The fragility of it, the natural way of things that took Mary and her boy, they wait for her too. And Anne can do nothing.

The guards still bring bread and beer, but she pushes it away, waiting for an easy end. Anne tells herself it is for the baby, that it is the right thing to do. But she does not convince herself, and lies down on her bunk again to sleep away the empty hours, and to chase the thoughts from her head. Let life happen to her for once; and if death comes for her, then so be it.

The world has lost its colour, and she is quite sure it will never return to what it was. This sand-grain existence is all that is left, and the hourglass has begun to empty one crystal grain at a time.

She thinks she hears Mary scold her in her dreams, tells her the baby will come to claim life with or without her help, for it is nature at its rawest, but when she wakes, hopeful and half smiling, Anne sees she is alone with only her poor self for company. Mary is dead, all of them are dead, and she has only the certainty of a squealing, dependent thing waiting to come. It cannot be long until it comes, and what then?

Anne turns her head sharply, think she sees something across the cell in the dark, narrows her eyes to try to focus. Death winks at her from a corner, but she realises, with all that she ever was, that she is not ready for him yet. She struggles to her feet, unsteady and weak, for she will be damned if she lets the guards see her lying on the ground.

And then a little voice, a whisper at first, that becomes more insistent. What if she were to write to her father? Does she not have a responsibility to bring this life into the world, this evolving thing inside of her, that has insisted on its own existence despite the bloody reality of what lies outside? To give her a chance at life? She admires the bravery of her unborn girl, for bravery is certainly needed. No child of hers will be timid, thank God, for the world would eat it alive.

When the fat guard next shuffles in, and she tries to speak, her mouth dry and voice cracking, she finds that she has changed her mind. She cannot ask her father for help. She clamps her mouth shut to keep the traitor words in, and feels her old self spark inside her as she reaches for the bread and beer. She is, she realises, ravenous.

As she chews the stale bread that tastes like nectar, the baby kicks hard inside her for the first time, though in relief or anger she cannot tell.

Chapter 66

It is unfortunate that the letter from Governor Woodes Rogers – following his meeting with James Bonny – has taken such a circuitous route to its recipient. One must assume a servant's ability to carry out simple instructions, but it is naïve to trust that fate is always on our side.

Samuel Blagg, the servant in question, has become a little too partial to Madeira from the master's cellar in the weeks prior (taken from the furthest reaches of the store, of course, where it is less likely to be noticed), and has found the perfect hiding place to enjoy it and then sleep it off in that same cellar.

He has not done this lightly, for to be found out is unthinkable, so he has fashioned a door of sorts from discarded wine crates, and squirrelled away a blanket for his further comfort. Here he can pursue his enjoyments in peace and comfort, a rare experience in this all too noisy life.

Unfortunate, then, that said servant was the one to be entrusted with the missive from Governor Rogers bearing the appalling news that not only was a woman an active member of Jack Rackham's crew, but that said woman was the daughter of a respected family known to them both.

The note had been written in haste by the governor (such was its urgency), sealed with hot wax and stamped with a ring from the governor's own finger, and after a little wafting to cool, handed off to the servant in question. So obsequious was he that the governor would not have recognised Mr Blagg's face had he seen him again, merely the top of his wig as he bowed so low. Sam had felt a stab of pride at the thought that his master approved of the low gesture, for not nearly enough of his staff grovelled so well as Sam Blagg.

The Governor would not, however, have approved of what happened next. Samuel adjusted his wig and slid the letter into his pocket, fully intending, it must be said, at that moment to carry out his duty. It was hardly arduous, and he is employed in a good position that he should like to keep. Alas, we are all sometimes thwarted in our best intentions.

It cannot be said to be his fault that he was distracted by the thought of Madeira. Just a cup or two, perhaps, before he delivered the message. What harm could come of that? What harm indeed. As he was imagined to be engaged in his errand, Mr Blagg was in fact to be found slurring filthy songs quietly to himself and expressing his undying affections for the bottle he draped himself around.

The letter had slipped from his pocket beneath the racks of wine as he finally slumped in a heap on the floor of his hiding place, the bottle now sadly empty. Sam Blagg's brief dreams were happy ones until his snoring alerted the cook, who, appalled and angry (though not, admittedly, surprised), roundly boxed his ears and kicked his arse out of employment that same day, with 'sling your bleeding hook' and other such encouragements ringing in his ears.

That the letter would not be found for several months, the nervous servants, after much whispered discussion, agreeing it would be best to send it on its way without further comment, for why distress the master? There is relief in sending it. And after all, no harm is done.

Chapter 67

Sir Nicholas Lawes has ignored the letter from Governor Woodes Rogers since it arrived this morning. He greeted its appearance with a great sigh, for Rogers is a bitter man who wheedles and whines to the letter of the law, a fine soldier once who has become an exceedingly dull civilian. New Providence is not the excitement it once was.

His letters are always a trial. The words are dry and brittle, parched into efficiency. Sir Nicholas has not met the governor in person, but he imagines that he is dusty, crackling as he moves.

It is at the urging of his clerk that Sir Nicholas reluctantly agrees to take up the letter at all, the parchment smelling strangely of Madeira and mould, sighing deeply at the expected torrent of pedantry and legal verbiage. But that is not what he finds.

As his eyes follow the words on the page before him, his illustrious eyebrows shoot skyward as he chokes on his brandy, the explosion of it firing the amber liquid across his papers. Surely not – that the woman in the cells, the one still alive – has a maiden name he recognises.

A prickling horror creeps over him – that the creature he has sentenced to rot in his own cells is the daughter of a gentleman. There was no hint of it, for she is unlike any woman he has ever met, thank God. He hopes that whatever has caused this woman to change into the unnatural thing she has become is not catching. He thinks of his own daughters, who cannot bear too much reality, and determines to stifle them even more to the limits his title and wealth will allow.

He says a silent prayer and crosses himself before he picks up a pen and, with only a little hesitation, writes to a Mister William Cormac, a gentleman of the Carolinas, ink carelessly splashing itself onto brandy stains in his haste.

Chapter 68

Charles Town
March 1721

Anne,

I had not expected to hear of you after all this time, and it is not something I had wished for.

It seems inevitable that this letter finds you in prison. We both have his excellency Sir Nicholas to thank for this missive, though I cannot say that I am pleased to be writing it.

A pirate, they tell me, and pregnant! Words can barely express my shame for what you have become, but as I have been reminded by my elevated friend, you are still my own blood.

As such, you are to be sent home to me. I do not want you here, it need not be said, but an old business acquaintance of mine (one who has found himself in dire financial straits – I should not inflict you on a successful man) has agreed to take you off my hands for a large sum of money. The arrangement is purely financial, so no affection is due from either party in this agreement.

On the messy legal point of James Bonny – your first husband, in case you had forgotten – I have settled on him slender – though sufficient – funds to ensure that neither I nor you need ever see or hear from him again. *You are officially divorced, and I need never again suffer another pitiful letter from that bloody irritant of a man. Governor Rogers has seen fit to employ him as a servant. It amuses us both that he has been returned to his rightful station in life, and I am told he is suitably fawning towards the great man.*

You were always your mother's daughter, God rest her soul, though I am glad for her that she is dead and not here to witness your shame. That at least we must be grateful for.

You have cost me a great deal of money, embarrassment and inconvenience, and you should consider my charity exhausted. I shall expect your silence of these last years in your new life. It is a mercy you do not deserve.

Your father in name only,
William Cormac

PART FOUR

Anne

Chapter 69

Charles Town, South Carolina, 1724

It is a pretty captivity, with endless 'please' and 'thank you's and curt-seys as she passes. Anne moves from room to gilded room, dressed in rustling silks and ribbons supplied by her new husband's dowry. The whisper of silk, the tick of French clocks, the rarefied quiet of a rich man's house. Voices must stay lowered at all times to show respect for the vast amount of money it has all cost.

She wears a dress now, of course; a costume that suggests gentility, if you didn't know her better. She has a wardrobe full of them, though she longs still for trousers and shirts. She gives instructions to maids, to cooks, to the men who work the gardens, for, of course, she cannot have work of her own for it would not be proper.

She makes small talk with interminable guests who come to look at this unexpected new lady of the house, until she feels her face will break from smiling. She is asked to admire the needle-work of these unwanted new acquaintances, their singing, their ability to breed, as their names and faces blend into one another in her mind. How much more they would gawp if they knew who she really was, this Mrs Joseph Burleigh.

The story of Anne Bonny is quite the 'thing' after all. The balladeers have made themselves a pretty penny from the legend of Bonny and Read, and there are rumours there is a book to come. The lady visitors have gossiped about this terrible pirate and Anne makes what she thinks might be the appropriate noises and hides her smirk as she ensures that their coffee is sweetened to their taste, wondering how quickly they would faint away if the lady pirate of their stories were to make herself known. She thinks that any hint of real excitement might finish them off, for they know nothing of the world beyond this small backwater of Charles Town, a place she left like a fugitive.

Now she is back at the insistence of her father, the custody of her handed over in darkness and secrecy. Sir Nicholas glad to be rid of the abomination she undoubtedly is. Her father, Mr Cormac, glad that he has been able to offload her at such little cost to that old buffoon Burleigh. He would gladly have paid twice the price, so that at least is a blessing.

But of the time Anne has been gone from here? A lifetime of living and loss has been done in that period, and the Anne who has come back is not the Anne that left.

Anne sees now, for she has had ample time to consider it, that she was always running. She ran away from her father, from James Bonny and from Jack. She could not run from herself forever, and now she has had to stop: she has no choice. It will be the making of her, in the end.

It has taken time to regain her strength, and to feel more like herself again, the woman she was when she boarded *Revenge*. But she has been changed. It is as if she has learned again to walk, to speak, to think after everything she knew was torn from her. She is separated by acres of ocean from what she was before, the girl who was once Anne Cormac.

Her father thinks it an excellent joke that he has rescued her, knowing that it is the last thing she would have wanted. Whatever she might think about it, she is, at least, still here to tell the tale. And she is grateful at least for that.

The name Anne Bonny was hard won, but it is a tainted prize. Anne Bonny is not only a wanted woman, Anne Bonny is meant to hang. Marriage – in a church this time – has seen to it that the legal inconvenience of her previous name is gone. She is Mrs Burleigh now, wife to a man thirty years older than herself.

Mr Burleigh is in receipt of a handsome amount of money from Anne's father (a godsend since a foray into stocks and shares had ruined him) and has Anne now too into the bargain. He is more than content with the arrangement, and thanks his lucky stars each night before he retires to his own comfortable bed. He has been glad too to hand over responsibility for the purse strings to Anne, for he now accepts that he has never been good with money, and she has become quite expert at it.

As far as the world is concerned, Anne is now a lady. The irony is not lost on her. And she is a mother now too. Jack's child came into the world, as children will, and stayed. The girl is almost four years old. Her daughter. Her anchor. The curls of an angel and eyes like his. She will cause trouble as she grows this one, as she should. And Anne will be there to worry for her, to disappoint her no doubt, and to burn proud with how well she loves her. Anne loves her in a way she has been seeking her whole life. The discovery has changed her for the better, and she could not be more grateful for it.

The child has a fierceness that used to be Anne's. She is, after all, made of Anne and of what Jack once was. Her name is Mary, for there is no better name in the world than that. Anne has been surprised to find that she needs to find a new kind of courage for this new, wilful responsibility.

Little Mary seems to think the house a heaven. To her delight, there are always confections made of sugar which the cook excels in, coming as she does from France. That Madame Florette has an appreciative audience, and one so young and sweet, means she outdoes herself each day. Yesterday there was a kitten in pale sugars, today a lovebird.

Little Mary is wide-eyed and open-mouthed before she devours them, sugar turned into satisfaction and sticky fingers. The shapes of those fingers stain windowpanes and tabletops, making the housekeeper tut and scowl, though Madame Florette's beaming smile betrays her satisfaction. What she does with sugar, she tells Anne, is love made real, and Anne believes her.

Mary is very much herself. She is familiar and entirely unknown. Anne could not be more proud or terrified for her. She knows all too well what the world is like outside these walls, and only a small bit of it good. Anne has determined to bring out all she is in fierceness, stubborn and unrelenting. For that will keep her girl safe when she comes to leave this place. It will break Anne's heart, she knows it, but her girl must have her own adventures – her mother will never see her confined or restricted, even for her own sake. In the meantime, Mary is loved and she is wanted, and will always be so.

Her daughter is infuriating, contrary, vulnerable and magnificent. She is everything Anne is, and all she is not. In time, Anne will tell her stories about herself and what she has done, and the wonders she has seen and the mistakes she has made. And little Mary will make of them what she will. After all, Anne is a creature of her own creation, and little Mary must shape her own thoughts in turn. She will carve her path, no doubt of that, and grow into her name. Anne knows beyond a doubt that one day she will marvel at what her wonderful girl has become.

There is something of Anne's soul in her. She asks so many questions, pores over maps, demands stories of foreign lands and draws animals that Anne has neither seen nor heard of.

'Mama – Papa said that you have travelled on a ship?'

She is surprised he has told her this much, but is pleased. Anne tells her 'yes', and Mary looks at her with cautious, questioning eyes.

'And what is the sea like?'

What should she tell her? How the light plays upon it turning it to silver? How it can raise itself up like a giant to break ships to matchwood? That it is wild and unknowable? Or dark and wonderful? More than anything else, it is wonderful.

'When you are old enough, you will find out for yourself. I cannot tell you, for it would not be fair to what it is. But it will not disappoint you, of that I am sure.'

Mary is satisfied with that. Anne knows that she will make her own discoveries and map her own world some day. And she will be there to help her.

Anne has determined to teach little Mary to read, to write, to shoot a gun, and to be herself no matter what. She will teach her not to rely on a husband but to rely on herself, for there is nothing certain about any man. She will teach her that there are greater possibilities than men, for after all Anne has bound herself to three and knows there is far more to life than only this.

Mr Burleigh is a good man and has let Anne be herself. He does not make demands on her – which is wise as she would not bend to them – and is contented with his lot. Perhaps he is more than contented. He is not new to marriage. Burleigh's first wife was afflicted by more than her share of children – eight of them, all stillborn – though she had continued in her wifely duties until the end, bringing grief and loss into the world like a Christian until she was carried off by fever. And now there is Anne.

Burleigh had not expected to find himself with another wife, but he is glad of the company. That he has gained a daughter into the bargain has made him a happy man. Little surprise, for Anne knows that Mary is the finest child to have ever lived. The formerly staid man of business melts into smiles and silliness when Mary is around. He hides badly behind chairs or crawls under tables so that he can amuse her in games of hide-and-seek. He is wise to let her win easily for she has an impressive temper on her. She is still her mother's daughter, after all.

Little Mary is inordinately fond of her new father. She shrieks with delight as he lumbers after her like a bear, chasing her through the house and roaring, her laughter resounding around the place. She is hope made flesh, when Anne thought there might be no hope left in the world. Jack still comes to her thoughts unbidden, and there is always a whisper of regret that he did not get to meet this wonderful girl. But Anne likes to think that he watches over her, wherever he now is. And knows that Burleigh will be a better father to little Mary than Jack would ever have been. Burleigh does not have a restless bone in his body, and that gives Anne comfort.

When Anne first came here, Burleigh was all care and nerves. He seemed to think he had a female Bluebeard under his roof, dispensing bloodily with husbands and lovers, though neither of the ones before him had been dispensed by her hand. Anne could have reassured him that she had no plans to dispose of him just yet, but where was the fun of that? She has enjoyed his discomfort, but suspects that he would forgive her for the pleasure she has taken from it.

Burleigh has continued to count the knives away each night after supper, locking them into a strong wooden box with a small gold key he still carries in his breast pocket. He used to hide them, thinking Anne might slit his throat while he slept, and has continued to do so, though he is relieved to note that the feeling of imminent peril has eased.

They have been married for three years and in that time Anne has become less angry at him. Their domestic life has become less fraught, and he has become quite fond of her. Perhaps she has even become a little fond of him. Certainly, she has put aside all thoughts of murdering him, and we know of marriages that have been built on less harmonious foundations than this.

He is a kind man, and everything that Jack was not.

Anne had promised herself that she would not allow this new-found kindness to undo her, but it is not the worst that could happen. In her looking glass, she sees someone older, wiser perhaps, and she is a surprise. Anne had not expected to see her there.

Anne has all that Mary Read ever wanted, and the realisation is not lost on her. Every day, she whispers apologies to her dead friend in the darkness, though she knows Mary cannot hear. It makes no difference, for she is sorry nonetheless. Mary would make so much more of this, would enjoy the ease, the peace of it. Perhaps because Anne has grown used to it again, because her life was easy until James Bonny, and Jack. There must be something in chaos she craved, while Mary wanted a simple life and nothing more. Mary was right. But then Mary was always right.

Mary. There is only silence where she should be. Anne has been cut open, her heart torn from her chest. She was unmoored for so long: it was Mary, not Jack, who centred her. She had not known it when she was there, but now she is gone, Anne sees it all too well. She is sure she felt Mary with her when her time came, as little Mary tore herself forth into the world, Mary Read laughing and crying at the wonder of it all. The lack of her is a bruise, a pain that will not heal.

Her memories are precious for they keep Mary with her. A smile like an imp. Loud. A temper to be reckoned with. She had seared herself into Anne, and she misses all of her. Little Mary will hear all about her namesake until she can picture her clearly for herself. It would be a disservice to them both to do less.

Life has moved on. Anne watches the same stars, seeks out the shapes and stories above her. The same constellations are there, but there is nothing certain beneath them. Experience has taught her uncertainty. The world as she knew it has gone, and she is not the person she believed herself to be. Anne is more like other people than she ever knew. She fears. She grieves. She looks for reassurance and certainty that is not there. She has lived a life already, and is unsure about the one to be lived still.

And now?

She writes her journal. She reads books from her husband's library. He has not mentioned it, but from the early days of their marriage, books would appear where she might happen upon them, books that speak to her and fill her heart. Books of seafarers.

Travellers. Adventurers and their discovery of the world. A book of astronomy that has told her more about the heavens than she ever thought possible. There are so many wonders still to know. This, for now, is enough. The world will still be waiting for her when the time is right.

And this morning she wakes to find a new delivery from the bookshop, wrapped in crisp white parchment and tied with a ribbon. It is a gift left for Anne at her breakfast table, unremarked, and so she opens it.

The rough black leather of the book's cover is embossed with gold letters:

A GENERAL
HISTORY
OF THE
PYRATES

The surprise of it takes her breath, her heart beating loudly.

So Captain Johnson was as good as his word. The hack of Bart Roberts they met on that ill-fated day. It seems so long ago.

She opens the pages and there they are, Anne and Mary, etched in time. The publisher has chosen to show them bare-breasted – could God not have granted men more imagination than this? – but she swallows her annoyance for now. It is still Mary Read, and there she is, alongside her as it had always been.

Anne feels Mary breathe again, scowl and wave her sword. And she reaches out to her, touching the picture, Mary captured by a drawing that looks only a little like her.

Anne takes the precious book with her to the library and finds the room's furthest hidden corner. She sits on the wooden floor, the planks oiled and spotless, her back against a tower of books. The smell of leather and warm dust surrounds her as she sinks down, lost in memories as she reads about Jack and Mary, their stories written down in black and white. She is greedy for the words, returning over and over to the pictures as if they might be stolen from her. But they remain, a reassuring constant.

The Mary in the story is a poor substitute for the one Anne knew, but the words are better than nothing at all. She is still magnificent – that at least Johnson got right. Anne reads about her three times over and finds that she has cried, though she is smiling too. She remembers all too well what Mary was. A force of nature made flesh and blood.

And when she has read all she can for now, of Mary, of Jack, Anne turns the page to read her own tale. She is a strange one, this Anne Bonny. Mercurial, thoughtless, restless. Familiar and yet nothing that she recognises. And when she reaches the end of the chapter, she finds that she has no final act, no ending. She is at a full stop.

It seems that she must complete her own story. She realises that she has always known it must be this way, and is so very grateful for it.

She looks up from the book to see that the light has shifted. She has lost track of time. Reluctantly, Anne stirs herself and leaves the library, the book still held tightly to her, for it is a treasure, the past made real. It tells her that she has lived and lost, but reminds her too that there is still a life to be lived.

The song she had heard about them both – 'The Ballad of
Bonny & Read' – has played loud in her head since she heard it:

Oh terror of women upon the seas,
And they did sail and they did please
Themselves alone as they did steal
Men's lives away with ease.

They painted oceans red with blood
Let women cry and they will grieve
And pay the price with widowhood
When they will take their leave.

Hellbound, they care not for the price
They'll pay for crimson deeds.
The Devil sees and rolls his dice,
For damnèd Bonny & Read.

Such a strange, sad song. Such daring women. But it was a different world, and she does not recognise herself in the words now.

The late-afternoon sun sits heavy on the garden wall, its warmth
cooling into evening. There is birdsong, the sound of insects, and
the distant call of church bells. There is the heavy scent of flowers, the green sharpness of the trees. There are gulls overhead,
calling out. It means that there is poor weather at sea. Ezekiel
Moore told her once that gulls house the souls of dead sailors,
and she has known too many of those. She is still here when so
many are not.

She hears the distant cannon fire of thunder, and then, approaching from the east, heavy clouds that promise drenching rain that will wash everything clean. She watches until it is over-head, until rain drums hard against the earth, and lets it soak into her hair and clothes as she looks up into the storm.

She is still Anne. She will soon be twenty-six years old, an old married woman now, given birth to a child and killed six men. Her ability to bring life into this world has not kept pace with her ability to dispense with it, and we should not record a final tally until she is dead and buried.

But history does not concern itself with married women, and so she will step back into the shadows, unnoticed. Anne Bonny is no more, and Mrs Burleigh has begun. She will live, grow old and die unremarked. It is a luxury she may not deserve, but she will accept it gratefully. She will do it for those she has lost, and for Mary Read most of all. Perhaps it will be an adventure in its own way – if she lets it.